Praise for JoLyn Brown's *Run*

I have to say I was not expecting this. This is a story that pulls you in and never lets go. Intriguing and emotional, this book will make you laugh and make you cry. . . . These are timeless emotions that we all experience in life. This book is extremely well written and the characters are well developed. —Wanda

Run *kept me reading without wanting to quit. Jolyn Brown did a wonderful job keeping the story interesting.* —Rachel Hert

WOW! This is an intense book. . . . I loved the running analogy throughout. [T]he growth of the reader and the characters is truly phenomenal. Keep a box of tissues handy. Seriously good. Forgiveness and letting go to move on. A faith-promoting experience. —Teya Peck

I liked the emotions this book envoked. The characters were developed and evolved. Good read. —Karen Briggs

Every girl can relate to Morgan and the stress of parents, school, and boys—and that is one of my favorite things about her in this book. She feels real! . . . The author, JoLyn Brown, does a wonderful job of developing the characters, helping you understand and love them, and creating a fantastic storyline that entraps you with adventure, emotions, and love. You'll laugh and cry, cheer and boo, and thoroughly enjoy this tale of Morgan's summer journey. A five-star read for me! —Marci Preece, *Stand & Shine Magazine*

Wow. JoLyn pulled me into the mind of a crazy, emotional, unhappy, good-hearted sixteen-year-old like magic. The character development in this book was fabulous. The plot was interesting and the twists kept me hooked (I read it in two evenings). . . . I not only got the thrill of a good story but also got to take away a feeling of peace and contentment that I can't quite explain. Thank you for a beautiful book, JoLyn. —Tessa Dior Jensen

Stunning! I have recalled parts of this book days after finishing it; the twists in the storyline were rather unexpected. In addition to all the rugged twists and turns, this story expertly explored an age-old wonder: What will my life end up like? —Nicole Whipple

With an emphasis on the importance of family, honesty (with oneself and others), and navigating one's place in the world, this story takes us into the head of a young woman who feels entirely abandoned by her parents. . . . The cast of imperfect characters is highly loveable and engaging. Each is unique and you'll find yourself thinking, "Oh yeah, I totally know someone like that." My only gripe with the story is that I wanted it to keep going. . . . Highly recommended. —Crystal Collier

Run has great elements of mystery, and page-turning excitement. Morgan and her cousins come across as real teens with real problems. Yet, through it all, you don't feel weighed down by the problems, but anxious to solve the mystery of Morgan's nightmares. —Cindy Beck

I laughed, I squirmed, I cried, and I cheered Morgan on during her summer of adventures. Most of all, I found that I could relate after all: the emotions of a teenage girl, the large, crazy extended family, the realization that what you believe of others is not always true, understanding and experiencing the hand of God in our lives, and the feeling of wanting to run away from everything. My only complaint is that I didn't want to say goodbye to the characters; I want to know what comes next! —Cheri Larsen

Run by Jolyn Brown is as quick-paced as the title suggests. Morgan, who discovers she likes to run, doesn't realize that she is already running—running from the memories of her past, leaving them back at the day when events changed her life. . . . At moments I cried, and others I thought, "oh no, they (he/she) didn't," because the characters were real. —Susan Dayley

BREAK

BREAK

JoLyn Brown

WALNUT SPRINGS PRESS

For Grandma and Grandpa Nielsen,
who never give up

Text copyright © 2017 by JoLyn Brown
Cover design copyright © 2017 by Walnut Springs Press
Interior design copyright © 2017 by Walnut Springs Press

ISBN-13: 978-1-59992-178-5

Printed in the United States of America.

Acknowledgments

The first time I sent *Break* to my critique group, I stayed up until 5:00 in the morning pulling together a mess of thoughts and ideas. I wasn't even sure how to end the book. That same week I'd experienced an unexpected personal loss and I couldn't find it in me to face anything but the words on the page and a promise I'd made to send the manuscript no matter how bad it was. Rachel, Emily, and Jacque, thanks for reading this when it was raw and unedited and then reading it again.

I'm grateful for Jordan, Cynthia, Madeline, and Jeff for being my beta readers. I also could have never figured out the story without countless friends who encouraged me and listened to me, especially Sheri. I'm grateful for Joyce for walking with me morning after morning, loving this story from the beginning, and giving me so many great ideas.

Kaylee, Trevor, Lydia, Davis, and Stan, thanks for your help with the fountain scene. It was fun experimenting with you. Rebecca, I'm so grateful for your personal experiences and inspired ideas. Many thanks to Elena for helping me create Luna, and to Kathleen and Stan for sending dog photos. Ryan, I appreciate all your therapist advice and guidance about dealing with mental health issues.

Mom and Dad, thanks for being my biggest fans. Linda, thank you for believing in me as a writer and editing like crazy. Finally, my love and gratitude goes to my husband, Jacob, for helping me through all the ups and downs, and to my children for understanding my need to write. Thank you for advising me to include a food fight and helping me remember to laugh. You are my greatest blessings.

One

Sammy sat on the end of my bed, breathing into the silence. His shoulders were hunched in the lightening shadows, his eyes deadlocked on my face.

I jerked the rest of the way awake. "Sam, it's creepy to stare at someone when they're sleeping."

My brother waited several seconds before he spoke. "Preston?" His tone set off a trail of worry from my head to my gut. I pushed up onto my elbows. "You okay?"

He rocked back and forth, making the bed bounce beneath us. His tongue jutted between his lips. "Are they really coming today?" His eyes were bloodshot, his voice more slurred than usual.

I slid my feet to the floor. "Yeah."

"Last night I realized we don't have a bedroom for them." Sammy flopped back with a rattle of springs, and the bed knocked against the wood-paneled wall. "Will we have to share a room?"

"Maybe. But they aren't living with us till after the wedding." I didn't add that we might have to move.

Sammy grunted and rubbed both hands over his head in a furious motion. Now the short strands of his brown hair stuck straight up.

Not wanting to upset Sammy so soon after our friend Bryan's death, Mom had been gradually sharing the news of her engagement and the changes that were coming. Her plan wouldn't work. It wasn't like using a generic-brand washer fluid or wearing the same socks to football practice all week. Marriage wasn't one of those things you slipped into a person's life and hoped they didn't notice.

Sammy rolled to his side. "What if the girls don't like me?"

How to deal with stepsisters—three of them—wasn't the sort of stuff I knew about. I couldn't guarantee they'd like my brother, but most people got past his Down syndrome pretty quickly. After that, Sammy had a better track record for making friends than I did.

Scooting back, I slumped against the wall. "They will." If they didn't, they'd better keep it to themselves.

Sammy popped upright and bounced around me to sit on my pillow. He swiped something off my nightstand and tucked it against his leg. Before I could ask him what he'd taken, he whipped back toward me. "What'll happen to all my stuff?"

I sighed. "Nothing."

"Both of us won't fit in my room."

"Don't worry about it, Sammy. If it happens, I'll make it work."

"I wanna go hang out at the Powells' now." Sammy jumped to his feet and crossed the room while my sleep-sodden brain tried to keep up with the change of subjects. The Powells were our nearest neighbors—Bryan's family.

"Not today," I said. "I've got work, and you're going with Mom to help at the animal shelter."

"We have an hour." Sammy crossed his arms, rocking on his heels near the door.

"Later." I didn't feel like going to the Powells' house, with everyone still in shock over losing Bryan. It'd been a little better when his cousin Morgan was still there. She had been staying with them for the summer when the accident happened, but now she'd gone home to Orem.

"I'll go by myself," Sammy said.

He disappeared into the hall. Seconds later, the back door slammed shut. A glance at the nightstand brought an alarm screaming through the fog in my head.

The three-wheeler keys were gone.

He wouldn't!

I sprang from the bed and tripped over my own shoes. I hit the wall near the door and pivoted into the hallway. *Don't let me be too late.* The prayer rolled automatically into my head with the same words I used the day Bryan died. Fear shot through me.

The door to the hall closet smacked my arm. I stumbled forward but picked up my pace as I reached the kitchen and bolted around the table. Everything in the house conspired to block me. Two chairs connected with my hip and crashed over before I reached the screen door to the back porch.

"Sam!" The door slapped closed behind me with a jolt that shook the kitchen window.

In our dusty back yard, Sammy straddled the red three-wheeler. "You can't stop me," he said.

Seeing him on the ATV set a war off in my gut. "Get off."

"You're not in charge."

"I don't care." The smell of gasoline had been in my nose for three weeks. Every breath reminded me of Bryan.

Sammy shoved the key into the ignition. The ATV roared to life. I jumped off the porch and dove at him. He shrieked and slammed his round fingers over the key. Straddling the three-wheeler behind him, I pried at his hand and turned the key. The engine cut off. His elbow whipped into my chest, taking my air with it. He yanked the key free of the ignition and clamped it to his stomach. I worked my arm around his waist and pried under his arm until I wedged my hand under his and the jagged edge of metal met my fingers.

"Let me go." Another swing of his elbow caught me in the gut.

I buckled forward, groaning, and Sammy shoved me to one side. Ignoring the throbbing in my midsection, I wrapped him in a headlock and dragged him off the vehicle. His weight took us both to the gravel, which dug into my bare knees. I rolled him to his back and inched my fingers under his.

He threw his head back. "Get off me! Stop it!" His wail hit me straight in my ear. Like a siren. I hated that sound, but this time it didn't stop me.

My fingers circled around the key.

"Preston Troy Bensen!" Mom yelled from the porch. "What are you doing?" Her tight, dark curls were a wild mane, her eyes fierce.

I freed the sweaty key and rolled off Sammy.

"Give it back!" He sat, dirt clouding off his green T-shirt and brown hair. Tears made streaks down his round face.

"What's going on?" Mom asked, looming over us.

Sammy wiped his snot on his arm. "He took the key."

Mom's gaze softened at once. "Preston." She drew my name out as if trying to read something inside me. But there was nothing there to read. I was empty.

I got up and brushed off my shorts, avoiding her frown.

"Give me the key," she said. Her hand appeared in my side vision, palm up, waiting.

I lifted my head. "He's not driving it."

"I know this is hard for you, but when Sammy drives the three-wheeler again needs to be my decision." Mom's green eyes fixed on mine. "Give me the key."

My fingers shut around the key like they'd been cemented in place. When *Sammy drives the three-wheeler again.*

Sammy could *never* drive the three-wheeler again.

Mom's gaze traveled to my tightening fist. My voice jammed in my throat. I had nearly a hundred pounds on her, and a half a foot in height, but I'd never defied her like this before.

I inhaled and braced myself. "No." I pushed around her and went inside the house.

I had enough presence of mind to grab my shoes before slipping out the front door and into my truck. Three weeks ago, I'd have gone straight to the Powells' house. I drove by it and didn't even slow. The last thing I needed was more reminders of Bryan.

I drove to Carter's. After I parked, I jammed my truck keys in my pocket next to the three-wheeler key and grabbed my Carter's Feed polo from the floor of the truck. I yanked the shirt over my head as I walked in the front door. The feed store smelled of barn and wood dust. Grain hung in a thin layer in the air, and tiny slivers of hay were scattered over the concrete floor.

Mr. Carter stood at a display of miniature plastic farm animals. He held a cow in one hand and a brown horse in the other. "You're early." He scanned me up and down, his eyes lingering on my basketball shorts streaked with dirt. "Rough morning?"

I hadn't changed into the right pants. Heck, I hadn't even brushed my teeth or combed my hair. I pressed a hand to the brown curls I'd inherited from Mom. A matted portion caught under my fingers.

"Since you're here, I might as well put you to work." My boss's gruff tone couldn't mask his concern. I'd never shown up half-ready like this. I tried to be reliable—I needed the job.

"Kathy ain't had any luck selling those rabbits of hers." Mr. Carter nodded toward the notice board near the entrance where people posted about animals or equipment they were trying to sell or get rid of. "Told her she could bring them over here this afternoon to drum up interest. Why don't you haul some rabbit food and a couple of fancy hutches up front? I ain't sold much rabbit stuff since Easter."

I mumbled an okay as I walked by him, passing the checkout counter. At least he hadn't wanted to put me to work there. It was the first thing that had gone in my favor all morning.

Three hours later, sweat ran down my back and soaked into the band of my shorts. I heaved a bag of rabbit food onto a shelf and stopped to wipe my hand over my forehead. With the swamp coolers going full blast, the August heat still leaked into the building. Swamp coolers added a mugginess to the air that made me wish I could be outside, even though it was ten degrees hotter.

"Preston." Mr. Carter came around the metal shelving at the end of the aisle. "Your mom's on the phone. She didn't know if you were here or not. Didn't you tell her you were going to work?"

At the edge in my boss's voice a few customers glanced over, an audience to the wash of red that flooded my face. My tongue stuck to the roof of my mouth, casting a guilty verdict by virtue of no protest. Getting myself to talk had been worse lately—just when I'd thought I'd started to get over the stupid thing.

I knew a year ago that getting a job meant I had to talk, especially when Mr. Carter put me on the register. So I'd figured out how to speak to the customers. I didn't have to say a lot. It worked until three weeks ago. Then people started saying stuff like "I heard you were the first to get to them—that must have been awful," or "It's terrible what happened to Bryan . . . he was a good kid," or—and this was the worst—"How's Sammy takin' it?"

If the customers weren't standing behind Mr. Carter, if I hadn't told Mom no a few hours ago, if Bryan hadn't died . . . There were too many ifs. But if I could shift all that junk a little bit, I wouldn't be standing there like a guppy.

Mr. Carter's dark-gray brows furrowed. "Better go straighten things out with her."

I got to the phone and clenched it to my ear, but since there were at least five customers within hearing distance and my boss had followed me, I couldn't do anything but breathe.

I guess Mom knew my breathing, because she said my name. I retreated away from everyone, the yellowed cord stretching over the counter and knocking over a cup of pens. They spilled to the floor, hit in an echoing clatter, and rolled under the checkout stand. My hand grew sweaty on the phone. *I'm not doing this. I'm not going to stand here like a mute.* It took way too long, but I finally forced the word through my lips. "Yep?" I wanted to tell her sorry. I wasn't trying to make things hard for her, but nothing came out.

She didn't wait long for me to try. "Are you okay?"

"Yeah."

Silence followed as if she was trying to work out how to handle me. The three-wheeler key in my pocket felt heavy against my leg. Maybe it was an illusion, a false sense of control in the face of things that were really only in God's hands, but the key was all I had.

"I know now isn't a good time," Mom said softly, "but when I get home, we need to talk about what happened. Right now, I need your help with something else. I got a call from Alex. His van broke down. He's only twenty minutes from Kanab, near the turn off to the slot canyons."

I braced for what I figured she'd say next. Alex, my mom's fiancé, wasn't the sort of guy who knew about fixing cars, but I did.

"You're only working a half day, right? Do you think Mr. Carter would let you off early so you can drive out and look at it?"

I dropped my elbows on the counter and leaned over them. "Can't you call a tow truck?"

She went quiet, as if surprised I spoke at all. Meeting up with Alex without her there freaked me out more than the entire store of listening ears. I liked the guy okay. I had since I met him at an art festival in May, but in the last four months he'd gone from the cool guy I talked to about art to the guy my mom got engaged to. My problem with speaking got worse around him. My elementary school counselor would've told me it was connected to the way I'd taken on unnecessary guilt over my dad. Knowing that didn't loosen my tongue, no matter how much I wanted it to.

Mom finally spoke again. "Even if we call Sterling's Tow, someone will need to go get the girls. There's not enough room in Sterling's truck for them all."

What on earth did she expect me to do with three girls?

Mom clicked her tongue. I could almost see her face scrunched up in thought. "Do you have much longer on your shift?"

Hope flickered alive in me. "I'm supposed to work till noon."

"I didn't realize you had two hours left." Her tone changed to the matter-of-fact voice she used when she needed to solve a problem. "We have the public open house at the animal clinic in half an hour, and I promised Joe I'd be here to help with adoptions and fosters. Hmm. Maybe I can get a hold of someone to take my place for an hour, and then I could get back here before things get too crazy. Plus, Sam might like the chance to meet the girls sooner."

He might, but Sammy took things seriously when he went to work with her. If she dragged him away from any of his favorite jobs, it could easily turn into a full-on meltdown. That would mean a second tantrum in one day. I already left Mom to deal with his first one this morning. The one I'd caused.

What could possibly be so intimidating about a guy that didn't know how to fix his own van? I'd talked to him fine before he started dating Mom. I could do it today. "Don't worry about it," I told her. "I came in early. I can go."

After a pause, she asked, "Are you sure?"

"Yeah."

"Thank you." Relief filled Mom's voice. "Sam and I will try to get away early, all right?"

"Yeah."

She always meant well, but I knew better than to count on that happening.

TWO

Mr. Carter didn't know about Mom's fiance and his daughters, but he waved me off before I figured out how to explain. "If your mom needs you, she comes first. I'll see you Monday."

I headed out to the parking lot. I'd learned most of my mechanic skills trying to keep my great-grandpa's truck, Old Blue, running. It hummed like a freight train and rattled just as much as I bounced out to the road, but it had two side-facing seats in the back and would hold all the girls if it came to that. The highway wound away from Karlon toward Kanab, the air above the blacktop wavering in the heat as I passed the park where I'd first met Alex.

Technically, it was my fault Mom and Alex even met. I'd gone into his art booth at the fair and gotten distracted. Talking with him had been easy and comfortable, something rare for me. The next thing I knew, Sammy had crashed into a table of paintings and ripped a gaping scar through the biggest and most expensive one. In the chaos that followed, Mom showed up to figure out how to pay for the damage. She and Alex hit it off from the start. It shouldn't have come as such a shock when they started dating, but it did. And it tripped a switch inside me.

Since then, nothing about my conversations with Alex had been comfortable. The last time I'd seen him, a day or two before Bryan died, I'd perfected my grunts and nods like some stone golem from one of Sammy's video games.

In the canyon behind Kanab, the tree branches reached toward the road as the red rock walls drew closer around Old Blue. Somehow, the drive from Carter's to the turnoff for the slot canyons seemed shorter than normal. A gray van with its hood propped up came into view.

I eased down on the clutch and shifted before making a U-turn. Old Blue grumbled like he wanted to fall apart as I pulled off the road behind the van. Heat rushed through my open window. Fresh drops of sweat beaded on my forehead before I got out.

Alex came around the side of his van. He was only slightly taller than me, with a slimmer build. A smear of black dirt ran up the side of his usual tan slacks. His short, thinning blond hair lay plastered to his head, and sweat rolled down his face and neck. He closed the distance between us too quickly. Breaking eye contact, I glanced into the bed of the truck to find my toolbox.

The old rules I'd picked up from the elementary-school counselor rolled through my brain on a fast track, as if trying to make up for not coming earlier. *"Step one for dealing with social anxiety: plan out what to say beforehand. Think of things you can talk about and how to respond to possible questions."*

Yeah. Not going to work this time.

"Thanks for coming." Alex stopped behind me, talking at my back. "I don't know what's going on. The windshield wipers came on, all the lights started blinking, and the engine stalled." He stopped, then added in a tense voice, "Luckily I was already slowing down or we might have missed that last turn."

My eyes flickered toward the drop-off on the opposite side of Blue, but I didn't let myself dwell there. Hadn't I read some stuff about that happening with newer vehicles, something about a fancy fuse box? I'd never even seen anything but an old-style fuse box in the vehicles I'd worked on. I probably couldn't do a thing for it, but I wasn't ready to commit to bringing the girls home, either.

I grabbed the toolbox so I wouldn't have to take the oil-streaked hand Alex held out to me. His striped, button-down shirt had sweat marks under the pits, and a yellow stain on the sleeve.

Three girls with staring eyes huddled on the side of the van farthest from the road. I went the other direction. I hadn't met them yet and preferred to keep it that way as long as possible. I dropped the toolbox on the gravel and ducked under the hood. Inside, everything bore the sleek, tidy look of modern engines I'd only glimpsed in the outdated *Mechanic's Weekly* magazines Mr. Carter passed on to me. A black plastic cover encased the engine.

A teenage girl a few inches shorter than me with a head full of frizzy, blond hair ducked under the hood on the other side. She adjusted her glasses and flashed a grin. "I hope you know more about this than my dad. He could hardly get the hood up."

Shaking his head, Alex stepped between the girl and me. "I'm glad to see you have so much confidence in me, Hannah."

She shrugged. "You poked it with a *stick*." In the next breath, she spoke to me. "Can you fix it?"

I stalked to the driver's side and yanked open the door. There were no keys in the ignition. *There's no way I'm going to get through this without talking.* I turned around, my arms stiff at my sides.

"Step two for dealing with social anxiety: Take calming breaths and try to relax your body."

I forced a longer breath through my nose and unclenched my hands.

Alex handed me his keys. I sank onto the edge of the seat, shoved the van key into the ignition, and twisted. Nothing. I turned the ignition once more and scanned the touch screen, music system, and various types of outlets between the dashboard and center console. The armrest on the door held switches for everything from the windows to heated seats. It was one sweet van. Minus the not-working part.

I popped open the glove compartment. There, tucked under the registration, was the owner's manual.

"Dad already tried turning it on, after he poked it with the stick." Hannah said, leaning through the passenger-side window. Her pale arms hung inches from my head.

I sprang upright. The owner's manual hit the seat and slipped to the floor. The registration fluttered beside it.

"To make sure you take deep-enough breaths, count slowly to five before releasing the breath for another count of five."

"Who is he?" A girl's voice in my ear made me jump, my recently drawn-in breath exploding outward on a count of one.

I whirled around. A second girl, a small one with straight blond hair, had climbed between the bucket seats behind me.

"Preston. He's helping us." Alex pulled the girl out of the van. "You need to stay out here. It's too hot inside."

He could say that again. My shirt stuck to my skin where it had touched the leather seat. Not to mention the whole vehicle reeked of urine.

Hannah moved from the window to talk to the little girl. I snagged the owner's manual off the floor and I flipped to the pages I needed. Back under the hood, I located the fuse box and worked the top off to reveal a grid-work of fuses.

Hannah popped up beside me again and laughed in a sudden burst. "Nice. I didn't realize that opened. Maybe you do know what you're doing."

I wiggled some of the fuses and found the one for the heated seats and the windshield wipers. A few more minutes passed as I went between the owner's manual and the fuse box.

"So, it's fixable, then?" Hannah inched closer. My fingers stiffened over the fuel-pump fuse.

I backed out from under the hood. As much as I wanted to examine every inch of the van, including all its high-tech details, I didn't have the knowledge or parts to fix it. Alex and the girls couldn't stand in the heat while I played around. I forced myself to meet his eyes.

He frowned. "I'm going to have to call the tow truck, aren't I?"

I nodded.

"Will you put the number in?" He passed me his phone. "It's Sterling's, right?"

Relieved Alex made it easy not to talk, I nodded again and punched in the number I'd memorized when Old Blue had one too many problems this summer. Alex took the phone, and I walked around to the side of the van where the girls waited. I'd better see what the last one was like. Now that there wasn't any choice, I wanted to know what I was getting myself into. Hannah followed me.

The little girl Alex had pulled out of the van sat on a rock, swinging her feet and playing with an almost-empty water bottle. The third girl—the middle one, judging by size—sat on the ground, hunched over herself, blond hair around her like a blanket. An untouched water bottle lay beside her. She peeked up at me. Worry sparked over her face before she ducked down and tightened her arms around herself.

"That's Bonnie." Hannah stepped between me and the middle girl, her own water bottle swinging in her hand. "She's in a bad mood. It's better if you don't bother her now."

I didn't want to bother anyone, but I was worried about heatstroke. I pointed to the water bottle. "She needs to drink."

Hannah shrugged. "She won't."

I stepped around Hannah, scooped up the plastic bottle and opened it, then squatted near Bonnie's untied blue canvas shoes. "You need to drink."

She jerked away, unfolding like a spring and scooting back. She blinked at me with wide, frightened eyes. The smell of urine flooded my nose. A caking of red dirt clung to her pants and snaked down her legs, a clay replica of trails left by liquid that had since dried up. She sucked in a tiny squeak, following my gaze to her legs. She wrenched her knees to her chest and buried her face.

Alex's voice, a murmur in the background, cut off midsentence. He stared down at Bonnie and me.

Great. A flash of heat blazed over my face.

His frown flipped between Bonnie and me. "Yeah, that's right," he said into the phone. "It's never done this before. I thought these vans were supposed to be some of the safest out there."

I hated when people stared at me, but you didn't mess with hundred-degree weather. I shifted around and sat beside Bonnie. She was probably ten years old or so—old enough to reason with.

I rolled the cap between my fingers. "It's Bonnie, right?"

She scooted an inch away.

"Do you know what heatstroke is?"

She scooted again.

This time I scooted too. "Look, it's over a hundred out here and you've been sitting in the sun for probably thirty minutes. Heatstroke can put you in the hospital. Fast. The last thing I want is to drag you to a hospital. There ain't nothin' I hate more than hospitals."

She lifted her head. Strands of dark blond hair stuck to her cheeks. Her hand shot out and snatched the water from me. She downed half of it while still glaring. I stood. The water would help, but I still needed to get the girls out of the sun.

I walked to the truck and opened the doors, then slid the front seat forward and moved all the junk off the back seat. Between Sammy and me, the back seat had become a dumping place for everything from sweatshirts and running shoes to takeout napkins and old homework. I stuffed the junk into plastic grocery sacks and shoved them under the seats. The heavier stuff I dumped into the truck bed, leaving an old sweatshirt on one back seat for Bonnie to sit on.

When I got to the van, Alex stood with the phone cupped to his ear, rubbing his sweaty hair. "Are you sure?" he asked the person on the phone. "If it's too much trouble, he can drop the girls off at the rental house."

He must have called Mom. A bit of hope rose in me. It wouldn't be so bad if I could leave the girls at their own place.

Alex glanced at Bonnie and spoke into the phone again. "Okay. You're right."

Hannah lifted the tangled mess of her curls off her neck and frowned at me. "Will we all fit in your truck?"

I shrugged.

Alex joined us. "Preston, your mom wants to talk to you."

I took his phone and stepped away to where the side of the road dropped, forming a V with the canyon wall. "Yeah?"

"Preston, I told Alex you'd drive them out to our place while he gets the van to the shop," Mom said.

"Can't I take them to the rental?" Alex had mentioned that. And Hannah was old enough to watch her two sisters.

"They're all a little shook up from the van breaking down. He's worried about leaving them alone after triggering memories of the other accident."

I dug my shoe into the dirt. Alex's first wife and two of his kids had died in a car accident maybe four years ago. I'd been trying not to think about that. My stomach crawled as if tiny creatures were climbing around in it. It would have been so easy for the van to slide off the side of the canyon road, down into the tree-and-rock-strewn gully beside me, just like Bryan's ATV slid over the side of a red ravine in an avalanche of mud, plastic, and steel.

"Nothing is unpacked at the rental, and they don't have any food yet," Mom continued. "They'll be more comfortable at our place."

A tightness spread into my chest. I dragged my attention from the gully, refocusing on what she'd said. They didn't have food.

If I reminded her that we hadn't gone grocery shopping either, she would probably send me to buy food. Just what I needed—crowds, checkout clerks, and the impossible-to-avoid, small-town scenario of running into someone I knew and being forced into a conversation.

Mom kept going. "Also, if things take longer than—"

"—I'll drive them to the house."

"Oh. Okay. That's perfect. Thanks, Preston. I love you."

"Yeah." I hung up and handed the phone to Alex.

He studied Old Blue with more than a little concern on his face. "Will a booster fit in the back?"

I pulled a pink booster from the van, carried it to the truck, and shoved it into the narrow bucket seat in the back. Hannah peered around me as if she didn't quite believe it fit.

The youngest girl peeked in, her nose just high enough to see into the truck. She pointed to her booster. "Are you taking that?"

Hannah flipped her curls over her shoulder and laughed. "No, Edith, you're riding in it."

A high-pitched scream came from behind us. Alex crouched beside Bonnie and spoke quietly to her. I knew that voice. He'd used it on me right after I pulled Sammy off the ruined painting at the art show. I'd thought I might vomit when I saw the price tag. We'd never be able pay for it. Not if we wanted to do stuff like eat and keep the electricity on at our house.

Bonnie grabbed her hair and pulled it around her cheeks before clamping her hands over her ears. Alex'd had a bit more success with me. He had told me he could fix the painting. I'd calmed down somewhere between the soda he handed me, and the drawing pad he pressed into my hand with a suggestion to draw for a bit.

Now he scanned the three of us at the truck. "Preston, do you have something for Bonnie to sit on?"

I nodded.

"Shut up!" Bonnie shoved her father, knocking him off balance.

My pulse kicked up. I rolled my shoulders and tried to shake it off. I should do something. Talk to her, maybe. Tell her it wouldn't be bad at the house, that I didn't care if she wet herself. Like when I had to calm down Sammy. I could do that. My heart sped like I'd already moved, but my feet fused themselves in place.

Alex caught Bonnie's chin in his hand, tipping her face up to his. "Are you walking? Or am I carrying you?"

This time, something final lined his voice. It did nothing to stop the tension hardening my shoulder blades. Sammy and I had that much in common. Both of us got uneasy when people started fighting. Of course, I didn't start screaming the way he did, but it didn't mean I didn't want to sometimes.

Bonnie yanked Alex's fingers from her chin. He reached for her arm. She screamed when he hauled her up. He pinned her body to his chest and caught her legs with his free arm. Her hair tangled in their arms and hands. I didn't know how her dad held on to her, but he got her to the truck and into the back seat, then buckled her in. The second he let go, she reached to undo the seatbelt. Alex closed his hand over hers. "Bonnie, you can't stay out here in the heat forever, and the alternative is riding with me in a tow truck. If you don't want everyone at the repair shop to know you wet yourself, you need to go with Preston." Alex let her go and she slumped forward. "Hannah and Edith will be with you," he told her. "You'll be fine."

He moved out of the narrow space between the front seat and the back and looked through the truck to where I stood by the other two girls. Clearly worried, he said, "Maybe I *should* keep her with me."

Bonnie gasped and her head popped up, terror widening her eyes and stopping her tears. Somehow I didn't think Sterling would take kindly to pee in his tow-truck.

I scooped up Edith and plopped her onto her booster seat. She gaped up at me as I wrapped a seat belt around her and locked it into place. After sliding back the passenger seat for Hannah, I stalked to the driver's-side door.

Alex caught my shoulder. I jerked at the touch. He reversed a step, his hands half raised. "I just wanted to make sure you were okay with this."

Way to stay calm, Preston. Real cool. "Sorry. It's fine." I grabbed at the steering wheel and got into the truck. The door slammed between us. I forced myself to make eye contact with Alex through the open window. "You have water?"

One side of his mouth lifted and a soft laugh escaped. "Yeah. Don't worry about me. Hannah has a phone if you need anything."

My fingers tightened around the wheel. *These girls can't be worse than Sammy.*

Three

Wind rushed through the open windows, blowing Hannah's hair around her head like a cyclone. Her curls, a tangle of frizz that whipped at her face, were tighter than Mom's and mine. Hannah didn't even try to tame hers. The wheels hitting the main road through town were like pressing the start button on her. Words spilled out of her faster than I could process. She lost me as she began some story about cowboy boots and Edith. The truck bounced by the last building in town, Carter's, and into a long stretch of nothing.

Hannah glanced at me. "Where are we going?"

"That was Kanab, not Karlon," I said.

"Oh, is our house in Kanab or Karlon? I think it's in Kanab. The rental, I mean. *Your* house is in Karlon."

Her chatter might give me whiplash.

"Karlon must be way small," she continued. "How far are your neighbors? Do you have any? We lived in a townhouse in Payson. I don't mind neighbors, but one guy next to us didn't like Eddie. He said she screamed too much." Hannah stopped talking to check on Edith.

"Who's Eddie?" I flinched at my question. After all that Hannah had said, I should've come up with something more intelligent.

"That's Eddie." She pointed to Edith like I'd missed something obvious. "Edith . . . Eddie. It's a nickname."

At the turnoff to Karlon, I rotated the steering wheel a little sharper than intended.

"Wheee!" Edith squealed. I glanced back. Her booster had tipped to one side. It settled back into place as I straightened out.

"Do it again!" she said.

Hannah laughed and set off chattering again. She talked about the potholes, the old brown church, and the four blocks of town that gave way to twisted orchards. She mentioned the Powells' "cute" white house, which was actually old and faded.

We pulled into the driveway at my house. Hannah's voice cut out at once. I followed her stunned expression to the house. I'd grown used it—almost forgotten how bad it was—but now I saw a crooked, brown, wreck of a place with a broken window and a cracked front door. Rusting parts, wooden pallets, and a bent plow were behind and under and through the overgrown bushes. The grass that once grew in the front yard sat dead and yellow.

If the girls were planning on a palace, they'd gotten in the wrong truck.

I got out and pulled my seat forward for Bonnie. Her mouth hung open. "You've got to be kidding!" She spun on Hannah like it was her fault. "The townhouse was bigger than that! We left it for this?"

Not wanting to hear more complaints about the house, I hurried inside. I got the swamp cooler going and closed the bedroom doors so the cooler air could wind from the kitchen to the living room instead of getting lost in the rest of the house. Then I peeked out the window. Hannah lifted Edith out to the gravel beside the driveway. Edith danced from foot to foot, clutching between her legs. Bonnie remained inside the truck, slouched down in the seat.

"Bonnie, come inside." Hannah's chipper tone carried through the duck-tape-patched window.

"Leave me alone," Bonnie shouted.

Hannah glanced at the house again. "It's not that bad."

"Everyone in the whole world is going to know I wet myself, and all you will do is try to find something good about it! And the worst part is I'm stuck in this outfit because Dad had to fill the entire trunk with painting supplies and you had to fill the entire back seat with medical supplies!"

As much as I hated Bonnie's hysterics, I could understand her frustration. I doubted we had anything that would fit her. I found a pile of clean but unfolded clothes on Mom's bed, including a pair of drawstring basketball shorts and one of mom's smaller T-shirts. I snagged them and headed out.

Hannah stood in front of the bathroom, blocking the hallway. As I got closer, Edith's voice carried from within. "I'm scared."

"What?" Hannah leaned in to get a better look.

I knew what she'd see. A cracked sink I'd filled in with a line of caulking. The wooden toilet seat sitting crooked on the hinges, and the bowl stained with rust. Near the tub, the linoleum peeled back to reveal wooden floorboards peeking from under two ragged rugs.

My fingers twitched at the urge to pull Hannah back. I never intended to leave the bathroom like that. Just till we got enough money . . .

"It's fine." Hannah, still oddly cheerful, pushed Edith closer to the toilet and stepped out into the hallway.

"No!" Edith flung herself at the door, hanging onto the knob. "There might be spiders! Or snakes." She twisted, slamming her back against Hannah's legs and pushing her into the hallway until she bumped into me. As Hannah spun around, I squeezed by the two girls and headed toward the living room.

No Bonnie.

I glanced at the van. Her feet dangled out the door. My seat was still pushed forward, with her blond hair just visible around it.

I dropped the clothes on Mom's high-backed rocking chair and jogged out. Bonnie glared at me as I approached. "You can't stay out here," I told her.

"Watch me." She snarled the words like a cornered cat.

The girl either had a death wish, or no concept of heatstroke. Maybe it was the heat, or maybe plain frustration, but I reached up, pulled Bonnie out of the truck, and slammed the door. I faced her toward the house. "Go inside." My voice held a plea I reserved for Sammy.

"I'm not going in there!" She pointed at the house.

It had to be better than sitting in pee-covered pants in the heat until you died. I clenched my teeth, grappling with my anger. How did you reason with a ten-year-old girl? Maybe you didn't. Alex had simply hauled her to the truck. "I can't leave you out here," I said finally. "Walk in yourself or I'll carry you in."

She dropped to my feet, her arms crossed around herself, her hair trailing in the red dirt, and her furious face tipped up toward me. "You better not touch me or I'll tell my dad. You can't touch me if I don't want you to."

"I can't leave you out here to die, either!" If Alex wanted to get after me for dragging her out of the sun, let him. I caught Bonnie's arm, lifted her to her feet, and headed for the house, pulling her along. She dug in her heels and put in a mean fight for such a lightweight kid. Several kicks and scratches later, I got my arm around her waist, lifted her up the stairs, and pushed open the door.

After prying her fingers off the doorframe, I shut the door with my foot and blocked her escape route. Then I locked the door behind me.

She staggered back a few steps, her face sweaty and flushed, and stomped her foot. "I want to wait in the truck."

"The air inside a vehicle is ten times hotter than the air outside," I said. "You'll roast to death in that truck."

I didn't know the exact math, but it had to be close. When she stepped back farther into the house, I circled her and grabbed the clothes off the chair. Hannah stood in the kitchen archway, frozen with a plastic smile on her lips.

Expecting to have to chase Bonnie down at any second, I stepped into the hallway and motioned for her to follow. "Come on."

To my surprise, she blinked at the front door and then took a few steps toward me. Taking it as a sign of compliance, I headed down the hall. Her feet stomped after me, with Hannah's close behind. I opened the small cupboard near the bathroom, pulled out a faded blue towel, and handed it to Bonnie, along with the clothes. She stood in the doorway while I grasped the shower tab on the tap, yanking it up and to the left to turn the water on. The water hissed, gulped, and spat into the tub, spraying out both the shower and the tap. I wiggled the tap and flicked the water on and off. The loud sputtering faded as the rest of the water redirected itself out the showerhead.

I stepped out of the bathroom and frowned at Bonnie. "Okay?"

She hugged the towel and clothes to her chest and dashed inside the bathroom, then slammed the door shut between us.

A loud voice called from the kitchen, "Hannah! I need a bowl."

"Edith." Hannah jerked around and rushed to the kitchen. I sprinted after her.

Edith stood on top of the counter near the sink, a cupboard door open. She'd put the last egg and the pitiful remains of the milk on the island behind her.

"They are heavy." She pointed to Mom's best glass bowl, which sat on the edge of the shelf.

Hannah dashed toward her and stood on her tiptoes to brace the bowl. It slid into the safety of the cupboard. I let out the breath I'd been holding. Hannah lifted Edith to the floor. I circled to the fridge and put the things on the counter back inside.

"I'm cooking!" Edith said in a shrill voice.

I froze with the milk halfway to the fridge. Her arms were rigid at her sides. My whole body braced as the storm inside her visibly unfurled up her tiny frame.

"You are messing it up! Stop messing it up!" She stamped her feet, shaking the contents of the cupboards and drawers as she charged toward me. "This is *my* found kitchen. You go cook on a fire."

Hannah choked on a laugh. I gaped at Edith.

Edith whirled on Hannah. "Stop laughing. This isn't funny. Make him stop!" She jabbed a finger toward me. "You both stop being mean, or I won't let you have any of what I make. Not one bit."

I put the milk back on the counter.

Edith lowered her finger. "Where's the egg?"

I got the egg out of the fridge.

Edith took a deep breath and exhaled slowly. Her body relaxed. "Good. Now someone get me a bowl. We've been starving for weeks, people. We don't have time for this."

I sent a questioning glance at Hannah. Her cheeks flamed bright pink as she admitted, "I maybe—sort of—told her we should pretend like we'd been stranded in the desert and found this place."

Great. Now my house is a hermit cottage someone happened upon. My stomach growled in complaint at having missed breakfast. I got out a plastic bowl.

Five minutes later, with a few suggestions from Hannah, Edith had created a bowl of white batter. She stood on a stool beside the counter, frowning. "It needs something else."

Hannah closed the lid on the bucket of flour and passed it to me. "To be cooked?" she said. "Do you have a griddle?"

I opened a cupboard under the island. Hannah managed to pull out the black griddle covered with scratch marks and attached the cord I handed to her.

Edith clapped. "Sprinkles!" She danced around on the chair. "Hey, you, Boy Preston, do you have sprinkles? Pink ones?"

"No."

"Okay. Purple ones, then?"

"We don't have any sprinkles."

Edith sighed. "Well, we can't expect to have everything, can we? It's lucky the people who used to live here left what they did." She frowned into the batter. "But I will miss the sprinkles."

Bonnie appeared in the hallway, tugging her fingers through her wet hair, which hung to her waist. She wore the shorts and T-shirt and held a towel-wrapped bundle. The shorts reached to the middle of her calves. "Everything doesn't need sprinkles, Edith," she said.

"Yes, it does." Edith licked some batter off her finger.

"The washing machine is in there." I pointed to a door off the dining room.

Bonnie bit her lip, sliding into a chair at the table. She settled the towel bundle on her lap and picked at the tabletop with her nail.

"She doesn't know how to use a washing machine," Hannah said. She rubbed a little butter on the griddle and handed Edith a clean measuring cup. "The edge is hot."

Edith scooped up an overflowing cup of batter and poured it dead center on the griddle. "I know. Don't tell me."

Hannah pulled open two drawers before she found a spatula. "Dad does the laundry," she said.

"Come on." I headed toward the laundry room. Sammy and I had been doing our own laundry for years.

Bonnie's chair squealed away from the table. She stomped after me again. "You're really bossy, you know?"

No one but Sammy ever told me that.

The pancakes turned out good enough, despite Edith's concerns about sprinkles. I figured that would pass for lunch. While the girls picked through an old arrowhead collection of Grandpa's that Sammy and I had added to, I started to clean up the kitchen. I didn't even get everything to the sink before Edith slid off her chair, dashed down the hall, and slammed open Sammy's door. Hannah raced after her, knocking the box of arrowheads to the floor in the process.

"Sorry!" she shouted over her shoulder.

If Edith broke something in Sammy's room, he'd have a cow in the form of a whole-body-throwing, mouth-gaping fit. I followed the girls down the hallway. In the bedroom, Hannah was trying to talk Edith into putting down one of Sammy's die-cast motorcycles.

Oh no. He knew every time they got touched. I grabbed the bike from Edith and put it on his bookshelf.

"I was playing with that!" She tore free of Hannah's grasp and came at me. "You have to share!"

This had better not be how Alex expected things to go, because no way was I letting these girls into Sammy's stuff or mine whenever they wanted.

Hannah shook her head. "Edith, it isn't yours and you didn't ask first. Let's go to the kitchen and pick up the arrowheads."

She glared between us. "I want to play with that!" She jabbed her finger at the motorcycle.

"It's Sammy's. This is Sammy's room." I herded Edith and Hannah out and shut the door behind me.

If I thought Bonnie could throw a tantrum, it was nothing compared to Edith's high-pitched, brain-engulfing wail. She collapsed on the floor in the middle of the hallway.

The pounding on the front door didn't register until I heard a shout. "Preston! Is that Sammy screaming?"

Jesse. He was Bryan's older brother and my best friend. Jesse and I had endured more than our fair share of Sammy tantrums.

The knock came again. "Preston? You all right?"

I met Hannah's eyes. "Don't let her go in there." I pointed at Sammy's room.

Hannah flinched, but I didn't have time to feel bad about the snap in my voice. I headed to the kitchen, wondering if I should relocate Bonnie, or tell Jesse to go home. If he said something about her unusual wardrobe, it would set her off again. Of course, telling Jesse to leave pretty much guaranteed he'd stay.

Bonnie's empty chair sat to the side of the table. I checked behind the kitchen counter and glanced out the back window. No Bonnie.

The lock rattled on the front door. In twenty seconds Jesse would have his student ID wedged between the doorjamb and the lock. I sighed. There was only one relatively undisturbed place in the house, and usually the darkness kept people out. If it was me . . . I pushed open the door next to the laundry room, revealing the rickety wood stairs to the unfinished basement.

Bonnie sat only two stairs down, her legs tucked up under the shirt, her back pressed against the support beams holding the stairs in place. She glared as light spilled over her from the kitchen, but the scowl couldn't hide the fear on her face.

I flicked the light switch on the wall twice without any results. I'd been meaning to replace that. The front door opened.

I closed the door to the basement, leaving Bonnie in the dark.

Four

Jesse emerged near the hallway to the bedrooms, his thick brown hair sticking up all over. He wore his stained football shirt and paint-splattered basketball shorts. He gaped at Edith screaming on the floor, and Hannah standing over her. A grin slid over his face. "Where'd you get the girls?"

"They're Alex's."

Jesse's expression went blank. He reached up and braced his hand against the overhead archway to the kitchen. Taller than me by a good three inches, he was as lanky as a pole. He twisted his face in mock thought. "Nope. Not coming back to me. Who's Alex?"

"The guy my mom's marrying."

"What?"

"Alex is the name of the man my mom is marrying," I repeated slowly, even though I knew it wouldn't help. I'd told Jesse a while ago—before Bryan—but it wasn't the kind of thing I wanted to talk about, so I hadn't mentioned it since.

"Huh," Jesse said. "When's that happening?"

"October."

He dropped his hand from the archway and turned to Edith. "Her lungs are almost as good as Sammy's."

As if to prove her screaming abilities couldn't be rivaled, Edith let out another banshee-like shriek.

I frowned at Hannah. "Can't you stop her?"

Hannah studied Jesse, her lips dipping in the first frown I'd seen on her. "Probably not." She stepped over Edith and headed into the kitchen. "Where's Bonnie?" Real concern lined Hannah's voice.

Jesse blinked at me. "There's more of them?"

"Bonnie?" Hannah yanked open the back door.

"She's fine." I stepped toward the basement. "How do you get her to stop?" I pointed to Edith, hoping to distract Hannah.

"She's mad at you." Hannah bent over to check under the table.

Jesse cracked up. "Nice." He wandered to the kitchen and angled a chair so he could see the hallway, then settled down to watch.

I frowned as Hannah moved closer to the basement. I need to get Jesse out of the kitchen so I could bring Bonnie up from the creepy-like-a-horror-movie basement before Hannah gave her away.

Before I could do anything, Hannah yanked open the door to the stairs. I let out a garbled sound. She closed the door and glanced at me, then Jesse. At least she seemed to get it.

I stepped over Edith and squatted beside her.

"She's like a mini version of Morgan who screams louder," Jesse said, obviously amazed to find another girl as emotional as his cousin. But Morgan was nothing like Edith. I could calm Morgan down.

Hannah came around the table and stepped right on the spilled mess of arrowheads. She grabbed the chair but overbalanced, taking herself and the chair to the floor. Her squeal and the following crash cut off Edith's screams for a few seconds, but when I jumped over the younger girl to get to Hannah, Edith took up yelling again.

Jesse stood and peered at Hannah over the table. "Eh. I've seen better falls. Maybe a 6. Try squealing a little louder next time."

Hannah's lips twitched. I braced myself for tears, but instead she busted up laughing. She sat up and rubbed at her thigh and then her elbow. Her smile landed on Jesse. "Six? Is that some sort of injury-rating system?" She slid off her flip-flops to examine the bottom of her foot. "Do I get more points for bleeding?"

"Maybe." Jesse rounded the table to her. "But it has to be more than a couple drops."

I knelt by Hannah. Per the calculations of blood-damage points determined by Jesse, myself, and our brothers, she'd earned four more points. The arrowhead left a decent-sized cut and a modest amount of blood. I went to pull the first-aid kit off the top of the fridge.

"Does she need stitches?" Jesse asked. "That will put you in a whole new level. We'll have to start the scoring over again. Jordan has the record for the fifteen stitches he got trying to climb a tree with a pair of scissors."

Hannah's mouth fell open. "Really? Didn't anyone tell him that was a bad idea?"

"It's Jordan," Jesse said like everyone should know what he meant.

I grabbed a clean rag and wet it under the tap. "You don't tell Jordan not to do things. It makes him want to do it more." My brain skirted around Edith's wails. More than once, Jesse and I had resorted to this "ignore-the-screamer" tactic with our younger brothers. Usually they got bored and stopped screaming to figure out what we were up to.

I tossed the rag at Jesse, who caught it and dropped it on Hannah's halo of a hairdo. "Heads up," he said.

"Who's Jordan?" Hannah tugged the rag off her head and dabbed at the blood.

"My brother, or at least one of them." Jesse grabbed the kit from me, then crouched down and popped it open.

"How many brothers do you have?" Hannah asked.

"Five." Jesse's flippant tone made me sure he'd replied without thinking—without remembering Bryan.

"Wow." Hannah pulled away the rag. "Older or younger?"

"All younger." Jesse rummaged inside the kit, spilling out cotton balls and disposable gloves.

Hannah's foot had already stopped bleeding. But letting the girls play with sharp arrowheads definitely hadn't been a good idea.

Jesse dug out a bandage, opened it like he might for one of his little brothers, and waved it in Hannah's face. "You think you can handle the rest?"

She grabbed the bandage dangling under her nose and cocked her head at him, her smile growing even bigger. "Yeah. I've got it."

"Preston?" said a voice from the front door Jesse hadn't bothered to close.

Dread washed over me. Alex walked down the hallway and stopped at a still-screaming Edith, who renewed her hysterics with vigor. "What's going on?" His tone was only curious, but my whole body clamped up.

I backed away from Hannah. She was bleeding, Edith was screaming, and Bonnie was sitting in a pitch-black stairwell. When I opened my mouth, nothing came out. Guppy kid, all over again.

Alex rolled Edith over. "Eddie? What's wrong?"

She twisted away from him, screaming harder. She hadn't cried a single tear, but Alex might not have realized that.

"Preston. Is. Mean." Edith spit each word.

Alex's gaze traveled to me. Before I got the breath back in my lungs, Jesse stood between Alex and me, blocking my view. "If you're all done using Preston's babysitting service, we'll take off." Jesse stepped over the arrowheads, clamped a hand on my arm, and pushed me around the back of the table. "If you don't need anything . . ."

"Actually, I do need a little more help, if you don't mind." Alex lifted Edith in one arm and frowned at Hannah's foot. "What did you do?"

She grinned and waved the foot she'd finished bandaging. "I stepped on an arrowhead. Apparently, it only scored a 6, though."

"Ten." I muttered, then silently cursed the word that mattered least for coming out first. "The blood." Wow. I was on a roll.

Hannah grinned. "Nice. That's not bad, then."

Jesse released my arm and shook his head. "It's a 25-point system."

A snort exploded from Hannah. "What kind of system is that?"

Alex stepped closer and held a hand out to Jesse. "You must be Jesse. I'm Alex."

"Yeah," Jesse said stiffly. He cast a weirded-out expression at me.

Had Mom told Alex about Jesse? Or . . . wait. I had. The first day I met Alex. I'd told him how Jesse made fun of me for wanting to take art in junior high, and how I'd dropped the class instead of standing up for myself.

When Jesse didn't take the extended hand, Alex dropped it and asked, "Where's Bonnie?"

Silence met his question. Hannah's gaze slid up to Jesse at the same time mine did. I winced. *Subtle, Preston. Make it obvious that Jesse is the reason Bonnie won't come out of the stairwell.*

Alex followed our looks.

"What?" Jesse flung his hands up. "I don't even know what the girl looks like. She's been missing since I walked in."

"Oh." Alex shifted the whimpering Edith, nodding his head as if he understood everything. "Well, Sterling let me borrow a car. Convenient that he owns a towing company *and* a car rental place. Anyway, with the delay, I had to have the landlord open the house for the movers and then send them off without getting everything in the right rooms. I'm going to need some help moving stuff around, if you're up for it."

Jesse glanced at me. He hated helping people move. He would complain the whole time. If you wanted a good job done without complaining, you needed to get Bryan—

"Sure." The word blurted out of me as if in response to the unwelcome thought. I instantly regretted it.

Jesse rolled his eyes at me. "Fine. Whatever."

"Great." Alex pointed out the door. "Oh, your mail was falling out of the mailbox."

Pretty much everything in the house was falling apart, but I had tried to fix that mailbox. Unfortunately, my first attempt at welding hadn't looked so good and apparently hadn't worked so well.

"I was going to grab it when I heard Edith screaming." Alex patted Edith's back. "Maybe you and Jesse can help Edith pick it up and give me a few minutes to grab Bonnie before we head over to the rental house."

Edith's head popped up from Alex's shoulder. "I don't like Preston. He's mean."

Alex ruffled her hair and then passed her to me. Too stunned to do anything but take her into my arms, I let out a few garbled sounds.

"All right. I'll meet you out front." He stepped to the side, and my feet headed out the door.

Getting away from him lifted the crushing sensation from my chest. Jesse followed me down the front stairs with a stack of pancakes in his hand. He rolled them in a ball and shoved half in his mouth.

Edith stared at Jesse, the anger draining off her almost at once. "He ate all my pancakes."

I cocked my head, not sure if she was done screaming. It had ended as abruptly as it started. "Well, they were really good pancakes."

She grinned at me. "I'm good at cooking." She looped her arm around my neck and kissed my check. "Let's be friends again."

I went stiff. Edith wriggled out of my arms and took off to gather up junk ads a mysteriously absent wind must have blown around.

Jesse snorted around his mouthful of pancakes. Ignoring him, I stopped at the mailbox. The front door hung on one hinge, and the black dome of the box was dented and scratched. It took me two more seconds to realize the pounding I'd heard last night was more than Sammy hitting rocks like he'd claimed. He had broken the mailbox last time, too.

Jesse's left hand came down hard on my back. He licked the last crumbs off the fingers of his other hand. "You ain't scared of Alex, are you? He's just some city dude, ain't he?"

I shook off Jesse's hand and stalked over to dig through a bush with an envelope inside. The branches bit into my arm and left scratches over the skin. Jesse followed me, still talking. The sound faded when I saw the return address.

Arizona. My dad's address. I hadn't been to Troy's place in years, but I knew his address and scrawling script like I knew my own. He used to send letters once a month with the child-support checks. The checks that didn't cover nearly enough of the living expenses and didn't even touch Sammy's hospital bills. The ones that turned Mom's face gray and made her cry at night.

I hadn't seen a letter from Troy since last winter when he wrote to say he couldn't help with Sammy's most recent hospital bill, from the heart surgery. It seemed that letter meant Troy would also be unable to cover child support. Around that time, I realized I'd have to quit basketball in order to get enough hours at Carter's to really help out.

This envelope was bigger than the ones Troy sent checks in. It was one of those manila folders for mailing important documents.

"From your dad?" Jesse's voice broke through my thoughts.

I shoved the letter under a second envelope, probably a bill, then stood up to check on Edith. She danced around, scooping up ads.

"So, what's the deal?" Jesse asked. "How does Fancy Clothes know my name, but I didn't even know your mom was getting married?"

"I told you they were getting married."

"Yeah, but you also acted like it wasn't a sure thing."

"Well, now it is," I replied.

"And you didn't tell me?"

I shrugged.

"Does my mom know?"

"My mom kept it quiet at first. We didn't tell Sammy until two days ago. She might've told your mom. I don't know. She might not have wanted to bother her right now."

Jesse frowned at my veiled reference to Bryan. We hadn't even said his name to each other since Morgan left.

After Jesse thought for several seconds, his face cleared. "Oh, yeah, I remember now. He's the guy with the crazy-expensive painting Sammy ripped or something. The one that drove down every couple of weeks to take your mom out." Jesse stared at Edith, who'd dropped her stack of mail. She held a handful of something tiny she kept stooping to dig up. "So, he has lots of money or something?" Jesse asked me.

My whole body went still. I couldn't even draw in a breath. The letter cut into my sweaty palm, and a buzz filled my ears.

"It's not like your mom's one to marry some guy for money, right? She probably really likes him."

Sometimes Jesse didn't know when to stop.

"I guess that's good for your family," he went on. "Maybe you can play football this year after all." He finally looked at me, a half grin melting away. "Hey, I didn't mean anything by that."

I shook myself and headed for Edith. We didn't need Alex to pay for my family's bills. We took care of things fine on our own.

Five

By the time Jesse and I maneuvered Edith back toward the house, Alex had gotten Bonnie back into her own clothes, which were now clean and dry. We followed his rental car to the home in Kanab.

Jesse let out a whistle as we drove into the richer section of town and passed rows of new houses. Then he grunted as if he'd suddenly realized something. "You ain't movin', are you?"

I gripped the wheel tighter and turned right, trying to stay on Alex's tail. "Don't know."

Jesse fidgeted, his knee bouncing a couple times before he grabbed a tape measure from the top of the dashboard, unrolled it, and let it spring back with a zip. "Well, you don't need to, right? You could make things work at the house . . ." The tape measure snapped inward again and he sat there staring at it. "You can't move. Tell them you'll live with me."

I shook my head. "What about Sam?"

"He can come too."

"Even if your mom was willing to put up with that kind of stress, my mom wouldn't go for it. I can't come if Sammy can't. He's already worked up enough about the marriage and everything else." I didn't say Bryan. Why couldn't I say Bryan?

The truck bounced up a long drive to a two-story, narrow house with gray stucco siding, green grass, and two young trees as thin as golf clubs.

Jesse groaned. "Well, there goes the 'make-your-house-work' idea. This place is crazy nice." A scowl pinched his thick brows together. "That sucks." He got out of the truck and slammed the door.

I took a deep breath and said a prayer for help. I couldn't keep avoiding talking to Alex. The question "What room do you want this in?" played through my mind. Moving directions were all I needed in there. I got out and followed Jesse inside.

I stepped into an open, tiled entryway with vaulted ceilings. To the right, boxes and furniture, stacked edge to edge, filled a living room space. A hallway led deeper into the house.

Jesse flicked the closest box with the back of his hand. The tiny thump echoed off the vaulted ceiling. "Great. I'm still sore from football practice, you know. Coach is working us hard."

Leaving him staring at the boxes, I made my way farther in. It would've been nice if I'd been able to tackle more than just Sammy this morning.

Inside the kitchen at the end of the hall, the sleek silver appliances and white stone countertops reflected a bright glare of sunlight streaming through a wall filled with large windows. Bonnie stomped across an open area under a low-hanging, elaborate light fixture, and headed straight for a stairwell off the left side of the kitchen. Edith ducked into a cupboard under the kitchen island.

Someone moved behind me. I turned as Alex made his way down a second hallway that branched off to the left of the kitchen. "There are two bedrooms up here." He waved at the door closest to me. "I think I want Edith in that one. We can put the other girls in the downstairs rooms for now. Eventually I might move Bonnie up here as well, but that can wait until . . ." He came to a stop a foot or two from me as unspoken words died on his lips.

Glancing away from me, he pushed the door to Edith's room open. "Well, we'll see what happens, but let's do that for now." He surveyed the white-walled room and nodded.

For now. We were all tiptoeing around it, but Jesse was right. It made no sense for us to stay in Grandpa's old house. Alex seemed to already know that. Mom said we might not have to move, but maybe she'd said that to keep me from worrying, same as she'd kept things from Sammy.

"Can we get this over with?" Jesse said. "I sort of have plans later."

Alex smiled as if he hadn't noticed Jesse's impatient tone. "I need to run down and check out the light in the family room. This is the first time I've actually seen the place. Natalie thought the space down there might work for a studio." He circled Jesse and me, heading for the stairs Bonnie had disappeared down.

Jesse grumbled under his breath and trailed after him. We both stopped at the top of the stairs and stared down, waiting for Alex.

Jesse nudged me. "Fancy Clothes needs a studio?"

"He paints."

"You need a studio for that?"

I sighed. "Yes, if you paint for a living, it helps to have a place to do it in."

"Well, it can't be all that complicated, can it? Puttin' paint on a paper? The little boys do it at the kitchen table."

I shook my head.

From the foot of the stairs, Alex said, "I think this is going to work really well." He jogged up.

We got to work moving things out of the living room. The house's wide-open spaces shrank under the tide of stuff. Alex and I maneuvered an old double sofa down the stairs and settled it along one wall in the studio. Alex surveyed the room. A line of wrapped paintings half-buried the glass French doors that led to a small yard.

Bonnie came down the stairs with another paper-wrapped canvas and dropped it by the others before scurrying up the stairs. Alex moved in and bent over to carefully peel back the wrapper.

A mix of orange and purple paint formed a hazy sunset in what had to be Arches National Park. Human faces, a woman and a man, blended into the orange hues of the rock formations. They merged with the shapes and tones in a fluidness that made them almost part of the stone. Alex hummed to himself, checking the painting for damage before rewrapping it and coming out of his crouch.

He almost knocked into me. I stumbled back, not sure when I'd gotten closer. A hot flush burned over my neck as he blinked at me. I retreated another step, my eyes darting to the short-fibered carpet under my feet.

Alex moved away from me. The crinkle of paper sounded again. "Come see how this one turned out."

I lifted my head. He stood a few steps away, unwrapping a second, much-larger painting. This one had a thin forest with sunlight cutting sharp lines through the branches of aspen trees and striking against a pebbled bank and a white-foamed river. On a large boulder sat a teenage boy leaning back on his elbows, with one leg kicked out.

"You fixed it." The words rushed out of me, half breath, half sound.

I shifted closer again, searching for a sign of the ripped corner that'd plagued my dreams since May. Nothing remained of the damage. Close up, the brush strokes took on another level of texture. The light-yellow paint of the boy's hair rose from the canvas in short, staccato strokes that gave a rather accurate portrayal of curls that now seemed uncannily similar to Hannah's.

"I told you I could." Alex laughed, then stepped around me to set the canvas on an easel behind me.

"I thought you were saying that so I'd stop freaking out." I went around the easel to the back of the canvas. From that angle, I could see a thin patch running from one side to the other.

Alex's smile faded. "Have you been worrying about it this whole time?"

I shrugged off a rising discomfort. "It crossed my mind. Can you sell it like this?"

"Probably. It's got a really good story to go with it now. People like that. But I might end up keeping this one. I think Sammy would get a kick out of it if I hung it up somewhere."

A smile tugged at the side of my mouth. "Yeah."

"Hey!" Jesse appeared at the bottom of the stairs with three boxes stacked in his arms. "What's up with me doin' all the work?" He stomped toward us and dropped the boxes at Alex's feet. A scrawled script over the top box read "Studio." Before either of us responded, Jesse leaned in and frowned at the painting. "You paint this?"

Alex gave an amused smile. "Yes."

"Huh." Jesse's eyes darted to me. "I guess it's a mite bit better than Benji's latest snake drawing."

A strangled grunt wedged in my throat.

"Who's Benji?" Alex asked, unfazed.

"My two-year-old brother." A challenge hung in Jesse's voice. This time, he intended his comment to carry every inch of the implied insult, though if I knew Jesse it actually might have had less to do with Alex's career, and more to do with the idea of Sammy and me moving.

Jesse removed all doubt in his next breath, spinning to face Alex head on. "Sam and Preston have lived in their grandpa's house practically their whole lives. It was in Natalie's family a long time before that. You ain't plannin' on selling a family heirloom out from under them, are you?"

Alex's smile faded to a tense frown.

I reached for Jesse's arm. He shrugged me off and stepped toward Alex. "Well?"

Alex folded the wrapping from the painting in half and then in half again. He set it on top of the boxes Jesse had brought down. "We haven't made any decisions yet, but when we do, it will be a joint decision between Natalie and me. I'm not going to sell anything out from under anyone."

"And Preston and Sammy don't get any say?" Jesse's voice rose as if he was firing up for a battle.

I needed to speak before he said something worse.

Alex's eyes narrowed. "They do get a say, but we will all need to sacrifice a little. It's how families work."

"If you think this fancy house" —Jesse waved around the basement room with his hand— "is going to make your family work, you're wrong. Money ain't going to buy Preston and Sammy for you. It won't make them your kids." Jesse stormed toward the stairs. "Come on, Preston. He can move his own boxes."

A ringing in my ears made my movements sluggish and weak, like moving forward through water as I rounded the easel. I didn't know what to do. Alex's eyes shifted from the stairs to me.

"I—he—don't . . ." I faltered. *Great. Say something intelligent, something coherent.* I steeled myself. "Bryan . . ." The name spilled from my lips, a stain on the air.

Bryan. I hadn't said his name aloud to anyone in weeks. Now I'd vomited it up for Alex.

Alex's face softened. "It's okay, Preston. I understand."

I peeled my eyes from Alex toward Jesse's trail up the stairs.

"I'm good for now. Take Jesse home," Alex said, coming up beside me. His hand hesitated near my shoulder. I stiffened.

"Thanks for all your help today. You did great with the girls." The hand dropped without touching me.

I took a deep breath. "Between the crying, bleeding, and a dark basement, I think we got off to a rather bad start." I let myself glance at him.

Alex grinned. "I'd call it a good start. They aren't easy. You kept your cool, so thanks for that. We'll see you again for dinner. Okay?"

I nodded mutely and bolted for the front door. I drove half a block to catch up to Jesse, who had decided to start walking home rather than wait for me. The truck pulled up beside him, and he climbed inside without looking at me.

He slumped against the seat. "He's a jerk."

"Maybe we can make our house work. My mom's been saying we can."

Jesse snorted. "Yeah, right. It'd take a boatload of money to fix that place up. He's really that rich?"

I slammed on the brakes. "Jesse, shut up. Okay? My mom's not marrying him for money. That's stupid. She really likes him." Part of me knew that was true, but another didn't know what to do with the idea of Alex's money.

"Yeah, well, she liked your dad too, didn't she?"

My breaths smashed together, inhales and exhales caught in one painful clash. I almost kicked Jesse out the truck door. Instead, I accelerated again.

A vision skirted through my brain—Troy, a telephone in his hand, sucking up great gulps of air, trying to push a sound between shaking, drained gray lips. A sheen of sweat glistened on his forehead. Red rimmed his bloodshot eyes. He grabbed an open beer can and upended the contents into his mouth. The smell of yeast hung in his clothes, on his skin. I slid from his lap, the smell a twist in my gut. When a word came out into the mouth of the phone, it slurred. The scent of beer coated Troy's breath. He ended the call and slammed the phone down, then hunched over into the sofa. When I tried to climb back up, he pushed me away. "No, Preston, go find Aunt Jaclynn. The more you are with me, the worse you get. You are going to end up just like me."

~

When we got to my place, Jesse hopped in his truck and drove off in a cloud of red dirt. He'd get over it eventually.

Mom and Sammy got home around 6:00. Sammy smelled like dog from helping in the kennels. Mom sent him to shower and told me Alex wanted to meet in town for dinner. At a restaurant. I didn't do well with restaurants.

Mom dumped her purse on the counter, then grabbed the cordless landline phone and navigated though the vocal menu to access messages. It was the first thing she did every time she got home. I had a tendency not to answer the thing.

Sammy yelled that he couldn't get the shower to work.

She tucked the phone between her shoulder and ear. "Preston."

I headed for the bathroom.

Her voice followed me down the hall. "When you get it started, come back. We need to talk."

I grimaced. I didn't want to talk about the three-wheeler keys, or pretty much any of the other things she might have on her mind, including the fact that my best friend had yelled at her fiancé. I pushed open the bathroom door and grabbed the shower knob to coax it into working.

When I slid into a chair in the kitchen, I kept my eyes on the table, to the right of the mail stack. Mom closed a cupboard, putting away the rest of the dishes I'd washed after getting back from Alex's.

"Morgan left a message. She wants you to call her," Mom said. "Didn't she call yesterday too? I thought you were going to call her last night."

I shrugged again.

Mom stepped in front of me, blocking my view of the mail. She raised her brows, her green eyes latching onto me and narrowing. "Hmm. Does she know about the wedding yet?"

I shifted away from her. My head twitched a no. I might have only given the bare facts about Alex to Jesse, but at least I'd mentioned the guy to him.

Mom settled in the chair next to me, the one dead center in the direction I'd shifted to get away from her. We were face to face again. "You should tell her soon, Preston. Otherwise, she'll find out from one of the Powell boys. I think she'd like to hear about it from you."

"Yeah."

Mom frowned, her lips moving over unspoken words. She shook her head and sighed. "Thanks for helping Alex."

I raised my brows at her sudden change of topics.

"It's been a pretty crazy day for you, hasn't it?" She put her hand on my knee. "Are you okay? What happened this morning?"

I shook my head. Why did she have to go straight to the thing I least wanted to talk about?

"You need to give me the keys to the three-wheeler."

"No."

The silence hung for long seconds. It itched at me, but I couldn't take it back. I wouldn't.

"I know what happened with Bryan—"

"Don't." The word lay thin on my lips, hard.

"Preston." Mom sighed my name as if trying to blow out an ember she had accidentally ignited, but it only fanned something in me.

If she wouldn't keep Sammy off the three-wheeler, I would. I'd spent the better part of my life wondering when he was going to die. Would it be his heart or some other complication from the Down syndrome? One thing it wouldn't be—it wouldn't be from a crashing three-wheeler.

Mom leaned toward me, her narrow fingers looping around my forearm. "I don't want to fight with you."

"Then don't." I pulled my arm away.

We went quiet. The silence pricked at me. She reached for the mail.

"There's something from Troy." It blurted out, a bomb on the table between us.

Her lip almost curled up, but the smile didn't make it. "I wrote about Alex." She found the large envelope, frowned, and started to open it. She stopped mid-rip, lowered it to her lap, and met my eyes again.

"I was thinking about school. It's your senior year."

"Yep. All year."

She smiled for real. "I know it's late and practice has been going for a while already, but I think you should talk to the football coach and see if he will let you on the team."

My spine stiffened. I wanted football, but if I played, I couldn't work. "I have a job."

She put her hand on my knee again. "I want you to cut back on the hours. I never wanted you to give up sports like you did. You know that. I want you to play football your senior year."

Jesse's words earlier hit me like so many linemen. *"So he has lots of money or something? Maybe you can play football this year after all."*

"No."

Mom leaned back. "No?"

"No."

Four times. I'd told her no four times in one day.

She took a deep breath. "I get the thing with the keys. I'm willing to let that go until another day, but I'm not going to let this one go. There is no reason for you to miss football this year."

No reason except Sammy. He'd hung out with the team during practices last year for a few days but soon got bored and wanted to go home. When he started doing that, Bryan volunteered to stick around and hang out with him. But Bryan was gone.

Then there were the medical bills piling up that we couldn't pay. If I didn't help pay them, Alex might. My cutting hours at work would do nothing to refute Jesse's idea about Mom marrying Alex for his money.

"They've already finished two-a-days. It's too late." I grappled at the excuse. Missing the twice-a-day practices was a big deal. It was how the team got in shape for the season.

The water stopped in the shower.

Mom smiled at me. "I'm pretty sure they'll make an expectation. They are always searching for more players. Go talk to Coach Mendez Monday." As if it was settled.

But I wasn't going anywhere but Carter's Feed Store on Monday.

Six

We got to the diner on Main Street in Kanab by 7:00. The smell of gravy drew my attention past the crowd to a steaming plate of mashed potatoes on the nearest table. My stomach felt stuck to my backbone.

"It's him. I see him." Sammy pointed to a table in the center of the room, where Alex sat with the girls. "Look, she has wings." Sammy's voice rose until on "wings," several people stopped eating to stare.

Edith stood on her chair beside Alex in a swimsuit and a pair of fairy wings. "Hey!" She pointed at Sammy. "Is that the boy with down feathers? *He* likes my wings. Hey, boy with down feathers, come sit by me."

Alex's skin flushed to match the red on my own face. He tugged Edith down in her seat. A lady sitting between us and Alex's table smiled into her napkin.

Mom grabbed Sammy by the arm. I followed them to the table. I sank down into a chair. The hunger squeezing my gut had been driven out by the anxiety tearing around like a bull inside me.

Once Mom got Sammy seated, some of my nerves settled and another rule for engaging in social situations made its reflexive trip through my brain. *"Focus on the people and things nearest to you to keep yourself from becoming overwhelmed by crowds or other sensations."*

On my left, Bonnie sat slumped in her chair. She wore long gray sweats and a hoodie. Maybe the girl *wanted* heatstroke.

Across from me, Mom sat beside Alex. He leaned over and kissed her cheek. I jerked my eyes away as the bull resumed its rampage through my intestines. I focused on Hannah, sitting next to Mom on the edge of her seat, her backpack still over her shoulders, and then Sammy, between Edith and me.

A curvy girl from the cheer team bubbled up to stand beside me, a pen and notebook in one hand. A smile flashed over her pink lips. "Hi, Preston. I can't believe summer's almost over. Are you playing football this year?"

I opened my mouth, but nothing came out. I'd talked to her before, after a game, but I couldn't for the life of me get a sound through my teeth. I couldn't remember her name, or anything except Jesse nudging me as we walked off the field last year. "She's cute, huh?" he'd said. "You like her? I saw you lookin' at her earlier."

Now a scorch of fire ran up my neck to my face. I shook my head at her.

"Hi, Lauren!" Sammy jumped in, taking her attention from me. His voice became a babble of sound in the background, blabbing all about Alex, Mom, and the girls soon to be our stepsisters.

The waitress's name was Lauren.

Hannah wagged her eyebrows at me, her eyes traveling to something in front of me. I dropped my eyes at the same moment as a rhythmic scratching noise registered through Sammy's chatter. I held my metal fork clenched in my palm, dragging it up and down the maroon tablecloth as if trying to shred the fabric. I dropped the fork and stared at my water glass.

Lauren began taking everyone's orders.

What is wrong with me? My anxiety hadn't been this bad in years. I might as well be twelve again, hyperventilating in front of half the class because Melody Crawford asked me to her birthday party, and I thought someone might make me go.

Lauren smiled at me. "What do you want, Preston?"

Before the fear morphed into something out of my control, I grabbed the menu, flipped it open, and pointed to the first thing in the dinner section. I didn't even read it. I couldn't focus on anything but the sound of the pencil scratching on the order pad.

"The chicken-fried steak?" Lauren asked.

I nodded.

"Okay. Salad or soup?"

Urgh. I rolled my shoulders and forced a word out of my mouth. "Salad."

"Dressing?"

I was ready for that one. "Ranch."

"And what side?"

I hadn't even read the sides. I leaned over the menu, my heart beating hard enough it seemed to drum through my chest against the edge of the table.

Mom saved me. "I liked the mashed potatoes when I had them before. I think you will too. Is that okay?"

I nodded, the heat on my skin ready to burn me to ash. *Stupid, stupid.* My fingers clenched at the tablecloth.

"The potatoes are great—you'll like them." Lauren scratched some more on her pad before moving on to Bonnie.

When Lauren left, Mom leveled her frown on me. I froze and grasped at the ice water near my spoon, avoiding the deepening pinch of her brow. "You *are* going to football Monday," she told me.

I choked on the water, Lauren's question blinking through my mind. *"Are you playing football this year?"* I'd shaken my head no. Lowering the glass, I counted breaths again. Five counts in, five out.

"What about football?" Alex asked.

"I want Preston to play this year, but he's being stubborn." Mom looked at me again. "I don't get it. You like football. You love it."

"I love football too," Sammy put in. "I'll come and help out like last year. You know, like on the sidelines and stuff. It'll be great."

"You got bored half the time last year before practice ended. I can't babysit you and practice." *Wow, I just said two full sentences.*

Sammy scowled at me. "I don't need to be babysat."

"Is that what you're worried about?" Mom paused, then said in a quieter voice, "That Bryan won't be there to distract Sammy this year?"

Sammy slammed his hands on the table and yelled with unusual clarity, "Bryan wasn't babysitting me. We were friends. He was my best friend."

A riptide slammed my guts against my lungs, snagging all my air before it could get free. The taste of vomit spread over my tongue as a soundless gag squeezed my body tight. I shoved back from the table and staggered out the door. The air hit me with a wave of heat, right down my throat into my heaving chest. I blinked at the light and weaved around the building to the rear parking lot where we left Mom's car. It was locked. I slid down the side of the car and leaned against it, staring at the brick wall of Joanie's Hair Salon and Tanning Bed.

Anger swelled up as I held my trembling hands in front of me. I shoved them to the pavement. Tiny rocks bit into my palms.

Why was I reverting like this? This summer I'd done crazy stuff. I danced with Morgan. I told Melody off for being a jerk because she wouldn't stop following me around even after I skipped her birthday party. I led the youth group in our ward. I planned stuff for Scouts. I worked the cash register at the feed store. I talked to the bishop about serving a mission.

Mom waited ten minutes before coming for me. She appeared around the car and crouched down in front of me. "Preston? I'm sorry. I shouldn't have brought that up in there."

I shook my head.

The gravel crunched under her feet as she shifted. "I guess I thought we had worked through all of it earlier. You playing football is really important to me. I never wanted you to give it up."

I stared at a spray of broken glass in a corner of the parking lot.

Mom lowered herself to the pavement beside me. After a drawn-out silence, she said, "I'm worried, Preston. You've been through a lot trying to manage things with your dad. A stepdad hits awfully close to all that. All this on top of Bryan . . . I know it's hard."

I pushed her words away. I wasn't backsliding. I *couldn't* be. "I'm fine, Mom. I just don't like restaurants. You know that."

She took a deep breath. "No one expects you to be fine right now. Bryan was your friend, too. That and the marriage—Alex and the girls—

it's all crazy, overwhelming, and complicated. It's so important to find a healthy way to deal with all of it. I don't want you to bury it the way you did with your dad. Please talk to me, and if you can't talk to me, let's find someone you can talk to. A counselor at the school, or we can try a professional therapist. Alex has done that for his girls and says it really helped. He's already looking for a new therapist for them down here."

My hands rolled into tight fists against my sides. "I'm not going to fall apart, Mom. I'm trying to process it all. Once I get used to everything, it will be fine."

She ran her fingers through her dark curls, closed her eyes, and sighed. "Football will help."

Football would help. I craved the whole-body workout that football gave me. My mind cleared to focus on the game and nothing else, pounding everything into the turf under my cleats.

But . . .

"I never intended for you to take Sammy with you to practice," Mom said. "Alex says he'll watch him when I can't. Sammy is really excited about spending more time with Alex and the girls. I think it will be a good thing for him."

Alex. I didn't want him to take responsibility for Sammy any more than I wanted him to pay the bills.

"Mom, I'm not going to do football," I told her.

She shook her head at me. "At least go Monday and see what the coach says. You can do that much. Right?"

I didn't move.

She sighed again. "Come inside and eat dinner."

"Nah. I'm not really hungry." My stomach growled a protest at the lie, but I'd fast all night if it meant not going inside the restaurant.

Standing, Mom crossed her arms. "Preston Troy Bensen, you either come inside now, or I'm calling the school counselor first thing on Monday."

I rolled my eyes at her. "I'm fine, Mom. It's been a long day."

"Prove you're fine. Come in and eat dinner with us." A dangerous cast darkened her green eyes, burrowing into me with her warning. She would find me a counselor. Maybe even send me to a therapist.

I dragged my feet under me and stood.

She slid her arm around my waist and hugged me to her side. "It's going to be all right. I know it's hard right now, but things are going to work out."

Mom released me and we walked back to the restaurant.

As I reached to open the door, Alex and the others streamed outside. He handed me a bag of to-go-boxes that smelled like fried chicken, looped his arm around Mom, and pulled her toward the parking lot. He carried a second bag of to-go boxes in his free arm. "The kids want to go to the house. Sammy's going to show Edith his motorcycle collection."

Relief rushed over me. Lauren waved from inside the restaurant near the cash register. I waved back, managing a sort of smile before I let the door swing shut again. I trailed after the others. Edith skipped beside Sammy, her fingers looped through his.

~

Alex and the girls showed up at our ward for church. If anyone in Karlon hadn't heard about Mom's engagement yet, they would now. I slouched into the bench and tried to ignore the stares prickling against my shoulders.

After sacrament meeting, Jesse met me in the hallway with "Hey, I'm supposed to tell you to call Morgan." He lingered near the glass doors of the entryway, frowning as he gazed out at the parking lot.

A new worry rose in me. "Did you tell her about the wedding?"

"Yeah. Girls are weird. She's all worked up about it. Kept asking why you didn't tell her. I mean, you hardly told me, what'd she expect? It's not like she's your girlfriend." Jesse snorted. "As if . . ."

I took a breath, hoping he didn't notice my burning face. Morgan and I weren't together—not like that—but talking to her, being with her, was comfortable in a way I'd never felt around a girl before.

Jesse inched to the doors. "Well, call her anyway. You know how she gets." The push bar on the door clicked as he backed through.

"Where are you going? We have class." I jerked my thumb down the hallway towards our Sunday school classroom.

"Nah. See ya around."

～

Mom had meetings with the stake Young Women's presidency after church. That left Sammy and me to fend for ourselves for lunch. Since I still hadn't mentioned the lack of food in the kitchen, our options were limited. Normally, I didn't have to say anything about getting groceries. Now, with Mom so busy, I didn't know how to bring it up without implicating myself in the shopping process.

We ate ramen noodles. Sammy cleaned his bowl and disappeared into the living room to play video games. I plowed through the rest of the dishes and skipped wiping off the table. Three hours of mandatory socializing had left my body in overdrive. Shutting my bedroom door acted like a muffler, quieting the chaos in my head and dulling the adrenaline rushing through my body.

I grabbed a book off my nightstand and dropped onto the bed. I opened the book, but the words on the page didn't register. The drawing pad Alex gave me at the fair hovered in my side vision, hanging out of the shelf under the nightstand.

I pulled it free. A pencil spilled out behind it to bounce across the worn carpet. After snagging the pencil off the floor, I scooted to the headboard, flipped open the drawing pad, and found a clean page. I'd nearly filled the whole book. I liked drawing. It felt good. Even after Alex started dating Mom, that hadn't changed. When the school told me I had an extra elective this fall, I'd chosen beginning art. I'd always been a little bothered I'd let Jesse talk me out of it before.

I scratched a line across the paper, then another. The dashboard and windshield of Old Blue appeared. I threw my attention into the details: the dial knobs of the radio, the chipped air vents, and the coin tray filled with interesting rocks Sammy found. I lifted the pencil and studied the empty paper through the windshield, but couldn't quite decide what to draw outside the cab.

The phone rang. I rolled off the bed and sprang upright. The pad fell to the ground. Sammy's thundering run to the kitchen rattled the walls. I willed him not to answer.

The ringing cut off.

"Hello?" he shouted. "Morgan?"

I dropped on the edge of the bed. Sammy quieted down, his voice flowing in a muted current from the kitchen. My fingers tightened around the pencil. Minutes passed without me moving—one, three, five.

Bang.

My body flinched.

Sammy beat his fist against the door again. "Morgan wants to talk to you!"

I forced my feet under me, dragged them to the door, and opened it an inch or two.

"It's Morgan!" My brother shouldered the door the rest of the way open and shoved the phone at my face.

My hands stayed limp at my sides.

He waved the phone harder. "Here."

I took it, if only to protect my face. It rose to my ear. "Hi." The word slogged out, thick and clumsy.

Morgan's voice surged from the phone. "Preston. What on earth? Why haven't you been returning my calls?"

I couldn't think to say a single word.

"I've called like five times!"

When I still didn't speak, she waited. I fought the rising uptick of my pulse, slowing my breaths and trying to think through the rush in my ears. *"I'm sorry." Say "I'm sorry."* Sammy wandered down the hall, leaving me to my inner battle.

Morgan broke the silence, her anger replaced with worry. "Are you okay?"

"I'm sorry," I said finally, way too late. I slammed my palm against my forehead and clenched my teeth.

"It's okay. I was just worried. Jesse told me your mom's getting married." Morgan sighed. "Why didn't you tell me? We're friends. You tell friends stuff like that."

I clicked the door closed behind me and leaned against it.

"Do you like him? Is he okay with Sammy?" Morgan asked, then stumbled with embarrassment. "I mean, I guess that was a strange thing to ask—"

"He's fine with Sam," I cut in. "The guy my mom is marrying— he's fine."

"Oh, good."

Neither of us said anything for a while. I rolled the pencil in my fingers.

"Uh, Preston?" Morgan said finally. "Did I upset you? Is that why you stopped answering my calls and didn't tell me about the engagement? Are you mad?"

"No." I paced the floor from the door to the nightstand, stepping over the drawing pad without slowing my stride. "I was going to tell you. I just . . . I made it weird and didn't know how to fix it." I stopped, my breath rushing in and out like I was running a marathon. "Can we talk about something else?"

Morgan paused. "Sure. Uh. So, school starts on Wednesday, right?" She perked up. "Jesse was talking about a football game next weekend. I forgot to ask him. Are you playing?"

I dropped into the chair by my desk and planted my head against my palm. "I think that's the second-to-last thing I want to talk about."

She laughed. "Sorry. I take it you won't get to play, then?"

"My mom wants me to play. She won't stop bringing it up."

"So?" Morgan drew out the word.

"So, I can't. We can't let him take care of all Sam's bills, can we? I need to keep working." The anger in my voice surprised me. I straightened in the chair and frowned at the poster of last year's football team over the desk.

"By 'him' you mean your new stepdad?"

"Yeah. Alex."

"Hmm." I almost could see Morgan's left brow quirk and her lips lift in doubt. "Does Alex know about Sammy's medical bills?"

"Yeah."

"Does he know your mom wants you to play football?"

"Yeah. He said he'll watch Sam."

"I guess I don't understand." Morgan's tone was expectant now, like she was waiting to drop the final line of a joke.

"What don't you understand?" Now I'd gone defensive.

"Your mom said you can play, your stepdad knows about the bills and is trying to help by watching Sammy, and if I remember right, you told me if you could play football, there wasn't a chance you'd let it pass."

Having my own words repeated to me brought me up short. Only a few months ago, I'd said them to Morgan. I'd meant them then. I couldn't understand why she wouldn't join the track team when she loved running so much. I'd been getting up every day knowing I'd soon be missing summer practice, two-a-days and football camps.

I sank in my chair and pushed my feet under the desk.

"Do football, Preston," Morgan said softly. "You'll regret it later if you don't."

"Maybe."

"You can pick up the hours at work when the season ends. If football is at all like running is to me, you're going to need it over the next few months."

I wasn't sure I'd ever loved football the way Morgan loved running. Once you saw her on the track, you realized you'd only ever seen her half-alive before. Running was the real her, exploded outward, nothing held back, the piece of her you didn't know was missing. Football was something solid underneath me. A place where life made sense. I craved that, maybe not the way she craved running, but strong enough to make me waver.

"I'll think about it," I said finally.

Morgan laughed. "Okay. That's a start."

Seven

Monday morning, I drove Sam to Alex's house. He disappeared inside before I got to the front porch. Bonnie stood in the doorway holding a fork. "Do you like omelets, Preston?"

The smell of eggs and onions curled around me until I moved forward like some cartoon drawing dragged inside by a wispy smell hooked under my nose. The oatmeal I'd eaten from cold storage that morning hadn't filled me up. I stopped at the kitchen table.

"You can have that one." Bonnie pointed at a plate of still-steaming omelet. Cheese oozed out one side. She sank into a seat and dug into her own plate of egg, cheese, and bacon—all the parts of an omelet in separate piles. "Dad's making more," she informed me. "After he gets Edith dressed. Eat that one."

I sat in the chair. Bonnie beamed at me. I'd never seen her smile. It made her almost look pleasant. *Weird.* I shook my head, cut into the omelet, and took a bite.

Suddenly Hannah dropped between us, her forearms braced on the tabletop. She rotated her head, her glasses sliding down her nose, and grinned at me. "What? I slip out for five seconds to comb my hair, and Bonnie gives away my breakfast?"

I choked, the fork clattering from my hand to the table. Hannah pounded her hand against my back, and I shifted away from her.

She laughed easily. "Don't worry. I didn't eat any of it yet." She handed me the fork and moved to sit on the other side of me.

Alex walked in and slid Edith into the chair next to Hannah. "Morning, Preston. Where's Sammy?"

"Downstairs," Bonnie said around a bite of eggs.

I'd let Sammy go downstairs! Alex's paintings . . . I jumped to my feet, but Alex caught my arm across the table. "Whoa, it's okay. Everything is put away. I've got Edith around, remember?"

I stopped moving, but the blood rushing double time through my veins took a little longer to slow down. Alex released my arm. I reversed a step, hit the chair with the back of my legs, and sat. Humming, Alex wandered to the stove and poured a bowl of eggs into the skillet.

I gulped down the rest of my omelet. After slipping downstairs to tell Sammy goodbye, I speed-walked to the front door. A strange tightening ran through my chest and froze my hand to the doorknob. A flash of fear pulsed near my forehead.

You can't leave Sammy. Something could happen to him.

I tried to shake the thought away, but it seemed stuck in my brain. *He'll be fine,* I told myself.

The day Bryan died, I'd let Sammy go riding with him and Morgan. If I'd been with them, maybe I would have noticed the washed-out trail. And maybe I could have . . .

No, I couldn't think like that.

Heavenly Father, help me calm down. Instead of the peace I expected after my silent prayer, the rush of anxiety swelled up in me, growing with each breath.

"Preston?"

My hand jerked, yanking the door toward me. I swayed back so it wouldn't hit me and caught it before it slammed into the wall.

"Hey, I was wondering what I could do to help with dinner tonight," Alex said behind me.

Dinner? I turned to blink at him.

"Did your mom tell you we are coming for dinner and family home evening tonight? We talked about a family meeting. She wanted to take care of dinner this time. I'm wondering if the girls and I can help out."

Great. Another evening with them. Mom had been in a hurry this morning. She'd gotten a call about a sick horse and wanted to see what the vet said.

When my only response was a shrug, Alex went on, "Okay. I'll text her. I thought you might have a better idea of what she might need. I get the impression she's been running from one thing to another all weekend. I thought I could help."

Mom probably could use help, but even if I was willing to let Alex do the helping, I doubted I'd be able to get the words out. They were jammed in my throat, wedged against one another like some old-school Tetris game.

Alex sighed as he watched me, frustration lining his brow. Frustration with me. I hadn't said anything to him this morning. "Okay, well, I'll let you go. Don't worry about Sam. He'll be fine."

I hurried out before he asked any more questions that required answers.

I slid into the truck and dropped my forehead on the steering wheel. I needed to go if I wanted to be on time for work, but I had to change into jeans. I'd worn basketball shorts to keep Mom from getting suspicious. It was stupid, really. If I didn't go to football, she'd find out soon enough. I drummed my knee and sucked in hard as the guilt knotted through me.

"Do football. You'll regret it if you don't."

I frowned at Alex's too-nice house.

An urge to hit something flowed into my arms. I tightened my hands in fists. Maybe football was the only place I could really blow everything off, before it erupted into something else. If I wanted Mom to believe I was fine, I had to find a way to deal with my anxiety. I had to talk to Alex. I had to go to football.

Adrenaline flooded through me with a flash of clarity. I had to ask Mr. Carter to give me the morning off. I started up Old Blue and peeled out in the direction of the feed store.

~

The glass door swung shut with the rattle of bells as I stopped behind Mr. Carter in the store's entryway. He stood at the notice board, removing the advertisement for baby rabbits. A new poster about free puppies had taken up residence next to it over the weekend. My boss turned, the start of a smile fading as he looked me up and down. "Are you making a statement about the work uniform, or are you out of clean jeans?"

I brushed a hand over the side of my basketball shorts. "No. I—" I dropped my eyes to the concrete floor. "My mom wants me to do football."

Mr. Carter chuckled. "You've missed practices all summer, haven't you?"

I shrugged. "I still might be able to get on the team."

"'Course you can. It's a bad precedent, but they need all the help they can get, don't they? What time is practice?"

"Now." I swallowed and forced myself to look up again. Mr. Carter raised his brows at me. "But I don't have to go today," I rushed to add. "I can stay until I find someone else to take my shift."

He shook his head. "Sort of short notice, ain't it?"

"Yeah . . ." I would have called him Sunday if I'd made up my mind earlier.

"Huh. Well, I can manage today without you. I guess we can work things out for the rest of the season, too." He clicked his tongue and walked over to the checkout counter. "You're a good employee. I'd like to figure out a way to keep you on the payroll until you have more time, even if it's once or twice a month until school gets out again. Did that for some other kids before, you know."

"I can work more after football ends."

My boss wagged his wiry gray brows. "We'll see. I hear your mom's getting married. That'll be a lot to juggle on top of school and sports. I just wanted you to know I'll work with you."

At least there was that. "Thanks."

"All right. Get going or you'll be late."

Coach Mendez had the team on the field when I arrived. A short man with sun-wrinkled skin and a muscular build, he shouted directions in a Spanish/English mix. Sweat had already beaded around his forehead when I wandered over from the parking lot.

The coach's eyes about bugged out of his head when he saw me. "Preston Bensen?"

I took a deep breath and stepped up to him. "I found out I can play. I know I missed two-a-days—"

Coach Mendez clamped a hand on my bicep and yanked me toward our defensive-line coach. "Johnny! Get Preston some gear. He's playin' this year after all."

Several guys let out cheers. Soon, I was in pads and a helmet and more than making up for being late.

In the middle of practice, the coach pulled me aside and shoved a water bottle into my hand. "Take it easy, Preston. You haven't been training out here like the rest of us. You aren't used to the heat yet."

I drank the water and said, "I'm fine. I've been doing lots of heavy lifting at Carter's."

He shook his head and pushed me toward the stands. "Sit out for five minutes. Cool down a bit." He scooped up a notebook. "You can go over the plays." I sat. Coach flipped open the book. "Hey, so . . . a few things. Remember your job is more than blocking out there. It don't do us much good if all you do is keep the guys from getting to the quarterback. You need to make passing lanes so we can get the football down the field."

"Sure."

He grinned at me. "You were good at that last year. We'll get you back in the swing of things." He tapped the playbook. "Study up."

The coach left me sitting there. For the first time since Saturday morning, my head didn't swarm with worry. A calmness settled in its place. Relieved to finally have a grip on my anxiety, I drank more water and looked through the playbook.

At the end of practice, Jesse caught up to me at my truck, his brown hair darkened with sweat. "Hey, Preston, you find out about the house yet?"

"No. They want to have some sort of family meeting tonight, though, so maybe they'll decide then."

Jesse leaned against Old Blue. "How can you be so chill about moving? Don't you care?"

"I'll still be in Kanab. It's not like we'll be moving across the state," I said as casually as possible. I didn't like the idea at all, but even if I fought Mom and Alex on moving, it'd be ten times worse trying to fit all of us in Grandpa's old house.

Jesse frowned. "It won't be the same. You won't be able to walk over whenever you want."

"I haven't walked to your house in years." I started driving over the minute we got the three-wheeler going. Since then it had been that or the truck.

Jesse shoved off Old Blue. "Fine. Whatever. But if you rethink any of that, you can still come live with us. It's only a year till you graduate. Maybe it will be a good way to transition Sammy to the idea of you going on a mission."

Before Jesse finished, I'd already started shaking my head. When he got to the mission part, though, my head stopped midshake. I'd been leaning toward going on a mission. I'd told Jesse I was going. Bishop Larkson had been talking to me about it for a year and had almost smoothed out all my worries. Money? *The Lord will provide.* Leaving Mom on her own? *She's stronger than you think. It will be hard, but she will be blessed.* Leaving Sam? *He's pretty strong too. You need to set an example for him. He'll understand.* Not being good at talking to people? *You've come a long way in the last few years. I am confident you will do fine.*

Check, check, check, check.

That was before Bryan died. I'd yet to drop that one on Bishop Larkson: "What if Sammy does something stupid and gets himself killed while I'm gone?"

I was sure there was a simple, gospel-grown answer for that too, but I didn't want to hear it right now. Something simple would never cover the gaping panic I felt thinking about Sammy dying in an accident I might have prevented if I'd been around.

Then there was the more complicated part, the part where talking to people had actually gotten worse. What kind of missionary would I be if I couldn't even speak?

"You ain't goin' on a mission, are you?" Jesse said.

"I don't know yet."

"Fine. But you aren't seriously planning on living with your mom forever. What about school? College? A job? You're going to have to leave home eventually."

"I know. I just need to make sure things go okay with Sammy and Mom and the new family."

Jesse snorted. "'Cause Alex is dangerous somehow?"

I yanked open the truck door. "Because it might fall apart, and I don't want Mom alone if that happens."

Jesse stepped in front of me, blocking the front seat with this lanky body. "You think it's about his money too, don't you? You think he'll figure it out and take off."

I met Jesse's glare. "Stop saying that." A sharpness edged my voice. "My mom isn't marrying him for his money. I just can't make plans for the future until I know for sure where they're going to be."

Jesse's brown eyes darkened. "You're being stupid. Now's the time to start putting in the distance. It'll only be worse if you don't. That's my plan."

I took an involuntary step back. "You're planning to distance yourself from your family?"

He looked away. "I guess so."

"So they'll be more prepared when you go on a mission?"

"Well, I never said I was going on a mission, did I? That was you. You were supposed to go." Jesse pushed around me and stomped across the parking lot.

Eight

Mom got home late. She dumped her purse on the counter and rushed by me as she picked up Sammy's shoes. "Hi, Preston. Did football go all right?"

"Yeah." I followed her down the hallway.

"Oh good." She tossed the shoes in Sammy's bedroom and leaned in the bathroom door. "Ugh." She grabbed Sam's and my toothbrushes off the toothpaste-smeared sink. "Washrag . . . washrag . . . hmm." She poked around under the sink and then pushed by me to speed down the hallway again.

I grabbed my razor off the counter and took it to my room before she mentioned my leaving it out. Next I found her in the kitchen, a pile of towels under one arm, shoving the mail—and our toothbrushes—into the junk drawer.

"Mom?" I opened the drawer and grabbed the toothbrushes.

She laughed a short, almost manic laugh and bustled toward the living room. "Oops."

I stared after her. Since when did Mom do stuff like put toothbrushes in the junk drawer? I took the toothbrushes to the bathroom. After splashing water around the sink to rinse away the toothpaste, I went to the living room.

Sammy was playing a video game. Mom climbed over and around him, picking up the extra controllers, remotes, and games he'd left strewn around. She still carried a bundle of towels under her other arm. "I forget how bad this place looks until I have to have someone actually come inside." She ran her hand over a break in the plaster on the wall behind her rocking chair, as if trying to smooth the twenty-year-old scar into the wall again. "I haven't even figured out dinner." Mom pulled out her phone. "I'll text Alex that I'm running late." She dropped the pile of towels and ran for the kitchen.

I picked up the towels and followed. They seemed clean, but I dumped them in the laundry room just in case. When I came out, Mom stood at the fridge with a bottle of mustard, staring at the yellowing insides of the empty shelves.

"Mom? You aren't planning on feeding them mustard as a main course, right?"

Another strained and manic laugh slipped out. She shoved the mustard back in the fridge. "I could make a sauce or something. To go over the chicken."

"What chicken?"

"The chicken we got Saturday night . . ." She whirled toward me, her mouth open. "When we didn't go shopping after dinner because Sammy wanted to show Edith his motorcycles."

I should have mentioned it. I'd thought she knew, but now that I considered it, she hadn't been home much all weekend. Apparently, she hadn't taken stock of the pantry in more than a day. "I thought you stopped at the store and that's why you were late."

"Oh no." She shoved by me and dug her wallet out of her purse. "You have to run to the store. We need chicken." She shoved a twenty in my hand and spun away to yank open the cupboards, the fridge, and the freezer. "Preston, what have you and Sammy been eating?"

"Oatmeal and ramen."

She whacked my arm with the back of her hand. "Why didn't you say something?"

"I thought you knew."

"You went to football on nothing but oatmeal and ramen? Did you eat that for lunch too?" She slammed each cupboard door closed with a thump. When I didn't answer right away, she swung toward me. "You did eat lunch?"

"Alex fed us before we came home. He gave us omelets this morning, too—when I dropped Sam off." I didn't want to admit to eating Alex's food, but she looked like she was about to break down over the thought of Sammy and me not eating well. I should have said something. After all my worry about being sent to do the shopping, I'd only made it certain she'd have to send me.

She deflated, her shoulders slumping and her head sagging forward. "Does Alex know we don't have food here?"

I looked away. "I didn't say anything." She cared more about the impression we made on Alex than I realized.

"He was in the house on Saturday. Did he get into the cupboards or something?"

I shook my head but paused. I'd been outside with Jesse for a while, and Alex had come back that night, too. "Maybe. I don't know. Sammy might have said something." My stomach rolled over. *Alex was feeding me out of pity?*

Mom raced to the living room. "Sam, Sammy, look at me." He pried his eyes away from the video game. "Did you talk to Alex about us not getting to the store for food yet?"

"No," Sammy said.

Mom breathed out. "Thank goodness."

The memory of Alex standing in front of me that morning shot through my mind. *"Can I help with dinner?"* He knew, I was sure of it, but I wasn't about to tell Mom now.

I followed her down the hall. "I'm so scattered lately," she muttered. "He might've thought we didn't have money for food. Honestly." She glared at me. "Oatmeal and ramen?"

She dug two fifties out of her purse. "If we are out of food, tell me. Don't just eat ramen and oatmeal." She shoved the money into my hand. "Buy enough food to make this place look like we aren't starving. Hurry. But don't get in a wreck."

She glanced up at the water-stained ceiling and around the walls of the dingy kitchen. "Oh my goodness. What am I doing?" she moaned. "This place is falling apart around us. No wonder people are saying I'm a gold digger. He's going to think the same thing."

"What?" I folded the money into one hand and reached for her shoulder. "People are sayin' that to you?"

She blinked at me like she'd forgotten I was there. "No. Yes. Maybe. I overheard something today. Oh, Preston. I wasn't going to say that in front of you. It's been a long day. It's okay. It will pass. People are stupid."

People like Jesse, and maybe me, but the question popped out before I could stop it. "Why are you marrying Alex?"

She froze, staring at me. The calm before the storm. Then she swept at me in a flurry. "Preston Troy Bensen, do you honestly think I would marry someone for money?" Her phone chimed a text notification behind her, but she didn't stop. "I get it from other people, but my own son?"

I caught her jabbing finger in my hands, the money pressed between her hand and mine. "Mom?"

She let out a sudden breath. Tears spilled from her eyes.

Mom cried occasionally. There were three main triggers. Spiritual stuff, getting stressed out about something, and receiving letters from Troy. I let God deal with her spiritual crying. With the stressed-out stuff, I usually hugged her and told her we'd be fine. If that didn't work, I broke out the ice cream. She always laughed when I handed her the carton and a spoon. The Troy stuff? I didn't really know what to do about that. She didn't cry in front of me when he wrote. She hid in her room, but some things were hard to hide in a house this small.

I wasn't sure if this was a purely stressed-out cry or if she was mad at me. Maybe I triggered a cry more like the kind Troy triggered. The thought didn't sit well. She'd seemed so chill with Alex taking over everything, but apparently she knew exactly how her marrying a man with lots of money looked, and it bothered her. I hesitated, not sure if a hug would help.

Footsteps sounded down the hall. Alex walked in, humming. I hadn't heard a knock. Sammy must have opened the door.

Mom took one look at him and collapsed to the floor in a sobbing mess. I'd never seen her do that. Alex dropped the groceries he'd been carrying and crossed the room in three strides to crouch over her.

"Natalie?" Alex gathered my mom to his chest, his hand caressing her hair.

I slid along the wall, my only coherent thought to get to my room before I saw more of Alex touching my mom.

"Preston, wait, will you?" Alex's soft voice sent a streak of guilt down my spine and slammed into my feet, pinning me in place.

I turned just as he went to his knees and pulled Mom closer. "What happened to her?" he asked me.

It was all sorts of messed up. I was supposed to be protecting her from him, but there he was rocking her on the floor, while I'd done the hurting.

His eyes widened as if he read the answer on my face. My breath dried as it slid down my throat, stalling in the intake.

"Did you . . ." He stuttered to a halt, shaking his head first at me and then Mom as if he couldn't quite believe I'd hurt her.

"It's not him. It's me. I'm a mess." Mom pulled away and rubbed at her eyes. "I didn't want you to see . . . I overheard this lady at work . . . He's been eating oatmeal and ramen." At this she stopped crying long enough to glare at me. "You can't live on oatmeal and ramen."

My body uncoiled. She was only stressed. I hadn't broken anything unfixable.

She wiped her tears, but they kept coming. "Oh, I'm such a mess. I knew it was a bad idea to keep going like I've been. I've needed a good cry for weeks, and now—boom, I'm ruining everything."

I couldn't hug her. Alex was doing that, and we didn't have any ice cream. Except . . .

I glanced at the grocery sacks in the doorway.

Mom saw the bags at the same moment. "You knew!" She hit Alex's arms away. "You knew there was no food in the house."

"I noticed Saturday," he admitted. "I started thinking about everything you'd been doing this weekend. When you texted earlier that you were still at work, I realized you didn't have time to go shopping, so the girls and I stopped and got some groceries. Is that okay?"

Mom sniffled, the tears slowing down. "You didn't think we were all starving, and I was marrying you to get your money?"

Her words were abrupt and honest in a way I'd been afraid to admit aloud. I'd never really doubted her motives in marrying Alex. I just hated how other people would see it and, ultimately, how he would see it if we kept expecting him to pay our bills.

Alex laughed. "No. I thought you were too busy to get to the store. Though I did wonder about Preston starving. At lunch, he ate as much as the rest of us combined."

The back of my neck went hot as he smiled toward me. *Stupid stomach.* It'd been so easy to accept stuff from the guy when it smelled like onions and was oozing cheese.

Mom burrowed into Alex and started crying again. The girls lined up along the wall in the hallway, staring into the kitchen like it was a war zone. I didn't have time to worry about putting burdens on Alex, not if I wanted to calm Mom down. I moved to dig through the bags and noticed Hannah and Bonnie were holding more.

Behind me, Alex kept talking to Mom. "I don't want money to be an issue between us, okay? I know you. I love you. We talked about this before. Right?"

She let out another sob. "I just started really seeing the house, like you must be seeing it. And Val. She's such an old gossip!"

What I needed was in Bonnie's bag. "Hey." I motioned for her to come over. She took a few halting steps. I crouched down, hooked the grocery sack on a finger, and stretched the plastic toward me. We both peered inside at a carton of ice cream. "Can I use that?" I asked.

She nodded, worry pinching her face.

I smiled at her. "Hey, she's all right. It's just tears. We'll get her fixed up." I pulled the carton from the bag, winked at Bonnie, and went to the silverware drawer to grab a spoon. Then I popped the top off the mint-chocolate-chip ice cream and knelt by Mom and Alex. I tapped Mom's shoulder. "Hey. He brought ice cream." I offered her the spoon and carton.

A laugh bubbled free and brightened her eyes for real. She took the ice cream, ate a spoonful, and sighed. "Wow. I'm so hungry." She blinked at the ice cream and took another bite.

Chuckling, Alex shifted to sit beside her with one arm over her shoulders. He grinned at me. "Ice cream's the trick, huh?"

Something hit me. "What have *you* been eating since Saturday, Mom?" I frowned at her, suddenly not so sure she'd been taking care of herself.

"Well, at the presidency meeting yesterday there were snacks, and I grabbed two granola bars from the break room at lunch. But I guess I really haven't been eating much." She sat up. "No wonder I feel like the world is falling apart." Her head whipped toward Alex so fast he leaned back to avoid her hair. "I'm not like this. I eat. I don't regularly forget stuff like this."

"I know." He took her spoon, got himself a bite of ice cream, and returned the spoon.

It took me a few seconds to realize how intimate the gesture was. I jumped to my feet, my skin crawling.

Mom laughed. "We're making Preston uncomfortable."

A smile spread over Alex's face. "He just needs to get used to it." He leaned in, caught her face in his hands, and kissed her on the lips.

My heart plummeted to the pit of my stomach. I reached for the wall, seized with the urge to vomit. Edith darted past, a blur of blue-glittered dress and tangled blond hair. She scrambled into Mom's lap and reached for the carton of ice cream. "I want some too."

Mom caught the carton before it landed upside down in Edith's lap. Alex's hands fell to his sides. I swallowed hard and my stomach settled.

"Preston, would you please get her a spoon?" Mom gave me a pink-cheeked smile.

In a daze I walked to the silverware drawer. It rattled when I pulled it open.

Hannah moved in from the hallway and shuffled her grocery bags onto the table. She produced a second carton of ice cream from one of the bags. "I've got cookies and cream." She grinned at Alex and Mom.

Shaking my head, I grabbed a pile of spoons and handed one to Hannah on my way to Edith.

Hannah planted herself on the floor beside Mom and peeled open the second carton, then took a spoonful and held the carton up to me. "Here, you want some?"

I shook my head and gave Edith a spoon. Bonnie remained where I'd left her, the bag hanging from her hand by one handle. She bit her lower lip while she studied Mom. I took the bag from her, wrapped her fingers around a spoon, and maneuvered her to Alex. He caught her around the waist and pulled her down between him and Mom.

Hannah's lips twitched as I backed away. "Why won't you eat any ice cream, Preston? Are you worried about getting our germs? It didn't bother you when you ate my omelet this morning."

"I didn't kn—"

Sammy poked his head into the room. "Ice cream!" He did a baseball-worthy slide, ending up in the dead center of Alex, Mom, and the girls. Hannah lifted her carton over her head as he flopped around to get settled. I passed him a spoon. He dug an enormous scoop out of Mom's carton and asked, "Is this dinner?"

"No." She reached around him to get some of Hannah's cookies-and-cream variety. "We're just having dessert first tonight."

"Oh." Sammy shoved a spoonful into his mouth.

When Mom leaned back, Hannah held the carton up to me again, cocking her head and raising her brows. "You started this."

I rolled my eyes, took the carton, and scooped out a bite at least as big as Sammy's. "Happy?"

Everyone laughed. I shoved the carton back into Hannah's hand and put the spoon in my mouth. Aside from an almost brain freeze, it tasted pretty good.

I headed to the table to unload the groceries. I didn't like the idea of Alex buying food for us, but seeing Mom upset was worse. That, and it meant I didn't have to go to the store myself. Relieved, I tucked the money Mom had given me into her purse.

Alex leaned over the table beside me to grab a package of chicken and several produce bags of vegetables. "Come make a stir-fry with me." He nodded toward the end of the table. "Bring the soy sauce, will you? And that bag next to it. It's got the rice vinegar."

He headed to the counter as if I'd said yes.

Mom and the others still sat on the floor eating ice cream. Edith had curled up on Mom's lap. Hannah knelt with one hand on Sammy's shoulder. Bonnie inched a tiny bit closer to Mom's side, and then another inch.

I grabbed the bag and the soy sauce and went to the counter.

Alex beamed at the food. "Great. Let's make your mom some dinner."

After dinner, Mom led us to the living room, where the girls and Sammy squished onto the couch. Alex came in behind us with two chairs from the kitchen. He handed one to me and sat the other next to Mom's rocking chair. I moved my chair to the other side of the room, near the sofa. My knee took up an involuntary drumming, but unless I focused solely on it, it wouldn't stop. The anxiety I'd worked out at football crept up from my drumming foot to my clenching stomach.

We sang a Primary song. Actually, I mouthed my way through the song. Mom said a prayer. Then Alex leaned forward and said, "All right. We want to talk about what's going to happen over the next six months or so. We also wanted to go over some of the expectations we have for the family. This is going to be a big change. We want to do everything we can to make this go smoothly."

He stopped for a moment and glanced at Mom. She took up the conversation as if they'd rehearsed it. "Blending two families is hard. We have two different ways of doing things. Alex and I are learning how to make this work, same as you, but we are trying to do our best to be fair to everyone." She slid to the edge of the rocking chair, which bent forward with her. "The current plan is for Alex to do his painting at home while I continue at the clinic. He will be home with you after school, and if you need something, he will be the best one to call during school.

"Even though we aren't getting married until October, Sammy will go home with Hannah after school. Preston, you can join him there after practice. We want to have dinners together, so you can hang out and get your homework done until I get back from work. Okay?"

I shrugged, but inside, my lungs felt too tight.

Bonnie gaped at Alex. "We're going to eat together *every* night?"

Her dad nodded. "Yes. In fact, that's one thing we really feel strongly about. We need to be together regularly if we want our family to work." He pulled out a pad of paper. "I thought we could make a list of Whole Family Requirements—things that everyone should be required to do, regardless of their age. Of course, sometimes there will be exceptions, but this can be a guide for us going forward." He scratched letters across the paper. "I'm going to put the first one on here, because it's the most important to me. No matter where we end up living, here or in Karlon, or even a bit of both, after the marriage, we need to be in the same house."

"I feel the same way," Mom said. "We need to start by acting like a family. That means even though we might have two houses at some point, and some of you are old enough to take care of yourselves, we are going to stay together."

Well, that meant Jesse's house wasn't an option. Not that I would've moved in with his family anyway.

Sammy raised his hand. Alex smiled at him. "Sam, you don't have to raise your hand."

Sammy's hand dropped to his lap. "Okay. So the next thing on the list is dinner. We have dinner together."

"Yes. Thanks. I'll put that down." Alex scribbled on the page.

"And everyone helps with the clean-up," Mom added.

Edith stood on the couch, her brows quirked. "Is this like chores? Are you trying to give us chores?"

"Yes, we are all going to have chores," Alex said, clearly trying not to laugh. "That's part of being a family, but we don't have to decide on them tonight. Really, we just want everyone to understand that we should work together and help each other if something needs to be done. I expect you to obey the adults in the house, just like you obey Grandma and Grandpa, or Aunt Erica."

Sammy bounced in his seat. "Cool. So Mom is like their mom and you're like our dad, right? Can I call you Dad?"

I let my head tip forward and locked my fingers behind my neck, my eyes pinned to the floor.

Alex chuckled. "You are welcome to call me Dad, but Alex is fine too. I want you to be comfortable."

"Comfortable" was not a word I'd use to describe how I was feeling.

Sammy kept going. "After the wedding, will I change my last name to Green, like yours? Will you be my real dad then?"

I peered up. Mom's eyes flickered to me and something warred over her face. I lifted my head farther. Alex was waiting on her, watching her for the answer. Was Mom going to ask Troy to let Alex adopt Sam and me?

A painful lump sprang to my throat, squeezing the airway. My legs drew under me, my body braced to move to the exit, mere feet away. But I couldn't walk out again. Not after the restaurant episode on Saturday.

Mom shook her head. "No, Sammy. He won't be your real dad. Your real dad will always be Troy, but you can still call Alex Dad. Troy won't mind."

Sammy's shoulders dropped just as the air broke into my lungs.

nine

School started on Wednesday. Sammy and I met Hannah getting out of Alex's rental car as we headed for the front entrance. She jogged over to us and swung her bulging purple backpack onto her shoulder.

Inside the school, Sammy and Hannah stopped in front of a display case near the office. The case held a memorial for Bryan, complete with a few medals for running, and photos from last year's yearbook. I averted my eyes, but Sammy shuffled closer, pressing his face to the glass and squinting in.

Hannah's usual smile faded away. "He was a runner?"

"Yeah. Me too. I ran with him last summer. Me and Morgan," Sammy said, his words fogging the glass.

"I can't believe he died," whispered a girl passing behind us. "I heard Sammy was there when it happened."

I turned. A second girl elbowed the first, nodding in my direction. They fell silent and hurried away.

I waited another half minute before I couldn't take it anymore. "Come on, Sammy. I'll walk you to your first period."

He didn't move. "I don't need you to take me to class."

"It's a new schedule. I want to make sure—"

"I know where my class is." He folded his arms, keeping his back to me.

"You can help me find my class." Hannah unzipped her backpack and yanked out a tattered paper. Her grin snapped into place.

I didn't want to walk around the high school with her. People already had enough to talk about.

She unfolded the paper. "I need to find my locker too."

I let out a sigh. "What's the locker number?"

"It's on here somewhere." Stepping into the center of the hallway, Hannah scanned the paper. "They said it was down the sophomore hall." As she spun around, a group of guys from the football team charged into her. Her bag launched forward, the contents spilling across the hallway. The tallest guy, Zach, shouted a "sorry" at her, but no one stopped. The football players disappeared around the corner.

Hannah gaped at the floor. "It's like I'm in a movie or something." Her shocked expression disappeared with a laugh. "It's a pure 'first day at the new school' moment, like a movie!" She threw her hands out, almost hitting kids on either side. "How awesome is that?"

I shook my head at her, bent down, and reached for the mess on the floor before it spread even more. She laughed again and knelt by me. I picked up a bag of bandages and passed it to her. She stuffed it inside her deflated bag.

I continued to gather up reading books, candy, a hairbrush, a book about origami, a stack of origami paper, notebooks, hair elastics, pencils and pens, at least twenty postcards, a photo book, winter gloves, a beanie hat, and two zippered fabric pouches whose contents I didn't want to know.

Sammy pulled away from the display case long enough to help with a few matchbox cars and a plastic pony that rolled behind the trash can. Hannah picked up the rest.

She dumped it all inside her bag, which she pressed to the floor, trying to get the zipper closed.

"You're going to break that," I muttered under my breath.

She flipped her hair over one shoulder. "Yeah. It's pretty full. I probably should have left the cars and pony home. They were for Edith anyway. I forgot they were in here." She twisted her lips in thought. "Did we leave out my schedule?"

I groaned. "Are you serious?"

She plopped down right on the floor and crisscrossed her legs. "It's the curse of the movie-like first day." She opened the bag again and dug through it. After a few minutes, she popped up with the crumpled paper from before, her glasses crooked on her nose. Her face broke into a wide grin. "Got it!"

I avoided the stares of passing kids. "Come on or we'll be late."

"Just a sec." Hannah began another fight with the zipper.

I dropped beside her again and held out a hand. "Here."

"Huh?" she said.

I pulled the bag away, pressed the open ends together, and worked the zipper closed. Shoving the bag into her arms, I stood. "Let's go."

Her finger ran along the closed zipper. "Huh. You do 'Impatient Big Brother' really well." She clamored to her feet.

I rolled my eyes. "I'm not your big brother."

Sammy came to her other side. "Yet. You will be in October." He considered Hannah. "When's your birthday?"

"January," she said. She flung the backpack over her shoulder. I sidestepped in time to avoid being clobbered by it.

"Cool. Mine was two weeks ago," Sammy told her. "I'm sixteen now. That means I'll be your big brother too." He lifted his chest in pride. "I can show you your classes and locker."

Hannah unfolded the paper. "Thanks, Sammy."

I took it from her and found her locker number and combination scratched in a corner under notes about a photography class offered next term. She and Sammy trailed after me down the sophomore hallway. The first bell rang before Hannah got her locker open.

By the time I'd escorted Sammy and her to first period, I was five minutes late to my own class. "Ah, there you are Mr. Bensen," said Mrs. Davenport as I stepped through the door. She peered around me as if expecting someone to walk in behind me. "Where's Mr. Powell? I thought he'd be with you."

I didn't even know Jesse and I had first period together. I also had no idea where he was. I stepped closer to the desk. The attention of the other kids itched at my skin. "Sorry I'm late. I had to help—" I broke off, not sure how to explain Hannah.

"It's okay." Mrs. Davenport's smile was strained with concern. "I'll give you a pass today. I figured it would be a hard one for you and Jesse."

She's thinking about Bryan. I didn't want special treatment because of him. I wanted to forget about him and be normal, but trying to explain that my crazy, not-yet stepsister made me late was just as complicated. I found a seat near the back of the room and willed everyone to stop looking at me.

～

Jessie didn't show up until lunchtime. He leaned against the locker beside mine and crossed his arms. "Sammy and Hannah are eating outside together."

I pulled my sack lunch off the shelf. "Yeah?"

Jesse yanked the brown bag from my hand, tossed it inside, and slammed the locker door. "Come with me to get a burger from the Junction."

"I can't." I dialed my first combo number on the lock.

He grabbed my arm. "I'll pay."

"You don't have to—"

"Shut up." He stalked down the hallway, his shoulders hunched.

I sighed at my closed locker, then gave in and strode after him. "Where were you first period?"

"Nowhere," Jesse growled.

I fell silent, but I couldn't help noticing he took the long way to his truck, entirely avoiding the front entrance and Bryan's memorial.

～

When I got to Alex's house after football practice, Bonnie opened the door with a book in front of her face. She didn't even lower it as she shut the door behind me and wandered off. I found Alex and Edith downstairs in the family room.

Alex had spread a tarp over the floor and set up an easel with a new painting. He stood in front of it, one hand rubbing at the top of his head. A paint palette sat on a high stool next to him. Edith knelt on the floor over a large piece of butcher paper, painting with her hands. Purple and pink paint streaked over her cheek and caked on the section of hair closest to her forehead.

Alex painted a smear of blue across his canvas. "Hi, Preston."

"Where's Sam?" My voice came out tight, accusing. I didn't intend for it to sound like that, but when I tried to say something to soften it, Alex spoke first.

"He went on a bike ride with Hannah." Alex lifted his watch. "Hum. It's been longer than I realized. They were going to be back at 4:00."

It was 4:15. "A bike ride?"

Alex set the paintbrush on the stool. "Let's go see if they're coming."

We headed upstairs. "Did they tell you where they were going?" I asked.

Alex stopped at the top of the stairs. "For a ride. Sammy seemed antsy."

"He has heart problems." I pushed around Alex and stalked to the front door.

"Hannah has a phone," Alex told me. "She'd call if something went wrong." He followed me outside to the sidewalk.

The last time someone with a phone called because something went wrong, it was too late. Bryan was already dead. I scanned the road. The empty street stretched in both directions.

"Let's give them fifteen more minutes." Alex's fingers squeezed my shoulder. "They'll be all right."

I shook his hand off and wandered down the sidewalk, squinting into the distance.

Alex appeared at my elbow again. "Come on inside for a bit. I want to make sure Edith isn't painting the walls."

I shook my head. "I'm going to go find them." I strode toward my truck and yanked open the door.

The truck door thudded to a halt against the palm of Alex's hand. His fingers tightened around the frame, holding it in place. "Wait. I'll call Hannah."

I moved away from the door. He closed it and slid his phone out of his pocket. Walking to the end of the truck bed, I frowned at the deserted streets.

"Hannah, where are you guys at?" Alex said into the phone, his voice casual. "It's getting kind of late."

A loud pulse thumped in my ears as I paced back to him.

"Okay. Sounds good. See you soon." He ended the call and lowered the phone. "They lost track of time. They're on their way now." He smiled. "All right?"

Even though I knew I should feel better, my heart refused to stop pounding. Instead of pushing by Alex and climbing in the truck like I wanted to, I trailed after him to the house.

I sat in the living room near the window. Alex went downstairs and carried Edith up at arm's length. A few minutes later, the sound of water rumbled from the bathroom down the hallway. The clock on my watch read 4:23 by the time he reappeared, soaking wet and dabbing at himself with a hand towel.

"They aren't here yet." I scooted to the edge of the couch and went to push myself up. "I'm going to look."

Alex stopped me in midrise. "Give them another fifteen minutes or so."

I sank down and he sat beside me. My knee bounced as I studied the road outside.

"I hear you're taking an art class," he said.

I shrugged.

"Can I see what you're working on?"

"We've only had one class."

"So you haven't started anything yet?"

"Yes, but it's not very far." I tried to get my knee to stop bouncing, but every time my thoughts strayed, it started back up. I stood.

Alex rose with me. "Preston, try to calm down. I know how hard this is. The first year after the accident, I couldn't let any of the girls out of my sight for very long without getting worked up. Living like that wasn't healthy for me or for them. I need you to trust me right now, even though it's hard. Your body is still coping with what happened to Bryan and it is overreacting. Hannah and Sammy are okay."

I didn't know how to respond to Alex's bluntness.

"Go get your sketchbook," he said. "Show me what you're working on."

I didn't want to do it, but I headed to where I'd dropped my backpack and pulled out the book. I found the page I'd started in art class—a basic shading of pots.

Alex took the book in one hand and studied it. "You're really good at this." He ran a finger over the stack of pages in front of the pots. "It's almost full. Is this the sketchbook I gave you in May?"

I nodded, worried he would turn the pages to find the terrible first sketches I'd done of Morgan running. I'd gotten better over the summer, but those first ones . . .

He passed the book to me. "Can you show me anything else?"

My shoulders relaxed half an inch. I turned to the picture I'd done of the inside of the truck.

A smile stretched over Alex's face. "You've gotten better. The truck you drew for me in May was nice, but you're really starting to pay attention to shading."

I showed him two more drawings and then the page flipped open to the last sketch I'd done of Morgan. I scrambled to avoid it, but my fingers stuck to the paper with a sudden sweat.

Alex stopped my hand. "Will you let me see?"

My fingers jerked away from his on reflex, revealing Morgan sitting on the grass, barefoot with her beat-up running shoes unlaced beside her.

He glanced at me and then at the paper. "I didn't realize you'd been sketching people. I'm impressed." He shifted the page toward him. "You are good at capturing expression. Makes you wonder what she's thinking."

A smile tugged at my lips. "She wants to be out on the track running, but she's afraid."

Alex tipped his head. "What's her name?"

"Morgan." It slipped out before I could stop it.

Alex stood. "I'm going to grab you another sketchbook."

He left me on the couch. I checked one more time for Sammy. Nothing. The worry set my knee to drumming again. I rolled the pencil in my hand and tried to force my mind to focus on drawing. I traced out a few short lines and curves.

The front door burst open and hit the wall with a crack. Hannah and Sammy stomped in, breathing hard and laughing.

"Dad! We're back," Hannah shouted into the house.

I came up in a rush. The sketchbook flopped to the ground. My watch read 4:45. I crossed the room in a few strides. "Where have you been?" The voice exploded from inside me, angry and sharp.

Hannah's brow furrowed. "Riding bikes."

Alex appeared at the end of the hallway. "Hey, did you have a good time?"

A good time? They were forty-five minutes later than they said they'd be.

Sammy's lips parted in a grand smile. "We went to this park. It's new. I made it the whole way."

Alex stepped between me and them. He pushed the door closed and patted Sammy's back. "Great job, Sam."

Hannah waved her phone around. "I got a ton of really great photos, Dad. There was this little lizard. It totally sat there until I was a foot away."

"Can I see?" Alex held out his hand. Hannah passed him her phone. Sammy and Hannah crowded around Alex, talking over each other to explain the photos.

That was it? Jesse's parents would have at least demanded an explanation for the lateness before letting it go.

"You were supposed to be back at 4:00," I shouted over them. They fell silent and blinked at me like they couldn't process what I was saying.

Alex took my arm, steered me toward the sofa, and said in an undertone the others couldn't hear, "Preston, let me handle it, okay?"

But he wasn't handling it. He was acting like it didn't matter. Being on time was how we knew if someone needed help. Out here, with all the wilderness areas and potential to get lost, letting someone know where you were and when you planned to be back was everything. I shook my head.

Alex put up a hand. "You're tense right now, and yelling at them probably won't help. Hannah is my daughter. I know a bit about her. Give me a chance to find out what happened. I've had some experience being her parent."

I wanted to say more, but I doubted any of it would change his mind. Instead, I clenched my teeth and waited until he backed away from me again.

If Alex ever talked to Hannah or Sammy about being late, I didn't hear it. They joined him in the kitchen to look at the photos and get dinner started.

Alex clearly didn't understand the level of danger Sammy and Hannah could've been in, but trying to explain wasn't going to work coming from me. Mom would have to tell him.

When she came in the front door, she didn't knock. Alex had told us not to bother, but I couldn't do that yet. She stopped in the living room to tell me hello. "What are you doing in here? Aren't you helping with dinner?"

I shut my math book and explained about Sammy being late, Alex's unconcern, and my worry about Sammy using a bike with his heart condition. "Anything could have happened out there," I told Mom, "but he didn't even mention them being forty-five minutes late."

She sat beside me on the couch and wrapped her arm around me. "This is part of the adjusting we talked about on Monday."

"They can't ride off without telling someone where they're going and when they'll be back. It's not adjusting. It's common sense. He should have told them that if he wasn't going to let me tell them."

Alex stepped into the living room, wiping his hands on a towel. "Preston, I didn't let you tell them that because you were yelling. Hannah isn't yours to yell at."

My mouth snapped shut at the tenseness in his jaw.

Mom shifted toward Alex. "Have you talked to them about being late?"

He let out a long sigh and walked over to us. "I asked Hannah to call if they were going to be late next time. They were—"

I came to my feet. "Did you tell her how important it is? Did you mention all the people that get killed or lost here every year because they don't tell someone where they're going and when to expect them back? Did you make it important enough that she doesn't forget?"

Alex tipped his head, his blue eyes darkening. His gaze drifted down to Mom. Mine followed. She glanced between us, her lips tightening.

Mom would tell him. She had been there when Jesse's dad told the stories of lost hikers. She'd even helped look for them. She knew about Bryan—how accidents happened even if you were following all the rules.

Mom took my hand and squeezed it. "Alex is right. You need to let us handle this. Why don't you go see if you can help with dinner?"

Her placating smile didn't begin to cover the whiplash of her words. She'd sided with Alex even though I knew she agreed with me. I'd seen it in her face.

"I'm going home." I grabbed my backpack and headed out the front door. The air had cooled, but not enough to take the heat off the frustration in my chest. I got to the door of my truck before Mom called my name and came running down the steps toward me.

"Honey, I know you're worried, but different ways of handling things is part of blending families. I know it's hard to back down when you've seen Jesse's dad get so worked up about this sort of situation, but I have to figure it out with Alex. We need to be united. It's important."

"More important than keeping Sammy safe?"

"I never said that, but I really think there is another side to this story. They went to a park, Preston, not on a hike through the Pit. You might be overreacting, but even if not, you still need to let us figure out the boundaries and rules. That's our job."

I opened the truck door. Mom caught it with one hand and grabbed my arm with the other. "Running away from this isn't going to make it any easier."

My shoulders sagged. "I need a break."

She glanced at the house. "Dinner is a whole-family activity."

"I've been doing family stuff since last Saturday. Please, Mom."

She released the door. "Fine. But just tonight." She gave me a half smile and a quick kiss on my cheek. "Please try to understand our perspectives. We're juggling a lot right now. Okay?"

"Yeah, I know. Sorry if I made stuff complicated."

"It's okay, Preston. I'll be home later."

I climbed into the truck. For the first time since Monday, I drove home to my own silent house where I didn't have to think about talking to anyone. It was the best thing that had happened all week.

Ten

We had our first football game Friday and had to leave at 2:45 to get to Beaver High School in time. Right before the kickoff, Mom, Alex, Sammy, and the girls made their way to the visitors' section of the bleachers. We won 14–7 and got home late.

When I woke on Saturday, I almost didn't want to get up. There was no practice, and Mom had asked me to take work off again. Alex and the girls were coming to help us get started on dejunking the yard, which had to happen whether or not we sold the house.

I rolled out of bed before 6:00 and drove the truck to the metal shed on the far corner of the five-acre lot. The shed was the one thing in the yard I cared about. Maybe I could get it taken care of before everyone else showed up.

I parked Old Blue near the entrance and opened the shed doors. I walked over to one of the work benches and pulled several web-covered boxes off the overhead shelves. Instead of seeing the junk inside the boxes, I heard Bryan in my head—almost saw him kneeling in the corner of the shed, still barely ten, glasses coated in a fine film of dust. Sammy knelt beside him, boxes of parts, screws, nails, and tools making a circle around them.

Bryan held up an old wrench. "Hey! You think you could use this?"

"Sure," Jesse said from where he stood behind Bryan, up to his armpit in another box.

Bryan tossed the wrench into the pile where he'd been stacking anything we might need for the three-wheeler. "When we get it going, I want a turn driving it."

"You're too young," Jesse told him. "I think you have to be twelve first, like us. You're so blind, you'd probably kill yourself anyway." I snickered.

"I don't have to help you, you know," Bryan said. For a minute, it looked like he might take off, but then the anger faded from his face and he went back to sorting, as if Jesse hadn't spoken.

Why had Bryan put up with so much from us?

I slammed the box down. Bryan could have touched every single thing in it. Maybe it was sorted in some Bryan-logical way. It had been a bad idea to start on this shed.

I stumbled out into the morning light and slumped down by the wheel of Old Blue. I hadn't *always* been a jerk to Bryan, but he'd been the little brother, tagging along, making life complicated for most of the growing-up years. When I only felt guilt for following along with Jesse's schemes, Bryan actually told us we were being idiots.

At some point after I turned thirteen, after Mom got the papers from Troy saying he wanted a divorce, things changed. Bryan went from annoying tag-along, to the kid that stuck up for Sammy and kept him safe. Instead of holding me back from doing something fun with Jesse, Bryan was my backup when I needed to talk Jesse out of it. And when Sammy was in the hospital in January, Bryan was the one who showed up every day to sit at his bedside. Bryan couldn't even drive, but he'd begged, bribed, and hitched rides with me, Mom, Jesse, or his parents every day.

Over half of those days I'd been sitting there with Bryan, listening to him talking to Sammy and wondering how he'd ended up more mature than Jesse.

I scrambled to my feet and stomped to the truck. The shed could wait. I didn't want to deal with it after all.

Jesse and his dad, Brett, rattled up to the house with both of their trucks and backed into the yard. I waited on the porch as they navigated around the rusting tiller and a large tractor Grandpa had used for the orchard that had now been dead for many years. Through the open screen door behind me, the girls clamored around the kitchen, chattering over each other. They never stopped talking.

A hand touched my back. I jerked and then relaxed as Mom stepped up beside me.

"Most of the stuff in the sheds I don't think I've even looked at since we got here," she said. "It shouldn't be hard to get rid of it." Forcing a smile, she patted my shoulder blade.

Jesse hopped out of his truck and slammed the door, striding toward us with Jordan on his heels. "Where's Fancy Clothes?"

A snort came from Jordan, Jesse's thirteen-year-old brother. His round belly stretched out an old baseball T-shirt that must have once belonged to Jesse or Bryan.

Mom let out a long breath. "Alex. His name is Alex."

"Yeah, so where is he?" Jesse searched the porch as if he thought we were keeping Alex under one of the cracked deck boards. "Aren't we going to get this party goin'?"

Mom waved toward the doorway behind us. "He's on the phone with the contractor we invited out to look over the house."

"Morning, Natalie." Brett reached the side of the porch wearing an old shirt from the travel lodge he worked at. He stood as tall as Jesse, but had an extra layer of muscle in his arms and shoulders that Jesse had yet to acquire.

Braxton, Jessie's nine-year-old brother, slid out of Brett's truck and ran toward us. Prickles rose along my neck. Braxton had cut his hair off—all of the wavy brown curls gone. A ghost-like reflection of Bryan lingered in the shape of Braxton's face, the clench of his jaw, his lean, narrow body.

"Did you say something about a contractor?" Brett asked. "You starting the remodel before the wedding?"

"I'd love to get it done before the wedding if we're going to do it," Mom said. "For now, he'll give us a quote on what it will take to fix up the house and get a functional studio for Alex in one of the sheds. He was supposed to be here already, but I think he got lost."

Brett chuckled. "That don't surprise me."

No. You had to really watch for the road or you'd miss it, and there were no alternate routes into Karlon.

"Fancy Clothes is going to put a *studio* in a shed?" Jesse got hung up on "studio," emphasizing it in a snooty voice.

Brett cuffed the back of Jesse's head. Jesse's face scrunched up in a grimace as he sidestepped away from his dad and rubbed a hand over his head. "What?"

Brett turned to Mom and me again. "Should we get started?"

She glanced at me. "Might as well," I said. Not mentioning my failed attempt at starting on the other shed earlier, I guided them toward the wooden shed closest to the house where Alex wanted to put the studio. I had serious doubts about it. If it stayed standing once we emptied it of the piles of boxes, I'd be shocked.

I opened the shed doors. Dust billowed around us. Jesse took in a mouthful and busted up coughing, waving his hand through the cloud as he staggered back. "Anyone think to bring dust masks?" he asked.

Jordan snickered, fanning the dust away from himself as well. "You ain't supposed to inhale it, Jesse."

Jesse rolled his watering eyes, still coughing. "Ya think?"

"I told you we'd need masks." Braxton stood away from the cloud billows, observing from a reasonable distance. I'd always thought he'd end up the smartest of the lot of them.

"Heh. Well, next time bring them, why don't you?" Jesse said, wiping his face on his shirt.

Brett tugged a bit on the top box nearest him, but didn't pull it out yet. "You even know what's in here?" The stack of boxes rose from floor to ceiling, spanning the space in front of us from the left edge of the shed to the right.

"Nope." I lifted one of the top boxes, wiggling it under the lip of the doorway to free it. The stack below swayed forward.

"Easy." Brett reached over me to brace the boxes.

"Yeah." I moved around him with the box.

"We're coming to help!" Hannah waved as she walked toward us. Sammy, Bonnie, and Edith paraded behind her.

"Great." The word slipped out under my breath.

Behind me, Brett chuckled. We started hauling stuff to the trucks. Brett leaned against the stack of boxes while Jesse wiggled them out. They passed them to us one at a time. I didn't open the boxes, just put them in the back of the truck.

"Hey, look at this!" Braxton squatted in front of a box with gnawed corners on one side. He poked a stick at a bit of debris hanging out of the box. "A mouse built a nest in here."

Hannah stopped midstep, right in front of me. I ground to a halt, my box bumping into her back. "Sorry," she said. She stepped out of my way and lifted her own box to examine its corners.

Bonnie moved to Braxton and the nest box. "Can I see it?"

He tipped the box. "See? It's a baby that didn't make it."

"Oh. Sad." Bonnie leaned close. "Do you think there are more in the shed? I mean live ones."

"Yeah, bunches. I already saw three dart behind that pile of scrap wood." With his chin, Braxton motioned toward the woodpile.

"Preston," Mom said, appearing around the side of the house, "come over here for a minute, will you?"

I brushed some dirt off my basketball shorts and strode over. The contractor and Alex waited behind her. They stepped to one side, making room for me. Mom put her hand on my arm. "It's probably a good idea if you walk through the house with us."

Alex grinned. By Thursday after practice he'd been his usual self and hadn't mentioned our argument. "I don't know a thing about most of what this guy is saying," he told me now. He waved at the contractor, who raised his brows and gave a short laugh. I recognized him from Carter's Feed but had never talked to him. *Bardell's Construction* was stitched over the pocket of his snap-front tan shirt.

"George, this is Preston." Alex motioned between me and the contractor. "Preston, George Bardell."

George held out a callused hand. I shook it with my own clammy one, hoping my firm grip would make up for the dampness.

Alex pointed to the house. "Should we go in the back door since we're here?"

George grunted a yes and they moved that direction. I followed them up the creaking steps to the porch.

The contractor eyed the decaying wood underfoot and nudged the plywood I'd nailed down over a large hole in the boards near the back door. "You wanna fix the back porch too?" His voice held a rough drawl that could rival Mr. Carter's.

Alex scanned the porch. "Might as well."

I could fix it myself if I had money for the decking boards. Which I didn't. I shoved my hands in my pockets as we moved through the kitchen door.

George crossed to the oven, opened the tan door with a rattling creak, and peered at the blackened insides. Mom sighed. Before she could say anything, he reached up and opened the cupboard over the stove. The door hung at a slant on one hinge, the finish bubbled and broken by the rising steam from years of cooking on the stovetop.

He straightened and dragged a flat-sided carpenter pencil and yellowing notepad from the pocket of his shirt. "You doing a full remodel in here, then?"

Alex opened his mouth, but Mom spoke first. "Our main concern is finishing the basement. We need at least two more rooms down there and a second bathroom and family room. We can make do with the rest of the house for now."

George grunted a *hmm*.

"If we are already doing construction," Alex said, "we might as well do the whole house."

"I can't live in this house with construction in every room. We can make it work with the basement, but the rest will have to wait." Mom's tone was final.

Frowning slightly, Alex studied her. My shoulders tensed. The last thing I wanted was more fighting.

"Let's take a look at the basement," he said after several seconds. "We can figure the rest out later." He headed toward the stairs.

I released my breath.

Under the light from the naked bulb I'd replaced Sunday, we descended into the murky smell of damp and mold. Mom rubbed her arms against the sudden cold, stopping at the foot of the stairs to let the rest of us ahead of her.

The contractor moved deeper into the basement, stepping around the Christmas storage boxes. We left Alex behind to have a whispered conversation with Mom.

George pulled the overhanging string for the basement light. It flickered on, dim and orange. He patted at his jean pockets. "You got a flashlight, son?"

I crossed to the shelf beside the stairwell and grabbed two flashlights. I flicked one on before passing it to him.

George shined the light into the spider web-covered beams overhead, around the concrete walls, and along the dusty floor. Walking by Mom and Alex, who had gone silent, George headed farther into the basement area under the upstairs bedrooms and bath. I followed.

He halted under the bathroom and shined the light at the underbelly of pipes and plumbing. "You have blueprints of the house?"

"Upstairs." I turned to go up.

Mom stopped me with "I know where they are. I'll get them." She headed upstairs.

"Shine that other light up here too, will ya, son?" George tipped his head, pointing his light on one side of a large pipe.

I turned on the flashlight and directed the beam up at the opposite side, further revealing the house's original plumbing in all its patched-up glory.

"Those give you a bit of trouble?" George lifted his chin toward the pipes.

"Yeah," I replied, avoiding looking at Alex.

The contractor chuckled. "I bet. You have leaks?"

"Sometimes." I let the beam of light fall to the floor.

With his light, George zeroed in on a short ladder I'd left on the back wall. After pulling out the ladder, he set it up under the pipes and climbed up.

My neck grew hot as he examined my repair jobs.

"You sure know how to make do, don't you?" George flashed a sudden grin down at me. "No wonder Hank Carter keeps you around. It's unorthodox, but it gets the job done, don't it?" George came down the ladder, chuckling to himself.

A mixture of pride and shame zigzagged from my chest to my gut, freezing there when George's smile faded to a serious frown.

"I'll be honest with you," he said. "If I start messing with these pipes to put a bathroom down here, I'm going to have to replace them all. Which means I'm going be interfering with the upstairs plumbing too." He faced me. "You know what I'm sayin', don't you?"

I knew, but it didn't mean I wanted to hear it.

"The electric original too?" George's flashlight beam shot to the wiring running to the light bulbs.

"Yeah," I managed to say.

He lowered his flashlight and stepped back to see both Alex and me. "It's a big project. You'll be lucky to get it done before October, especially if you're going to try to live here through the renovation. You might be able to do some of it on your own, but I'd recommend you hire professionals to replace the electric and plumbing." He pointed up. "How's the bathroom upstairs, son? 'Bout like the kitchen?"

I shook my head slowly. "It's worse." Alex needed to hear this—needed to know how bad it was. I faced him. "The whole house is worse than it looks. It doesn't matter what you do down here, the upstairs is one nail shy of falling apart. It'll escalate into more problems every time you touch something. It isn't worth it to try to fix it."

The three of us stood in silence, examining the basement.

At last, Alex turned to George. "Can you give me an estimate on the cost of overhauling the whole thing? A timeline?"

George shook his head as if he wasn't sure he heard right. "Yeah. If that's what you want."

"No. It isn't worth it," I spoke up.

Just as I was wondering if Alex had even heard me, he reached for my shoulder and said, "George, can you give us a second?"

The contractor nodded.

My skin crawled under the pressure of Alex's hand. I rolled my shoulder, but he didn't let go. He steered me toward the stairs. The tension I'd felt over Sammy and the bike ride rose like static electricity. Would I have to argue with him over this too? I didn't know if I could fight about something I wished I didn't have to do. Even in all its crumbling wonder, I didn't want to give up on the house.

Alex's hand dropped to his side and he frowned at the concrete floor. "Do you honestly want to walk away from this house?"

I didn't move, my body frozen between telling myself to nod and screaming not to. I'd put more than a little of myself into holding the place together. In the process, I'd learned a lot about my grandpa and the sort of guy he was. The house felt connected to me—a part of my pulse, my blood, and my family. If I had money to burn, I'd put everything into it. But I didn't. Only Alex did.

"Preston, you know this house better than anyone," he said. "You also know your mom and Sam better than anyone. What is best for them? What's best for you?"

When I didn't respond, Alex went on, "I have the money, Preston. We can fix this house. I'm pushing for the remodel because I think it's what your mom wants even though she won't admit it. The house means a lot to her. Her grandpa was a man she loved very much. Being here is important to her. I also think it's what's best for you and Sammy. Am I reading the situation wrong?"

Invisible ties wrapped around my tongue, pinning it in place. He'd read us right, even though I couldn't say it.

Alex stepped closer as if he didn't notice me stiffen. "The money I have was a gift from Heavenly Father, not something I deserved or was entitled to. It's meant to be used to help people, especially the people I love. That includes you and your family. I want to do this."

Warmth sparked outward, freeing my tongue and settling in my chest with a sense of reassurance. I recognized the familiar peace from the Spirit I'd come to rely on for help over the last few years. It was my connection to God. It brought me up short.

The last time I'd felt something like this in a strong way had been the day Bryan died. The Spirit had told me Bryan was already dead before I got off the phone with a frantic Morgan.

I blinked at Alex, fighting away the memory as the warmth faded a little. "We can't live here while the renovation is going."

"I know. We can wait until after the wedding to start. You guys can move in with us while they renovate. I know it's not perfect, but it's the best solution I can think of."

Alex *wanted* to spend his money on us. I didn't want him to, but it wasn't only me he was helping. Mom and Sam deserved better than my patch jobs.

My hands fell to my sides. "We'll be fine in Kanab for a while." I glanced over at the contractor, who'd gone up the ladder again. "Should we take him to see the rest of the house?"

The tension melted off Alex as he smiled. "Yeah, but I might need help talking your mom into this."

I grinned a little. "I can do it."

Eleven

Jesse overheard Alex and me telling Mom our plan to delay the renovation until after the wedding so we could overhaul the whole house. You'd think the fact that we were going to come back would make things easier on Jesse, but he only pointed out that we'd probably be in Kanab until most of the school year was over.

Around noon, Mom took Edith and Sammy to get lunch for everyone. Brett had to work, so he caught a ride with them to his house, leaving the truck in the back yard for us to finish filling with junk.

I found Bonnie and Braxton in the living room sprawled on their stomachs, talking to something under the couch. I wandered over behind them. Braxton glanced back at me, those too-large ears reminding me of Bryan. "Do you have a flashlight?" he asked.

Bonnie hissed "Shhh," without turning.

I crouched down to peer under the green sofa, but saw only dark shadows and a few popcorn kernels. "What's under there?" I knelt and planted my hands on the threadbare carpet to get a better angle.

"A mouse," Bonnie murmured. "Be quiet." She pushed a bit of bread under the sofa.

"Whoa." I snatched her hand. "A mouse?"

Braxton rolled to a sitting position and produced a weathered box he'd pilfered from the shed. "I was goin' to try to get it in here. We might have to move the sofa."

Bonnie huffed. "Will you two stop talking so loud? You're scaring it." She pulled her wrist free and pushed at the bread again. "Maybe it doesn't like bread."

"Or maybe it's wild." I grabbed Braxton's box and examined it. A flip lid was attached to the top of the box, where the letters of a brand had been ripped off by packing tape. It would do. I tipped the open box on its side and slid it toward the gap between the sofa and the floor.

Bonnie pushed the box away. "You can't put it in there. There's no air holes. And he's not that wild. I was coaxing him up the stairs outside, but he got scared when that mean fat kid tried to stomp on him. That's when he ran inside."

My mouth went slack. *She coaxed a mouse inside.*

"She's talking about Jordan," Braxton said. "He's the one who tried to stomp on him. It was the mouse that ran inside." Braxton took the box from me. "I'll make air holes."

I shook my head. "Don't bother. It's not going to be in there long enough to matter."

"What isn't?" It was Jesse's voice, much calmer than earlier.

I glanced up. Hannah had followed him into the living room. "The mouse," I replied, jabbing a thumb at the sofa.

Hannah squealed. "In the house?" She backed against the wall in the hallway. "Ugh."

"I take it you don't have anything in that bag of yours for catching mice?" Jesse smirked at the bag she'd slung over her shoulder again.

Hannah gulped and forced a smile into place. "Nope. Fresh out of mouse traps."

"You can't—"

I stood, cutting off Bonnie's high-pitched whine. "Jesse, help me move the sofa. Brax, when the mouse runs out, you try to catch it in the box."

"Okay." He shifted into a better position.

Bonnie stomped her foot. "No! It's my mouse!"

"It's not a pet," I told her. I grabbed the closest end of the sofa. The old thing, which used to Grandpa's, had heavy springs inside and a solid wood base. Jesse grabbed the other end.

Bonnie jumped on the sofa as we started to lift. "I won't let you hurt it!"

Jesse and I let out twin groans. The sofa, an inch off the carpet, hit the floor with a rattling clunk of springs and wood. Something small and brown darted behind my foot and ran along the wall, then disappeared around the short coffee table with a lower shelf we used for an entertainment center.

Hannah danced in the hallway, peeking between her fingers. "I can't stop watching. I want to hide, but I can't stop watching. Someone catch it."

Jordan, his T-shirt now smudged with dirt, appeared with a large shovel in one hand. "Where did it go? I'll squish it with this."

Bonnie launched herself off the sofa, locked her hands around the shovel, and pushed it from side to side. "Leave it alone, big jerk."

He yanked the shovel out of her grasp. "Chill out. It's a mouse."

She shrieked louder. "Murderer! Murderer!"

I wasn't about to let Jordan smash anything inside the house, which had enough problems already. I headed toward them.

"What's going on?" Alex's question filtered through the shouting.

Bonnie and Jordan froze, but Bonnie recovered first. "They are trying to kill my mouse. Tell them to leave it alone!"

Alex stepped into the room, a frown flickering on his lips. "So there really is a mouse in here? I heard the yelling, but . . ." He grasped the shovel handle. At first Jordan tightened his hold, but then he released the shovel and backed away from Alex.

"She's trying to make it a pet," Jordan said. "You can't have a mouse for a pet. It'll give you rabies."

"Shows what you know. Lots of people have mice for pets." Bonnie's chin lifted and she slid closer to Alex, as if she knew he'd take her side.

"Preston, help me move this." Jesse grabbed one end of the coffee table.

I went to the other end. Bonnie erupted again. "Stop! Daddy, make them stop. They want to kill it too. Preston said it didn't need air holes. He's going to suffocate it."

Actually, there were plenty of faster ways to kill a mouse. Suffocation wasn't what I had in mind.

Jesse wagged his brows at me and tipped his head toward the coffee table before nodding to Braxton. "Ready, Brax?"

He shifted the box around and knelt. "Yep."

"One, two—"

Bonnie pounced on Braxton. "Daddy. Make. Them. Stop."

Alex hauled Bonnie off Braxton and leaned the shovel against the wall near the couch. "Preston, wait a second."

I stiffened. *Really? It's a mouse. A wild, disease-carrying mouse. It's dangerous—an adult should know that.* "I'm not going to let a mouse run around my house. It could make Mom or Sam sick. Jesse?" I motioned with my chin to the table.

He grinned. "Three."

We lifted. The brown creature shot out, straight across the floor between Braxton and Jordan. For all his bravado with the shovel, Jordan screamed louder than Hannah. He jumped into Mom's rocking chair, knocking it against the wall. The drywall cracked.

Braxton threw himself after the mouse and landed on his chest, arms sprawled out. The box skated across the floor, while the blur of brown darted under the bookshelf in the corner between the sofa and the chair.

Bonnie escaped from Alex and dive-bombed Braxton, but Jesse leaped over them both and grabbed the box. He threw it to me and leaned his long body against the bookcase. "I'll tip it. You ready?"

I knelt. The shelf tipped. The mouse headed straight for me. I whipped the box down and missed by half a second. The rodent zigzagged around my hands and darted up the leg of my shorts.

"What the—" Something small and furry with tiny claws rubbed up my inner thigh. I clamped a hand over my leg, trying to block it from reaching anything higher up. A piercing yell burst out of my lips. I fell backward, clutching at my leg.

Jesse hooted with laughter, collapsing against the wall.

The mouse's claws snagged on my nylon shorts, which kept it from advancing. It tugged against the fabric, sending pinpoints of needle-like pain through the bottom of my boxers into my leg. I wriggled out of the shorts and tossed them a few feet away. Braxton pounced on them, pinning the mouse in the fabric.

I scooted along the carpet and rubbed at the red scratch marks on my inner thigh. The pressure of a large hand hooked around my arm jerked my focus to the right.

Alex knelt beside me. "Are you all right? Did you get bit?" His sincere concern took me off guard.

I gaped at him, my breath running in and out in a harsh flow.

Jordan lay balled up in the rocking chair with tears of laughter streaming down his face. Jesse tried to stand, but fell back down, gasping breaths between his own hysterical laughs.

Behind me Hannah's giggles were broken by moans. "I can't breathe. That was so funny."

Braxton grinned at me. "Well, we caught it."

From behind him, a trembling Bonnie said, "Leave it alone, or I'll, I'll . . . I'll kick you."

Alex leaned over and took the box, then scooped up my shorts and the mouse and closed them inside. "Bonnie, calm down a minute and let's talk about this, okay?"

"You can't seriously be thinking about letting her keep that mouse!" I didn't mean to shout it, but it came out loud and angry.

Jesse stopped laughing, his eyes wide.

"Preston, why don't you go get some pants?" Alex said.

Jordan hiccupped on laughs so hard he sounded like a cow. My face heated as I scowled down at my red boxers.

Bonnie hung off Alex's forearm. "You can't leave it in there! It'll suffocate!"

"No, it won't." A gentle smile matched the soothing tone of Alex's voice. He nodded at me. "Preston."

I scrambled up and navigated around a collapsed Hannah to get to the hallway. A pair of shorts lay on the floor of my room. I pulled them on before storming back out the door. Alex was crazy. He let Sammy ride bikes to unknown locations, he didn't care about his kids being home when they said they would be, and now he was going to let his ten-year-old keep a field mouse. Even its droppings could make someone sick. I knew one thing for sure—Alex wasn't putting that mouse in the same house as Sammy or Mom.

When I got back, he sat on the sofa with Bonnie beside him, the box on his lap. The others' laughter came from the front porch.

I stalked straight over to Alex and Bonnie. "It's not a pet."

Alex held up one hand. "Let me handle this."

"Like you handled Sammy and Hannah being late?" I said.

Alex closed his eyes for a second and took a deep breath. Then he looked at me again. "Preston—"

"No." I swiped the box off his lap and strode through the kitchen. The back door slammed over Bonnie's screams. A multitude of ways to ensure the mouse didn't come back inside ran through my head as I strode to the back of the yard.

"Stop! Preston!" The back door crashed open and Bonnie came sprinting across the porch. She jumped the stairs.

I'd have to settle for a less permanent solution. I opened the box. The mouse remained hidden in my shorts. I picked them up and shook them a couple times. The mouse slid out into the dead grass. It seemed dazed but managed to dart into the bushes behind the woodshed. At the same moment, Bonnie crashed into me. She shoved around me, grabbing first the box and then the discarded shorts.

"Where is it?" Her pale, wet cheeks were flushed a speckled red.

"It's a mouse!" My voice still came out in a shout, stuck somewhere between fury at the thought of Alex actually letting her keep the mouse, and alarm over the tears streaming down her face.

Bonnie threw the box and shorts at me. "I needed it!" Desperation cut through her voice. Her hands dug through the weeds in search of the mouse.

Alex's hand caught around my arm, pulling me back a step. "Preston, I asked you to let me handle this. Will you please go inside and give us some space?" He motioned to the house before he moved around me and grasped Bonnie's shoulders to pull her out of a bush.

She shook her head, her hair flying in a tangled mess over her face. "Get it back!" She shoved at her dad's chest.

His fingers wrapped around her wrists. "It's dead!" she screamed at him. "It's dead."

Alex pulled her into his arms.

"He killed it and now it's gone," Bonnie wailed. "How could he do that? It was mine!"

The other kids made their way around the side of the house, staring at us. Bonnie whipped her head between me and them. "Make them go away, Dad!"

Alex frowned at the other kids and me, then stood, bringing Bonnie to her feet.

Tears squeezed between her pinched eyelids as she shouted, "Make them go away!" over and over. Alex steered her toward the house.

My chest grew tight as her words slipped into a frantic plea. In a daze, I followed Alex and her into the house. This was more than just an angry, spoiled kid. This was something bigger. Something besides the mouse being gone was rising up out of her like a ghost.

Alex sat in a chair at the kitchen table and lifted Bonnie onto his lap. "Preston, I need you to go out." He spoke without turning.

When I hesitated, he turned to meet my eyes and said, "Now."

I retreated to my room but couldn't block out Bonnie's yelling. Her words carried through the walls. "He took it. It was mine. I needed that mouse. It was my pet. He just took it away. I don't want him to ever be my brother. He'll never like me, never love me. I could've gotten my mouse out, but he didn't let me. He pushed me away."

For a full ten minutes, Bonnie yelled about how awful I was and why she needed the mouse. Alex never said a word.

I paced my room, my fingers clenching and unclenching as nervous worry worked up me. Why didn't Alex say anything?

Bonnie's shouting died down a little at time until she sucked in on one last sob and fell quiet.

"You feel better?" Alex's soft voice brought my feet to a halt.

I strained to hear Bonnie's reply. "A little. But can we get my mouse back?"

I hesitated at the door and then cracked it open in time to catch Alex's response. "No. I know you loved that mouse very much, but it wasn't really a good pet. It could have made someone sick."

"We could have taken it to the vet. You said I could have a pet here."

After a pause, Alex said, "A pet, but not a wild mouse. I wasn't going to let you keep it. I could see how important it was to you, so I wanted to talk to you before you got worked up, but it still had to be let go."

Holding in a groan, I searched my memory. Alex hadn't mentioned anything about keeping the mouse. He'd only said he wanted to talk to Bonnie first.

I dropped onto the edge of my bed, every inch of my body alive with guilt. Outside, I heard Mom pulling up to the house and the rest of the kids shouting about tacos. I didn't move, even when she asked the others where I was. An explosion of laughter followed what must have been a retelling of the mouse running up my shorts.

A knock came at the door. I jerked my head up and managed a "Yeah?" The door opened and Alex entered. My knee started drumming. I leaned over it and pressed it down with my elbows.

The bed creaked as he sank down beside me. We sat in silence until he said, "Bonnie has a lot of anxieties. Some of it's just who she is. Some of it's because of the accident that killed her mom and brother and sister. Some of it's because she's almost eleven and suddenly growing up. Maybe it seems like I'm doing things wrong, or that I'm messing things up, but I am trying my best. And the reality is, I'm her dad. You're not."

I swallowed.

"So, in the future," Alex continued, "do you think you could trust me to do my job? I'll try to be more open with you. I should have found a way to explain what was going on with Bonnie, and I probably should have spent more time talking through things with you on Wednesday. However, I also need you to understand that your mom and I are the parents. If you're worried about something, it's perfectly all right for you to come talk to us about it. But you taking over the situation or yelling at the other kids is never going to be okay."

Still leaning over my knees, I frowned. No one had ever gotten after me for yelling before. In fact, I didn't usually yell at all. It always triggered Sammy, and I hated that. "I don't . . ." I rubbed at my hair and glanced at Alex out of the corner of my eye. "I don't normally yell."

He smiled at me. "You've been under a lot of pressure. I know you were worried about keeping people safe. Same as on Wednesday. I just thought I'd better talk to you, since it's happened a couple times now. And also because seeing Bonnie upset like that can be alarming."

"Is she still mad at me?" I asked.

"Yes. Being valued and respected is important to her. She feels you weren't listening to her."

"I wasn't."

Alex chuckled. "No."

I blew out a breath. "I'm sorry."

"It's okay." Alex put a hand on my shoulder.

I stiffened, but didn't shake it off. "Will she let me talk to her?"

"Probably not right now. Give her some time." Alex sat a little longer, but when I didn't speak, he stood and said, "Well, I think your mom has lunch for us, if you're hungry."

I was. I stood and followed him out of the room. We passed the living room, where the furniture was still a little out of place from the mouse chase. I scowled. "What happened to a normal pet, like a cat or dog? Something too big to crawl up a pant leg?"

Alex laughed outright. "Bonnie loves dogs. She just has a very finely developed concern for all creatures."

My lips twitched. "So I better not smash a spider around her?"

"Probably not."

That was good to know, but there had to be a better option. "I can get her a dog."

Alex paused with his hand on the doorknob.

"There are always notices for free dogs posted at Carters," I went on. "That or I can get one from the shelter."

Alex considered me. "You want to get her a dog? When?"

The sooner the better. "Today. Although the shelter is already closed."

Alex's smile returned. "Okay."

⁓

Jesse trailed after me, a bag of tacos in one hand, and shoved an open taco into his mouth. We climbed in the truck, and I reached over to fish a handful of tacos from the bag before he ate them all. He finished his taco and asked, "So where are we going?"

"To get a dog for Bonnie."

"Cool." He swiped one of my tacos, then pulled off the wrapper and shoved the taco in his mouth before I could stop him.

By the time we pulled into Carter's, we'd eaten all the tacos, though I had to fight for my five. Jesse had probably put away ten.

"What we doing here?" He nodded his chin at the feed store.

"Gettin' a number." Leaving Jesse in the truck, I ran inside to write down the phone number from the notice for puppies someone posted earlier in the week.

Back in the truck, I passed Jesse the number on a receipt Mr. Carter had given me. Jesse dug out his phone, an old Samsung with a dent on the side. He typed in the number and put the phone to his ear without waiting for me to ask him to make the call.

Thirty minutes later Jesse and I sat in the truck, staring at a small white ball of fluff. He lifted it and squinted. "You sure this is a dog?"

Its long tongue lolled out one side of its mouth. A small tooth jutted out of the other side. The dog looked at me with one eye, the other pointing off in the opposite direction, and barked. "She sounds like a dog," I said finally. "And her ears are droopy like a dog's."

"Yeah, but what breed is she?"

"Looks like a bit of everything." I shifted the truck and backed out of the driveway of the house where we'd gotten the dog.

"Including rat. Didn't you say you didn't want a rodent?"

I snorted.

Jesse grinned at me and put the ball of fluff on the seat between us. She darted into my lap and shoved her face to the window, her tail wagging like a motor. "You gotta hold her so I can drive."

Jesse took her back, plopping her on his lap. "That other one looked more like a dog."

It had. But something about this one seemed perfect.

"Hey, she's likes pickle-flavored popcorn!"

The dog gulped down a piece of popcorn Jesse dug out of a bag he'd left in the truck weeks ago.

"Don't let her eat that," I said.

He laughed and handed the dog another piece. She lapped it up before I could get it out of Jesse's hand. I grabbed the bag from him and stuffed it in the door on my side. The dog crawled onto his lap, licking his fingers.

"Okay, I like her." He pushed the dog's mouth away and settled into the seat. "Anything that likes pickle popcorn is good in my book."

When we got back to the house, the kids' voices came from Sammy's room. The puppy wriggled in my arms, her mouth curved up in a dog smile, marred only slightly by the odd tooth and too-long tongue. Jesse pushed into the house behind me with the bag of food we'd bought at Carter's.

In the space between the bookshelf and the couch, Bonnie sat curled over herself, her head tucked down, an abandoned book at her side. I crouched in front of her. Her head lifted a fraction and her eyes widened when she saw me. She pushed herself farther into the corner.

I set the dog on the floor in front of her. Bonnie's jaw dropped and her legs unfolded. Squealing, she swept up the dog and hugged it to her chest. "A puppy!" She pulled the dog back to look again as if she didn't quite believe it. "It's so cute." Then she kissed the animal's ugly face. "Is it mine?" Bonnie's head whipped toward me. "Can I keep it?" I nodded. "Thank you, thank you, thank you!" She threw one arm around my neck, still holding the dog in the other. "Daddy, look!" She shoved off me and scrambled to her feet with the puppy.

Smiling, Mom and Alex stood in the entry to the room. I rubbed the back of my head as Bonnie held the dog out for her dad to examine. He raised his brows. "Wow."

His gaze traveled to me. I shrugged. I didn't intend to bring home the ugliest dog—it just happened.

Bonnie pointed to a crescent-shaped patch of light-brown fur on the puppy's ear. "She has a moon on her ear. It's so cool. We have to call her Luna. Like from *Harry Potter*."

Jesse snapped his fingers from where he'd planted himself in the rocking chair. "That's it! She's breed of dog from the wizard world. That's why she looks like that."

Bonnie studied the dog. "That's so awesome!" Beaming she turned to me. "Preston, you got me a *Harry Potter* dog! How did you know I love *Harry Potter*?" Calling for Hannah, she hurried out of the room, with the dog cupped in her arms.

I sank against the couch. When I looked up, Mom and Alex burst out laughing. He collapsed on the couch next me, laughing so hard his shoulders shook. Mom sank against the wall and wiped tears from her eyes. "Oh my, Preston, where did you find that dog?" she finally managed.

Jesse grinned. "Preston was channeling his inner Hagrid."

I tipped my head back and laughed.

Twelve

As the second week of school started, my schedule was packed tight—school, football practice, dinner at Alex's, homework, bed, repeat.

Friday brought our first home game. The heat left me drenched in sweat before we even got on the field. Smells from the concession stand hung over everything like a deep-fried fog.

Jesse joined me off field as the special team lined up for kickoff. He nodded toward the stands. "Looks like they all turned up."

Midway up the packed bleachers, Alex and Mom were leading Bonnie and Edith to sit beside Josie and Brett. Jesse's brothers would be the four brownish-blond heads next to Jesse's parents.

My stomach dropped. "Where's Sammy and Hannah?"

"Don't know." Jesse waved at someone near the cheerleaders.

Lauren, her long legs and curves accentuated by a red miniskirt, waved back with a pom-pom.

I settled my helmet on my head as the ref blew his whistle. "I thought you were dating Mary."

Jesse put on his own helmet. "We broke up a week ago. She's too uptight, you know? Lauren's cute, though. If you don't get around to asking her out soon, I might do some asking myself." He grinned at me before shoving in his mouthguard.

The ball flew to the other team's twenty, and I didn't have time to respond to Jesse. Over the cheers and stomping in the bleachers, Coach Mendez shouted and motioned us out to the field.

Checking one last time for Sam and Hannah, I put in my own mouthguard and followed Jesse. Worried for Sammy and frustrated with Jesse, I tried to let the thunder of feet on bleachers and the clapping of pads against pads sink into me. All that mattered was a white line on the field, the sweaty bodies across from me, and the oval-shaped ball we needed to get to the end zone.

By the last quarter, Coach had me playing both offense and defense. When the game ended in a win, 21 to 7, a rung-out, muscle-throbbing daze hung over me. The crowd from the stands drained toward the parking lots. With my helmet swinging at my side, I followed the team toward the lockers.

"Good game!" Lauren said, bounding up behind me. She carried her cheer bag on one shoulder, her hip cocked out to support the weight. The stance emphasized the slender muscles in her tanned legs and the narrowness of her waist.

"Thanks." *That was easy. Maybe I* can *ask her on a date.*

She smiled at me with lips coated in flame-red gloss. An image of Morgan, her bare lips parted in a laugh, flashed through my brain. She didn't have Lauren's curves, but I'd already thought one too many times about what it'd feel like to kiss Morgan.

I shook the idea away. Morgan needed a friend more than a boyfriend, and I was hardly the kind of guy that made a good boyfriend anyway. I'd probably pass out before I got enough guts to kiss her.

But I did need to go on more dates. Mom kept telling me it would be good for me to get more experience interacting one on one with girls my own age.

"Lauren—"

"Have you—" Laughing, she broke off at the same time I did.

When I stood stumped one second too long, she rushed on. "I was just going to ask if you'd seen Jesse."

I choked, suddenly seized by a coughing fit.

"Are you okay?" Lauren asked, but her concerned expression morphed to discomfort as I continued coughing.

Wow, Preston. Good move. I pointed toward the locker room, hoping she'd figure out he'd gone in before me. Then I headed there myself. I was still coughing a little five yards later when someone yelled my name. Bonnie and Edith broke away from Alex and Mom in the dirt field being used as an overflow parking lot. They came racing across the street toward me.

"We won! We won!"

All the confidence I'd built up playing football was gone. After my conversation with Lauren, I was pretty sure my stomach was working on making ulcers.

Mom and Alex joined us on the sidewalk as Edith and Bonnie skipped around me, singing. Sammy and Hannah weren't with them.

Alex stopped the girls and kept one hand on each of their shoulders. "Nice game," he told me. "You played well."

My fingers tightened around my helmet. "Where's Sammy?"

Mom sighed. "Preston, the polite thing to say when someone compliments you is 'thank you.'"

What had Alex said to me? Probably not something about my brother. I fumbled for words and finally sputtered, "I didn't . . . I just . . . Thanks."

Alex smiled. "Sammy's with Hannah. They wanted to sit with the students. They're okay."

Does he really know that? Does he know exactly where they are? The stands were empty and the parking lot was growing sparse. I couldn't see Sammy or Hannah—not in the crowd of kids mingling near the school doors, or the larger group over by the field.

Mom put a hand on my shoulder pad. "Preston?"

"Huh?" I let her come into focus. Her brow furrowed, her eyes searching in that way that unnerved me, like she could see what was going on in my head when I hadn't said a word.

I forced my lips to smile. "Well, I better get to the locker room."

Alex stepped closer to Mom and slid his arm around her waist.

I stalked off. At the locker room, I stopped in the dark entryway. My teammates shouted and laughed behind a row of lockers, but I slid down the wall and let my head fall against the brick. Breathing was a chore. Keeping myself from running back out to find Sammy was a chore. I pinched my eyes closed and counted breaths.

He's okay, he's okay.
But part of me didn't believe it.

⁓

By mid-September, Jesse had moved on to a girl named Bella, also on the cheer team. After that, Lauren wouldn't even look at me. I probably should have cared more. Instead, I was relieved. The last thing I needed was more girls in my life.

After football practice, I'd spend the evening doing homework at Alex's. Then I usually helped Bonnie or Hannah with math. Watching Alex try to figure out math problems with them was beyond painful. Weekends were spent going through stuff in the house and deciding what would go into storage and what would come with us to Kanab. Even though we really didn't need the help, Alex and the girls still came over.

It turned out the problem with the van was common for the model. Rather than risk it happening again, Alex decided to get a new van. He took me shopping three times. Buying vehicles was one thing he didn't approach calmly. He spent the entire month of September looking. The first week of October he asked me to go with him to see a van two hours away.

I glanced up from a math problem I was working on with Bonnie. "Tonight?"

He put his phone on the table. "Yeah. Your mom said she could come home early from work."

"You got this?" I asked Bonnie.

She nodded. Luna sat in her lap, chewing on a pink fabric mouse Jesse had bought for her. It squeaked every few seconds.

I rounded the table to where Alex sat in front of his laptop. A silver van appeared on the screen. "That it?"

He turned the screen toward me. "Yes."

I reviewed the specs and then slid into the seat next to him. "That's pretty much the same van we saw the first time we went to the dealer in Kanab."

Alex frowned at the screen. "It is?"

I leaned over and loaded the page for the Kanab dealer. Once I clicked on the first van we'd test driven, I turned the laptop back toward Alex. He read the details and sagged in the chair. I waited a bit before speaking again. "So, are you going to drive the rental car to St. George for the wedding?"

He turned toward me. Behind him, Bonnie sat watching us both. I winked at her and she giggled.

Chucking to himself, Alex closed down the laptop. When Mom got home, I rode with him to buy the van from the Kanab dealer. With that taken care of, Alex went back to his normal self. Mom, on the other hand, got crazier the closer the wedding got.

One night as I dug through the fridge, she slammed her notebook full of wedding details down on the table and planted her forehead against it. "Ugh. Why, Preston?"

I closed the fridge, rubbing an apple on my T-shirt.

"No one will listen to me," Mom went on. "We wanted something simple for the reception. I called Aunt Rhonda to see if she could reserve her ward building. Instead, she wants us in her back yard. Now she's hiring a gardener, wants to know if I think a fountain would be a nice touch, and has decided I should wear Clare's old wedding dress." Mom rolled her head from side to side, still talking into the tabletop. "This was supposed to be simpler the second time."

I bit into my apple.

The phone rang. Mom jerked upright, pulled it around to check the caller ID, and moaned.

I wandered over, swallowing down the bite.

"It's Clare," Mom told me. "I told Rhonda no on the fountain and dress. I'm sure she's ordered every one of her girls to call me and tell me how nice a fountain will look and how sweet it would be if I wore Clare's dress. The phone is going to be ringing all night." Her thumb hesitated over the talk button.

I reached behind the phone base and disconnected the landline. The phone cut off mid-ring.

Mom's eyebrows rose and a smile twitched on her lips. She pushed aside the papers in front of her, revealing her cell phone.

I strode over, swept up the cell phone, turned it off, and tossed it back on the stack of papers.

She clamped a hand over her mouth, muffling her laughter.

"'Night, Mom," I said around a bite of apple as I left the room.

~

The last football game of the regular season came the day before the wedding. Mom didn't want me to miss it, and Alex didn't want to drive at night, which meant we'd be getting up really early to drive to St. George the day of the wedding.

Our team had won all but one game and looked good for the quarterfinals coming up after fall break. Eager to get on the field, Coach limited his pep talk to "Ándale!"

The players crowded out of the locker room. Jesse, who had shown up late, weaved to my side and said, "Morgan's here." He jammed his helmet on.

"She is?" A rush of nervous excitement shot through my chest.

We sped up to a jog as we headed toward the field with the rest of the team.

"Yeah. She's coming with us to the wedding," Jesse said.

Sammy had insisted on sending Morgan an invitation, but I hadn't really expected her to come. "She's at your house?" I asked Jesse.

"No, she's up there." He jabbed a thumb at the stands as we reached the field.

"Oh." The stands were crowded with people. Mom and Alex sat on the parents' side next to the Powells. They sat there every week, making it easy to pick them out, but Hannah, Sammy, and now Morgan were AWOL. Again.

I dragged my gaze from the stadium to the field. What mattered was the next play, the next move. I went from play to play until we won 14 to 6. The roar of pounding metal in the stands drowned out even the sound of Coach congratulating us.

After the locker-room celebrations, Jesse and I walked to the parking lot. I still wore my sweaty undertee and football pants.

Jesse waved at a brown-haired girl who stood near his truck. "You want to go hang out with me and Sarah?" he asked me. "We can bring Morgan."

I shook my head. "I can't go hanging out with you and your newest girlfriend tonight. They're getting us up at 4:30. I thought you were leaving early too."

"I'm not driving. Besides, don't you want to see Morgan?"

We stopped at the edge of the sidewalk that wound in front of the school. "Of course I want to see Morgan, but—"

"But what?" said a feisty voice from behind us.

I turned. Morgan stood in the light from the building, with Sammy and Hannah beside her. I couldn't make out Morgan's facial expression, but there was no mistaking her defensive posture as she closed in on Jesse and me. Her hair had gotten longer. The flyaways that had dangled over her pale checks all summer were tucked behind her ears.

She stopped in front of me and crossed her arms. "You don't answer my phone calls, and now you don't want to see me?"

"I was just saying we were leaving early in the morning, that's all. I wanted to see you, but I can't hang out long." The trail of words spilled from my mouth.

A smile broke over her stern features. She sprang at me and threw her arms around my sweaty neck. I was too stunned to return the hug. The next second, she jerked away. "Oh, gross. Preston!" She stared at her damp hands.

A laugh burst out of me. "What did you expect? I've been running around all night tackling guys."

"You smell awful."

Jesse pounded his knuckles into my upper arm. "Hey, you want to meet over at the Junction in thirty?"

"I can't," I said, more forcefully this time.

"Fine. Whatever. You know you suck, right?" He stopped long enough to look me up and down. "Might as well have already moved." In a long-legged loped, he took off across the parking lot.

Morgan frowned at Jesse's disappearing form. "What's that all about? Are you two fighting?"

"Nah." At least, I didn't think so.

Morgan's appraising look echoed my own doubts.

～◦

Within twenty-four hours, Mom would be remarried.

I stared up at my darkened ceiling and willed myself to stop thinking and go to sleep. Instead, images of Aunt Rhonda's house packed full of wedding guests played through my brain. *I shouldn't be thinking right now. I should be asleep.* I would need all the help I could get tomorrow. The wedding itself would be easy compared to having to deal with Mom's family—especially Aunt Rhonda.

I squeezed my eyes shut. *Please, Heavenly Father, help me get some rest.* But sleep wouldn't come. My brain paraded my worries one after another—Aunt Rhonda, the drive to St. George, the temple, the girls, the crowds of people I'd have to interact with. Morgan being around my extended family, Jesse being mad at me. Troy, and panic attacks I'd had after he was gone. And early in the morning, reruns of Bryan's accident.

When Mom came to wake me, I lay on the bed staring at the ceiling. She turned the light on. "Pres—" She cut off and frowned at me. "How long have you been awake?"

The clock on my nightstand read 4:46. I hadn't slept at all. Blinking back a groggy fog, I sat up. My room was bare but for the stack of boxes in the middle, and my bed. The dust-coated shelves overhead were empty. In the far corner of the closet, the carpet was worn through to the floorboards.

I jerked away from the memories of hiding in there. I'd been too long in my own head, and it was filled with the raw ends of things I didn't want inside me.

Mom left with a hurried "Get ready."

I was halfway through pulling on my clothes when Sammy's voice erupted in the hallway. "I don't want to be up! It's too early."

"Sammy, honey, we have to leave now if we are going to get there on time," Mom said in a soothing tone.

"I don't care!"

I moved to the hallway. My brother lay sprawled on the floor outside his bedroom, his old baby blanket over his head. He still wore his rocket-ship pajamas. He moaned and rolled from side to side.

Crouched at Sammy's head, Mom pulled back the blanket and said, "Alex is waiting for us."

Sammy let out a loud, fake snore.

"Why today?" Mom looked upward, imploring God.

My brain rooted around for a way to help, but instead it flipped through a hazy slideshow of other times Sammy had done this. The first day of my freshman year of high school, the morning of his stress tests for his heart, Mom's graduation from SUU . . .

I walked into the bathroom and grabbed my toothbrush from the gallon-sized bag Mom gave us to store our bathroom stuff in for the trip. Five minutes later, I returned to the hallway. Mom dragged her suitcase around Sammy's prone form, then continued down the hall and out the front door.

I crouched at his head. "Hey, Sammy?"

He swung wildly at me. "Go away."

I dodged his fists. If we were late for the temple, would they have to reschedule? I wandered into the kitchen. Alex had sent over some muffins for breakfast. I grabbed two and slouched in a chair.

Mom rushed by and scooped up two more bags. I picked the wrapper off a muffin and let my head fall into my hand. I wondered what her family, and Alex's, would say if we were late. Hopefully his family wasn't like hers. Maybe we could we go to the temple and avoid the whole extended family. Or maybe we could just skip the temple and send Alex home to Payson.

Mom ground to a halt in the hallway. "Preston!" I blinked at her. "What are you doing? Help me." Her hands waved over the stack of boxes and bags to load in the car.

"Oh." I left the muffins and grabbed at the closest thing, a box of what looked like vases. Outside, the car trunk filled fast. "Mom, why are we bringing all this stuff? I thought we decided I'd move the rest of the stuff to Alex's on Monday."

"It's for the wedding!" She popped out of the back seat. "I'm getting married *today,* or did you and Sammy forget?"

When I stared blankly at her, she growled and stomped to the house, grumbling. "Anything I let your Aunt Rhonda take care of turns into a production. If I want it to be a certain way, I've got to bring it with me. The first time I got married, she bought twenty fish tanks!"

I trailed after Mom. The last thing to haul out was a huge garment bag containing her wedding dress. I tried to squish the bulk of it down and fit it between the trunk lid and the pile of suitcases and the other garment bags that held suits for Sammy and me.

"Stop!" Mom shoved past me. She snatched up the dress, carried it to the back seat, and carefully laid it out. "You'll have to hold it on your lap until we get to Alex's house. I don't want it wrinkled."

It took both of us to drag Sammy to the car and get him into the front passenger seat. Mom tried to dust off his pajama pants. During all of this, he pretended to be asleep.

I crawled into the back seat under the wedding dress, doing my best not to disturb it.

When we arrived at Alex's, a much noisier scene spilled out their front door. Hannah was hauling out overnight bags, pillows, and blankets. Edith ran in circles on the front lawn, and Bonnie was throwing stuffed animals at Edith. I'd no sooner climbed out of the car than Mom and Alex had added four more garment bags to the back seat.

Mom motioned me to the bucket seat nearest the door of the van. I sat without thinking. Edith knelt in the seat next to me, singing the ABC song at the top of her lungs. Knee-deep in blankets and stuffed animals, I gaped at Mom. Was she really going to make me ride with Alex? "I can drive your car so you can ride with Alex." I put one foot out and tried to get around her.

"Preston, you haven't slept. You are really out of it. You can't drive like that." She grappled with my arms, caught both of them, and pushed me back into the seat. I was too dazed to put up much of a fight.

Bonnie cried out in the driveway, Luna clenched to her chest. "I have to bring her with me!" Each of her hysterical words hit my eardrums like a hammer.

"You were supposed to take her to Mrs. White last night, before the football game," Alex said in his most serious tone.

Bonnie retreated toward the garage door. "You never let me have what I want." She paused. "I'm not coming if I can't bring Luna!"

I sent a pleading glance at Mom. "Let's move the wedding dress to the van."

Hannah started the van and connected her phone into the radio. "You ever heard of Herman's Hermits?" She twisted in the seat to grin at me.

A man's British voice rang out of the speakers, and Edith and Hannah burst into song.

Seriously? I sprang out of the car.

Mom caught me again, pinning me against the front door of the van with her forearm across my chest, her whole body braced in a lean toward me. "Preston."

"Mom, I'm begging you, please do not make me ride in that van." I tried to keep my voice low, but the desperation in it carried far enough for Alex to hear. He glanced from Mom and me to the van, now blaring, "Second verse, same as the first" out the open door.

Mom took a shaky breath, but when she spoke, it was calm. "Alex, I left a small dog carrier in the garage yesterday." She turned to him. "My aunt has an old kennel on the side of her house. If Luna stays there, it will be fine. Rhonda just doesn't like dogs in the house."

For a long pause, Mom and Alex looked at each other. Then he smiled and they switched places, Mom heading toward Bonnie, and Alex heading toward me, like he and Mom had agreed to something neither Bonnie nor I heard.

I pushed my back against the door, my whole body seizing up. Alex put a hand on my shoulder and leaned around through the open side door. "Hannah, it's too early for music. Can you turn it off and put a show on for Edith?" He pulled down the built-in screen over Edith's seat and dug a set of headphones out of the chaos on the floor. "Or better yet, how about you let Preston ride up front? Then you can help Edith while we drive."

The door pressing against my spine got me to move.

"Excuse me," said Hannah, grinning as she climbed into the back of the van.

Alex raised his brows at me. "All right?"

I slid into the front seat. Hannah's backpack was jammed into my knees. I fished it out and passed it to her. Alex closed my door as Mom came out of the garage with the dog carrier. Within minutes we were on the road. Alex, me, three girls, and a cross-eyed dog named after a character from *Harry Potter.*

I was pretty sure I wouldn't survive the day.

Thirteen

Alex played soft classical music. The next thing I knew, we were pulling up in my great-aunt Rhonda's driveway, and I had a kink in my neck from sleeping against the door. I stayed in the van even after everyone else piled out.

Alex circled around to my door and opened it. "Feel any better?"

I felt like vomiting, but it was probably just the anxiety wreaking havoc in my empty gut. Two uneaten muffins still sat on the table back in Karlon. "You got any food?"

He chuckled. "There are muffins in the bag between the seats."

By the time I dug out as many muffins as I could carry, Alex had taken a load of stuff into the house. *Guess I should help.* I stuffed a muffin in my mouth and dumped the rest back in the bag, then piled as many things as I could into my arms. He returned and I followed him into the house and down Great-Aunt Rhonda's all-too-familiar hallway with vaulted ceilings and sleek, rug-covered wooden floors. When Alex stopped at the guest bedroom, I dropped my load by his, except for the bag of muffins. I ate another one before we returned to the van.

I managed the remaining trips from the van and car without any of the extended family seeing me. Keeping myself close behind Alex and my arms stacked high seemed to render me invisible. Several of Mom's cousins peeked around doorways or out of the kitchen, obviously wanting to check out Alex, but none of them spoke to me. I ate the rest of the muffins.

When everything had been unloaded into the guest room, Alex
stood with one hand behind his head, frowning at the bags. "Now
we've got to get it all in the right rooms. The girls' dresses are in those
bags." He pointed to the white garment bags on the bed. "I think I
got the wedding dress to your mom, but she wanted her makeup bag.
Which one is that?"

I dug around until I found two bags I recognized as Mom's. I held
them out to Alex.

"She's down in your aunt's bedroom," he said. "Why don't you
run them to her? The ladies went pretty nuts when I showed up with
the dress."

Still crouching, I lowered the bags. Alex and I stared at each other
for an uncomfortable moment. He reached for a suitcase, breaking the
tension. "I'm going to take this bag to the girls. My mom must have
been lying in wait for us. She's already attacking the hair situation."
He grinned. "Hair isn't really my thing."

"Where's Sam?" I asked.

"He grabbed his bag and headed off to change, I think."

I'd have to approach a roomful of my female relatives—alone.
Still, that didn't scare me half as much as the very good possibility
that one of those women would be Aunt Rhonda herself.

"After you take that to your mom, you'll probably want to
get ready too." Alex nodded at my basketball shorts. "And maybe
your hair."

He chuckled when I reached up to touch it. It was matted in the
back. *Great.*

He left with the girls' dresses and his own suit bag.

I closed the door, sat on the floor, and leaned against the bed,
taking long, slow breaths. In place of the sluggishness from earlier,
a reckless anxiety was attacking my tired body. Knowing the anxiety
was probably heightened by lack of sleep didn't make its effects any
less intense. This was the worst possible day for me not to have slept.

I forced myself to stand up and get dressed. The suit Mom
borrowed from a ward member held my shoulders tight and limited
the motions of my arms. With Mom's bags in hand, I braced myself

and headed for Aunt Rhonda's room. As I passed the open door of one of the other bedrooms, a female voice drifted out.

"He's totally loaded you know."

Slowing, I shifted the bags in my arms. One of Mom's many cousins responded, "How does an artist get rich? Aren't they supposed to be the kind that live on nothing in the name of creative expression?"

"I overheard one of Alex's aunts talking about it. I guess after his first wife died, his sister-in-law posted a bunch of his paintings online with the whole story about the accident. People started buying the paintings to help out with the funeral expenses and hospital bills. It turned into one of those viral things. The paintings were actually good, and it spiraled from there. Now he gets invited to all sorts of conferences and art shows."

No one had ever mentioned that to me. It hadn't even entered my mind to wonder how Alex made so much money painting,

"You'd think he'd have splurged a little more on the wedding," a third voice put in. "Aunt Rhonda's been killing herself getting things ready."

The first voice said, "I think it was Nat. You know how she is. She is probably worried he'll think she's marrying him for his money."

I shook myself and hurried on. The last thing I needed was to eavesdrop on that sort of thing right now. I already had enough to worry about.

Clare, Mom's closest cousin in age, pounced on me the second I appeared in the hall that wound to the master bedroom. "There they are! Nat, I've got the rest of your stuff!" She reached for the bags.

Aunt Rhonda poked her head out of the bedroom. "Preston? Well, what did you do, get dressed first? Honestly. Today is about your mom. Why are you making her wait?"

Clare went inside, but Aunt Rhonda stepped into the hall, her hard gaze traveling up and down me. I backed up two steps before she barked at me to stop. She stalked down the hall and yanked on the front of my suit coat. It strained over my shoulders as she tried to line it up the way she wanted. She adjusted my tie and dusted something off my shoulder.

"What did you do to your hair?" She licked her fingers and tried to go at my hair. I ducked. We ended up doing a strange sort of dance that moved me toward her room instead of away from it.

The unmistakable sound of Mom crying had me entering the room before I could think it through. Several women shouted protests.

At the foot of Aunt Rhonda's king-size bed, Mom sat dressed in a bathrobe too big for her. Her hair lay in a fuzzy tangle around her shoulders. Her cousin Shelly sat behind her with a comb in one hand. Clare knelt in front of Mom, trying to calm her down. Large tears poured down Mom's cheeks. One of the younger girls dashed in with a tissue.

Aunt Rhonda's long, witch-like nails dug into my wrist. "Preston, out."

"Why are you thinking about him today?" Clare asked my mom. "He's not worth it, Nat, you know that. All he ever did was hurt you."

Mom rubbed at the tears. "We had such a beautiful wedding. He let me buy so many lilies. You remember, Clare? They filled the whole car. We drove up with me practically in his lap. He was laughing so hard. I used to make him laugh."

My throat went tight. I was half ready to fight off Aunt Rhonda, half ready to run.

"Preston?"

The voice came from the other end of the hall. I turned. Jesse's mom held her shoes in one hand, a bag in the other.

The next thing I knew I'd reached her side. "She's crying." The words slipped from my shaking lips, a whisper only Josie could hear. She shifted her shoes to the other hand and inched the purse up her arm. Her free arm came around me, pulling me close to whisper in my ear. "It's okay. She's just nervous. I'll take care of her."

I nodded, trying to breathe.

Josie stepped back and smiled. "Wow, you sure are handsome, aren't you?" She winked at me. "Morgan and Jesse are in the living room. Your mom called and asked me to come over. They decided to come along. You and Morgan can keep Jesse out of trouble, right?"

I relaxed a little. "We'll try."

"Good boy." Josie hugged me against her plump side again. Then she scurried in to help Mom.

When I walked into the living room, Morgan's face lit up. She sprang from the sofa. "Nice, Preston. You look good in a suit."

With a snort, Jesse kicked his legs out where he sat in one of the reclining chairs.

I let out a loud sigh. "I'm glad you guys are here."

Morgan laughed and darted forward to throw her arms around me again. This time my own arms responded, circling around her and straining at the sleeves of my borrowed suit.

"Yay, you smell good." She sniffed at the lapel of my suit. "Well, like a car and some sort of cinnamon something." Grinning, she tightened her arms around me. "Much better than sweat."

It felt so good to hold her. I didn't want to let go.

She slipped back, grabbed my hand, and dragged me to the sofa. "Sit. You look kinda pale. Are you feeling okay?"

"I didn't sleep."

She'd looked good last night in the half light of the parking lot, but here, dressed up in a blue skirt and a flowered top with her hair falling around her shoulders in the bright light of the living room, she was beautiful. My anxiety slipped away like a shedding skin.

"Yuck. I'm sorry," she said. "Were you worried or something? About the wedding?"

So much about her was easy and comfortable for me. But talking about the wedding, talking about my worries—my real dad—that still wouldn't come. It stuck inside me. I couldn't give it to her.

Her smile faltered. I'd been staring at her.

"Preston? Are you sure you're okay? Have you eaten?" She slid closer to me.

I nodded. "Muffins. Cinnamon."

"How long is this thing going to take?" Jesse interrupted.

We turned to him.

"What?" Morgan said.

"This wedding. How long?"

Morgan stood, put both hands on her hips, and glared at him. "Honestly, Jesse, why did you even come if you're just going to be a jerk? No one made you come over here."

"Yeah, well, I was hoping hanging out with Preston would be more entertaining than sitting around the hotel. If I'd known you two were going to flirt and talk about feelings, I'd have stayed there."

Morgan went a scarlet that must have matched my own face. For a second, I thought she might slap Jesse. Instead, she took an unsteady step back from him. "What is wrong with you? You've been awful since last night, and all you did was fight with people the whole drive here." The red flush faded from her cheeks as she straightened her shoulders. "Maybe you're the one that needs to talk about your feelings. What's going on, Jesse? Why are you doing everything you can to mess things up? Huh?" She retook the step she'd given up and then took three more, planting herself in front of him.

To my surprise, Jesse shrank from her.

She slammed both her hands on either side of the armrests. "You want to tell me where you were last night when your dad was freaking out about you? You want to talk about how you made your mom cry when you got home? Do you? Huh, Jesse?"

A movement in the doorway tore my gaze away from them. My blood rushed, same as if she'd yelled all that at me. When I saw Alex standing there, eyes circling from them to me, my heart stopped pumping altogether.

"Crazy Girl. I'm sorry, okay?" Jesse said. "I'll be nice. Back off a bit." He placed both hands on Morgan's shoulders and pushed her away. "Overreact much?"

Alex chose that moment to enter. He picked up humming before he got far, jostling Morgan and Jesse out of their death stares with the sound. Then he plopped down where Morgan had been seconds before, next to me.

"I brought you food. You were eating those muffins like a starved kid." He pressed something into my hand—a plate of fried eggs and orange slices.

"You had time to cook?" I cast a skeptical glance at him.

"I cook when I'm nervous. Plus, no one seems to need my help except to ask me what bag I put stuff in. I wanted to make sure your mom was okay. Apparently she was crying, but your aunt Rhonda tried to hit me with a hairbrush. I don't get the big deal. It's not like she's wearing the dress to the temple. They have to put it on her there. And we're riding over together."

"Well, watch out," I warned. "When Aunt Rhonda hits, it hurts worse than it looks like it will. She can be brutal with that brush." I dug into the food as Morgan inched away from Jesse.

"She get after you a lot, then?" Alex said hesitantly.

My first instinct was to blow off his concern, but something deeper in his eyes stopped me. Maybe he thought Rhonda would go after the girls. After all, Mom and Alex were leaving us here tonight, since they didn't want me driving the kids home so late. Mom had said Aunt Rhonda wanted us kids to go to church with them and have lunch before we took off. Plenty of time for disaster to strike.

"I won't let her hit the girls," I told Alex. "Even if Edith breaks every plate Aunt Rhonda owns and then puts all the shards in her dishwasher." I'd have to be pretty diligent keeping an eye out, but it was nothing I couldn't handle.

Alex's lips parted in a little smile. "Yeah, okay." He clapped his hands on his knees and stood. "Well, I'll probably have a talk with her anyway. You ever tell your mom that your aunt has hit you?"

Jesse and Morgan gaped at us. I shifted awkwardly. "Nah. It'd just worry Mom. Don't tell her, okay?" I pushed the eggs around my plate and lowered my eyes.

"Yeah, okay. But Preston, you can tell Rhonda to back off, even if it's you she's getting after, not one of the other kids."

I pressed my fork into one of the oranges, sending a spray of juice over my plate. "That's stupid. It's not like she's going to hit me with her brush or something. I'm not ten anymore."

"I'm not talking about a brush," Alex said. "I'm talking about her words. You don't have to take it, and if she keeps at it, put the kids in the car and go home. I'm giving you permission to be rude if you need to be. Don't take the crap. You don't deserve that."

Relief spread through me, as if I needed permission to talk back to Aunt Rhonda. "Yeah, okay." I shoved another bite of egg in my mouth. When I finally looked up, Alex had gone. Jesse and Morgan still stared at me.

"What?" I held out an orange slice. "You want some?"

Jesse jumped out of the chair, grabbed the orange, and set to work on it while pacing the room. He didn't say anything, and neither did Morgan. Later, when we all started packing to head to the temple, they both stuck to my side like some convoluted winged shadow until I'd gotten into the van with Alex and Mom.

Fourteen

Jesse headed back to the hotel to watch the younger boys. He was going to meet us at the lunch after the wedding. I assumed Morgan would go with him so she could help watch the little boys, Jeremy and Benji. But when I got to the temple, Morgan met me as I climbed out of the van. I didn't ask and she didn't explain, but I could almost hear her and Jesse deciding I needed backup more than he did.

Hannah and I each took one of Edith's hands. Sammy fidgeted with his tie until it hung lower on his neck, and Bonnie pouted about having to leave Luna at Aunt Rhonda's place.

After begging us to behave, Mom and Alex disappeared inside the temple. We hung out at the visitor's center for a while. When the little girls started shouting and running, we went outside into the garden area and found benches to sit on. Not long after, the family that could go in the temple trickled out.

A new sort of disquiet hit me. Mom and Alex were married, sealed together forever. If he was also sealed to his first wife and all of their kids, including the two who died, then they were connected to Mom too. But Mom had never been sealed to Troy, so I wasn't sure where that left Sammy and me. Even if by some strange stretch Troy ended up joining the Church, he and Mom could never be sealed now, and Sammy and I could never be sealed to them.

The idea of eternal families had always been sort of a letdown for me, but now Mom had gone and gotten her eternal family without us. I was still trying to work out how God could make that fair one day, when a short woman with glasses, wildly curly gray hair, and a blissful smile strolled over to me.

"Hi, I'm Katie, Alex's mom. It's Preston, right?" She stepped closer and for one terrible moment I thought she might embrace me. Instead, she leaned in and whispered, "I'm so glad you are part of our family now."

I had no idea what to say. Technically, I wasn't part of her family, and coming after what I'd just been thinking, my brain tripped over itself and stalled out.

A hand clamped down on my shoulder. "Preston, it's polite to respond when people talk to you."

The smile faded from Katie's face as she took in Great-Aunt Rhonda standing behind me. "Oh, he's fine. I wanted to introduce myself," Katie said. She smiled again, then zeroed in on me. "And ask a favor of you, if you don't mind."

When I still didn't speak, she trudged on. "I didn't get a chance to ask you this morning when I told Hannah, but since I'm in charge of the luncheon, I thought it'd be so nice if you and Hannah each took some time to talk about your parents." At my lack of response, Katie pitched her voice higher. "You know, you about your mom and Hannah about Alex. It would be a good tribute to them. Maybe add a few words about how happy you all are for them, that sort of thing."

What? NO!

Aunt Rhonda shook my shoulder. Those nails bit down, the pain spreading even through the suit coat. Alex said I could tell her to back off, but what about if I couldn't get any words to come out?

"He'll do it," Aunt Rhonda announced.

Katie, whose smile had faded, tipped her head at Great-Aunt Rhonda. "I can't remember . . . how are you related?"

Rhonda straightened as if the words were the worst sort of insult. "I am Natalie's aunt. I practically raised her after her mom died, so she's basically one of my own. Her dad couldn't be bothered, could he? Unfortunate how girls tend to pick men like their fathers. Hopefully the second time around will produce better results."

Katie turned white, the wrinkled skin under her eyes on her otherwise rather youthful face standing out against the bloodless skin. "Oh, I see. You own the house where we got ready this morning."

"Yes. We've been helping Natalie plan everything," Rhonda said. "The reception's in the back yard. My gardener planted coordinating flowers for the event. Of course, he did that the first time around too, but you know, you can't help girls who go after their strays. Natalie's been doing that since before she started working at the clinic in Kanab."

"I see," Katie said again.

Clare pushed between the women, holding a flower in both hands "We need to put these on you for the photos."

One of Clare's girls—Anna, I think—appeared behind her with another flower. "This one is for Preston."

Someone took my hand and pulled me away. I followed, Anna trailing me. We stopped off to the side from the larger crowd, and I found myself standing in front of Morgan. She took the flower from Anna. "I can do it."

"Oh, okay. Thanks." My cousin studied Morgan with a perplexed frown. "Who are you? Some sort of special aid or something?"

Anger practically shot out of Morgan's eyes. I noticed, as if from some distant place, that she appeared to be swallowing her words. When she spoke it was tense and tight. "We're friends."

"Oh. Okay," Anna said before she wandered off.

With shaking hands, Morgan reached up to pin the flower to my suit. The pin she pulled from the stem had to be at least three inches long. My fingers moved of their own will, wrapping around hers. She went still. I tried to speak. Instead, I gulped air.

"It's okay, Preston."

Sure, it was fine. As long as I didn't let her try to pin anything with a three-inch-long needle to me while her hands shook.

Hannah and Sammy strolled up to us. Sammy pointed at his own flower. "Look, Morgan, it's really nice, huh? Mom likes this color."

It was a pinkish sort of orange, a color Mom wore a lot. The rose pinned between Morgan's hands and mine was white—the same color of the one I wore at Bryan's funeral.

"Preston? Are you okay?" Hannah put a hand on my shoulder, just like Alex did all the time.

My head nodded.

"What are you doing?" She pointed at my hands holding Morgan's in midair, the flower halfway to my shoulder.

"She's shaking. The pin is like three feet long." *Words. There they are.* I had no idea what would come out next, but I was talking.

Hannah laughed, a familiar sound from the last two months. My body unwound and the muscles in my shoulders relaxed. She wouldn't fight with me or yell at me. She never fought, never yelled. The girl was ridiculously positive and chill. She moved in. "Here, let me do it." I released Morgan's hands and she passed the flower over.

"They should be coming out soon," Hannah said. "I'm so hungry. I hope there's tons of food at the luncheon." She backed away. The flower was stuck to me now.

I wanted it off. It smelled of a casket and a stuffy room full of crying people.

"Oh, did Grandma warn you about her little speech thing?"

Hannah's words hit me like a full-body crush of a guy fifty pounds heavier than me. Desperate, I rounded on Morgan. "I can't do that."

"What?" said Hannah, behind me now. "Speak? It's not that big of a deal. Just say a few things about your mom. You can think about it while they take pictures."

Morgan gave me a half smile. "You can do it. You did fine with that sort of stuff at Young Men and Young Women events, right?"

Yeah. I did. But since Bryan died, I'd made someone else do all the talking. Every week.

Before I could protest more, people yelled, "They're coming!"

Mom and Alex emerged from the temple doors and descended to the walk. Mom glowed, her smile full and rich. The white gown added to the effect, as if more than her face glowed. A grinning Alex held her hand. He waved at me and Hannah. The next thing I knew, she was dragging me up to meet them.

~⌐

We arrived at the luncheon after everyone else. A full hour of pictures had given me plenty of time to think about what to say. It also allowed my frantic anxiety to morph into a rather large animal.

I had to do this. If I didn't, I'd ruin Mom's day with one more reminder of Troy. I'd prove that all the stuff Aunt Rhonda ever said about me was true, and I'd have Mom all over me about needing to get help with my anxiety.

The banquet hall had a private room set up for the meal, which was catered by a local restaurant. Round tables dotted the room, most already filled. After the prayer, everyone dug in. Katie slipped around to tell Hannah and me that we would do our "little talks" after dessert.

My foot drummed under the table, hidden by the white tablecloth. I breathed in, but the air wasn't enough. Someone put a plate of cheesecake in front of me. The room tilted. I'd black out if I stayed a minute longer.

I pushed away from the table and escaped out a door in the right side of the room. It closed behind me with a click, leaving me in a darkened and empty hallway. I slid down the wall and sat with my knees bent and my arms resting on them. The smell of the white flower pooled in my nose. I yanked the pin out and crushed the rose in my fist before chucking it away. As I leaned back over my knees, the reverberation of a microphone crackled through the wall. Katie murmured over the talking crowd, silencing everyone.

My heart skipped several beats.

The door beside me opened. I hunched over and prayed whoever it was didn't know me.

The person knelt beside me. "You aren't doing well, are you?"

Morgan. I jerked my head back and tried to take a deep breath. It slid like a hiss through my clenched teeth. Then out. And in. Until I heard my breath accelerate into a panic attack.

Full blown, right there. In front of Morgan.

She grabbed my hand. "Hey, hey. Preston. Calm down. It's okay. You don't have to do it."

But I did. I had to do this.

The static sound came again. Hannah laughed into the mike.

My breathing morphed into moans. Morgan's hand was the only solid thing beside me. I clutched it tighter and blinked hard. My mind spun until it reached to God. *Help me. I can't do this here. Please, help me.*

The door opened again. I released Morgan and brought both hands up to hide my face.

Sammy knelt in front of me. "Preston?"

I blinked at him through my wheezing breaths. Something wet spread though my eyes. *No. No. Please, no.*

He took my face in his hands. His fingers were round and short and too tight, digging into my skin. He pressed his forehead to my own, looked right into my eyes. "It's okay, Preston. You don't have to talk. I'm going to do it."

Sammy released me. When he entered the banquet room, Jesse slipped out. I hunched down, hoping he didn't notice, praying he'd be oblivious enough to not realize what was happening. He slumped down the wall next to me on the other side.

"Benji just spit pasta out his nose. Pegged one of those girls that were at the house. She about lost her own food when she saw boogers in the middle of the marinara sauce on her skirt." Jesse laughed to himself.

I grabbed onto the image of Benji pelting Anna with lasagna boogers and tried to block out everything else. Morgan's fingers, tangled in my own, were hot and sweaty. Jesse would probably give me crap about holding her hand, but I couldn't quite care enough to let go. The burning in my eyes passed.

Hannah wrapped up her comments to the lunch crowd. Silence spilled around Morgan and Jesse and me—except for my breath. It was loud and ragged in the absence of Hannah's voice. What if they didn't let Sammy speak? What if someone came out to force me in, and I had a breakdown in front of them all?

Jesse nudged my shoulder. "So then that girl was practically gagging, and Mom was trying to help her get the sauce off, and the rest of us were cracking up when Jeremy spit punch all over the girl's face. One of your aunts or cousins or something came over then and took the girl away." Jesse laughed again and it faded out on a pleased sigh. "I don't know why Mom always expects things to go different than last time at these things. She was all worked up about it, but honestly it was the best thing that has happened all day."

My ears strained for the first sound of disaster erupting inside. If I got dragged in there, it was a sure guarantee that no one would remember Benji's boogers or Jeremy's spit. My body rocked, my knee bouncing under my arms.

Sammy's voice spilled over the microphone. No one stopped him. By the time he finished, my breath evened and I stopped rocking. Exhaustion seeped from my head downward, draining out the former panic as I sagged against the wall.

Aunt Rhonda bulldozed into the hallway. She slammed her palm against the light switches beside the door, bathing us in light.

Frowning, Morgan blinked at Aunt Rhonda. On my other side, Jesse rolled away from the wall to his knees.

My great-aunt's eyes traveled to my hand, which was still looped through Morgan's. "Oh, dear, dear girl," Rhonda scoffed. "Don't you know it's pointless? No? He hasn't told you about his dad, has he? You don't want Preston. Not in a romantic way. He'll only hurt you."

I released Morgan. Shame swelled thick and deep inside me. I was going to suffocate or vomit. Jesse sprang to his feet and moved between Aunt Rhonda and me, blocking part of my view of her.

Alex emerged through the still open door—livid. Anger pulsed off the arch of his shoulders, the lean of his body, and the clenched fists at his sides.

I should've just gone in. A weight fell hard inside me, smothering any warmth left from Sammy's speech. Mom had only been married for a few hours, and I'd already started messing up another relationship for her.

I gulped hard. "Alex, I'm sorry."

Jesse glared at me before crossing his arms and stepping toward Alex.

Alex pulled Jesse to the left and leaned around him, pointing a finger at me. "No. You have nothing to be sorry about."

Jesse's defensive stance melted, his hands dropping to his side.

Alex moved to face Aunt Rhonda. "My children, including Sammy and Preston, will not be staying with you tonight. If you want me to bring them to your house for the reception, I suggest you apologize to Preston right now. And you had better not say another demeaning or hurtful thing to him the rest of the night. Preston is not Troy. No matter how much you hurt Preston, you won't get vengeance on Troy, but you will always be hurting Natalie, and you will always be hurting Preston."

Aunt Rhonda paled. For a long time, she and Alex stood glaring at each other. Then she turned to me. "I'm sorry. It's seems I misunderstood the situation." She skirted around Alex and disappeared into the banquet room.

Jesse frowned as the door shut behind her. "What a witch."

Alex stepped in front of me—right on the rose I'd thrown. He lifted his foot and looked at the smashed petals. Then he crouched down, scooped up the rose, and stayed there, holding out the flower to me.

"Roses are for funerals," I said.

Jesse let out a suppressed grunt.

"Ah." Alex's eyes flicked to Jesse, and he tucked the rose in his pocket. "I saved your cheesecake for you."

"Thanks." Emotions battled inside me. The way I'd felt, thinking Alex was that mad at me . . .

He let one knee down and dug into the coat of his tux. "Here we go." He pulled out a small notebook and pen. "Can you figure out something to do with that?"

My chin bobbed a fraction.

"Great. We'll take off in about thirty minutes. Why don't you meet us out by the van?" He stood, but stopped in front of Jesse to say, "You think your mom or dad could drive the van home tonight?"

I jerked my head up. "I can—"

Alex's hand lifted, stopping me. "You didn't sleep last night. I don't want you driving."

Jesse looked at me. "Yeah, they'd help. You need me to ask?"

"Nah. I'll find them." Alex disappeared into the banquet room.

Morgan and Jesse were unnervingly quiet. With Aunt Rhonda's words hissing through my head, a rush of anxiety bled out from my chest until even my hands shook. I opened the notebook.

Morgan slid closer to me. "What you doin'?"

I ran the pencil over the page, forcing my fingers to stop shaking.

She leaned against my shoulder. "I didn't know you drew."

"Jesse made fun of me for it, so I stopped."

He snorted and climbed around me to sit on my other side. "Since when do you care about what I think?"

"I was fourteen and stupid." The pencil lines grew more frantic across the paper.

"Huh." He leaned into my space to see the pad, which made me stop. "Why'd you listen to me? I was fourteen and stupid too."

"Jesse, you're still stupid." Morgan pushed Jesse's head out of my space. The pencil hit the paper again, trailing lead in an arc.

"Yeah, well, that's your opinion." Jesse pushed my hand aside to look at the drawing. "Huh. I guess you're good at it. When did you start up again?"

"I was at this fair this summer and met a painter who told me not to listen to you. I started drawing after that."

"So that's why you signed up for art this semester?" Jesse slumped against the wall.

I leaned over the notebook.

Morgan's hand rested on my knee. "Why didn't you mention any of that? I was here all summer. We talked all the time."

"Because the guy started dating my mom and it got complicated."

"Oh," Morgan said quietly. "Alex, you mean?"

"Yep." My hand twitched over a few quick strokes.

She sighed. "I wish you'd told me they were dating. You can tell friends stuff like that. I thought we were friends."

"I didn't realize how good of friends," Jesse interrupted. "How long have you two been holding hands?" He reached around my back and pushed Morgan away from me about five inches.

She shoved his hand off. "Shut up or go inside and leave us alone."

He slumped down. "Fine. I want to know too. He didn't really tell me either."

I stopped drawing. "I tried to tell you, Jesse." Though honestly I hadn't tried very hard.

He huffed.

Morgan leaned against me again. "But you didn't tell me. Why not? What's the real reason?"

I faced her. Her head was tipped back, her hazel eyes steady as they locked with mine. It didn't matter anymore. I had to tell her the truth sometime, and now she'd seen it happen. "Because I might've had to tell you about my dad."

"What about your dad?" Jesse asked. "What's he got to do with any of this? That Rhonda lady was talking about him too."

Morgan exhaled loudly. "Jesse, stay out of this for a second."

I broke eye contact, but she said, "I told you about my dad, how he was always gone. Didn't you think I'd understand?"

I curved a line around the face I'd been drawing—Sammy's. "What did you know about my dad back then?" I asked.

"That he'd left. Bryan said it was because of Sammy."

I scoffed at the pad. "It wasn't Sam. Not really. It was going to happen long before that. If one of us should be blamed, it's me."

Jesse shifted behind me. He didn't know this either. I'd never talked to him about my dad. I frowned when I got to Sammy's eyes, then flipped the page over and started a new drawing, one of a truck engine. It was simpler.

"Why would it be your fault that your dad left?" Morgan said.

"Because I was turning out like him and he was blaming himself. Kids are supposed to learn from their parents' example, aren't they? Half the time, he couldn't even leave the house."

Jesse scooted away from the wall. "You mean your dad has social anxiety too?"

"Yeah. But worse, okay?" I didn't want to have this conversation with Jesse.

"So that's what Rhonda Witch meant."

I glared down at the paper. *Fine. He wants to know, and Morgan wants to know. I don't have anything left to lose.* "Yeah, that's what she meant. Then Sam came along. Troy lost his job and started drinking, and he decided we'd be better off without him."

Morgan gasped. "He didn't . . . he's not dead, right?"

My eyes lifted, settling on her at last. "No. Just holed up in my Aunt Jaclynn's house. He gets jobs, has bad days, drinks, loses his job, drinks some more, gets depressed, does something to 'free us' from him, then gets help for a while before he does it again."

Morgan frowned. "What do you mean 'free you'?"

"You know—make it so we don't have to deal with him."

"How?"

Might as well go all in. "Mom learned that her family was willing to give her Grandpa's old place after he died. We were living with my aunt Jaclynn then too, and Troy, my dad, didn't have a job. Mom found the job at the animal sanctuary. She and Troy decided we should move into Grandpa's place and she could work at the sanctuary until he got back on his feet.

"When the day came to move, he didn't come. He told Mom he had stuff to take care of and would follow us down later. She had to be to her new job on a certain day, so she had to go if she wanted it to work out. We headed off without him, only he didn't come the next day. He went out and got drunk and decided we'd all be better off if he never showed up.

"After a few weeks, we went back to Arizona for him, but he wouldn't talk to me or Sam. He told Mom to go back to Karlon. He said if I kept spending time with him, I'd get worse."

I scowled at the paper. I was only five when that happened, but it was stamped on me, heavy-handed and dark, Troy closing the door in my face every time I tried to get to him.

The notebook fell to the floor. Morgan picked it up, pushed it into my hand, and guided the pencil to the paper. "Talk while you draw. So your mom gave up eventually?"

"She had to, or she'd lose her job. I think she would've stayed at Aunt Jaclynn's even with that, but . . ." I pressed a harder line over the paper and stalled near the spiral binding. "She found me having a panic attack. In a closet. I was freaking out because Troy wouldn't even look at me. I had Sam with me. He was trying to calm me down, but he couldn't. I heard her tell Troy. She was leaving because of me. Because I was getting worse."

Morgan leaned in again. "Preston, that wasn't your fault. It was his for ignoring you. That's what made it worse."

"Yeah. I know. I've had counseling and all. But that's what he does, anyway. At first, he swore he'd get help and come when he was better. Then he told Mom to move on. When she didn't, he sent the divorce papers. He's done nothing but hurt her for over twelve years. Aunt Rhonda, and several of my mom's cousins, hate him for it. It doesn't matter how much Mom tries to defend him or say she's forgiven him. And when she's not watching, they try real hard to make me aware of how disappointed they are that I'm so much like him."

The tip of the pencil ripped through the paper and snapped off. I tossed the pencil away and glared at my torn engine sketch. "But I'm not going to turn out like him." I lifted my head and met Morgan's eyes. "I'm not."

"I know, Preston."

How could she say that when I'd just had a panic attack right in front of her?

Fifteen

The only thing Mom mentioned about the speech was how much she'd enjoyed hearing Sammy. I got the impression Alex hadn't told her much. Maybe he wanted to avoid messing up her wedding day. I appreciated that. She seemed to think Jesse and I had talked Alex into letting us drive back with Jesse's parents. Although I'd never told Mom exactly how much Aunt Rhonda picked on me, she knew I disliked staying with her.

By the time we got back to Rhonda's house the majority of the back yard had been filled with tables, white chairs draped in orange bows, and an enormous lattice backdrop Mom and Alex were supposed to stand in front of.

Jesse, Morgan, and I found a spot in the shade not far from the kennel where Bonnie's dog was confined. Jesse popped three sticks of gum into his mouth and held out the package to me. I took a stick and passed the rest to Morgan.

A large group of men hauled a tarp-wrapped object around the side of the house. Mom and Alex came down the back porch stairs and walked toward them. Wearing a hat with a wide brim covered in feathers and flowers the same color as the ribbons on the chairs, Rhonda directed the men to the center of the yard, where they began unwrapping the tarps. A white stone statue of a naked cherub with a bow and arrow emerged. It balanced on a white stone basin that sat on a white stone pedestal.

About ten feet from the statue, Mom and Alex came to an abrupt standstill, their mouths slack. Jesse, Morgan and I walked over. The men hooked up a garden hose to the base of the statue and handed Aunt Rhonda a white remote. Flushed with excitement, she pushed a few buttons. Twin arches of water shot from either side of the cherub, rising over its head before splashing back into the basin. Pale lights shone out of the water onto the cherub's rear end, changing from pink, to yellow, to blue, and hitting every shade in between on the way. After the first round of lights, a sudden burst of harp music exploded outward.

Mom swore under her breath. Jesse choked on his gum. I slammed a hand against his back. Mom headed toward Aunt Rhonda, with Alex on her heels.

Jesse spit his gum in his hand and blinked at me with watering eyes. "Did your mom just swear?"

"Yep," I muttered, unable to recall hearing her do that before.

Morgan put a hand to her mouth but whispered around it, "Is that for the reception?"

"Looks like it."

We watched in silence as Mom confronted Aunt Rhonda. "I said no fountains." Mom took the remote and turned off the display.

Aunt Rhonda patted her arm. "I know. But once I saw it, I knew you'd love it." She sent a side glance at Alex. "Just because we are having a reception in a yard doesn't mean it can't be as nice as a venue. Do you really want the neighbors to think I don't take care of you? You're practically my daughter."

"What are you talking about? I haven't accepted a dime from you since I married Troy. I didn't want you to spent money on this. It was supposed to be at a church. It was supposed to be simple." Mom's voice rose to a shout, and she waved toward the fountain. "Tell them to take it back. I said no and you didn't listen. Again."

Rhonda gathered herself to her full height, snatched the remote, and stormed toward the house. "It's my house. The fountain stays."

Mom stood fuming with clenched hands.

Alex touched her arm. "You all right?"

She deflated, eyeing the fountain. "It's horrible."

He pulled her into his arms. "We'll only be here a few more hours. Hang in there."

She sighed and they walked to the house together.

I sank into a chair, and Morgan found one next to me. Jesse headed inside. Morgan and I talked a bit, but my body felt too drained to keep up the conversation. As much as I enjoyed the chance to be alone with her, I was kind of relieved when Jesse came back. Until I realized he held Aunt Rhonda's gaudy hat.

"Jesse?" I said, worried.

He examined the inside of the fountain and reached into the basin. Then he placed the hat on a chair and moved the chair until it sat a couple feet from the fountain. He sized up the distance to the fountain and shifted the chair another inch or two. Grinning broadly, he came over and dropped into the seat on the other side of me.

Morgan slid to the edge of her chair. "What did you do?"

"Nothing," Jesse said, but when I glanced at him a second later, he moved his hand enough for me to get a glimpse of the remote control for the fountain, clenched against his leg.

I studied the fountain-and-chair setup. The chair was positioned exactly across from one of the fountain nozzles. If all the water was forced out that one nozzle . . . "What did you plug it with?"

Jesse pushed his tongue against the side of his cheek. It took me another second to understand. His gum was gone.

People started showing up thirty minutes later. I went back and forth with myself about whether or not to stop Jesse. About forty people were milling around the yard by the time Aunt Rhonda made another appearance. Anna ran ahead of her, pointing at the chair Jesse had staged. "It's right there!"

Jesse's eyes lit up. I shook my head at him, dread sinking into my gut. I should've stopped this. The last thing Mom needed was another mess to deal with at her wedding.

The second Anna grabbed the hat, Jesse pushed the button on the remote. The arch of water shot from one side, high over the cherub, missing the stone basin and clocking Anna on the top of her head. Her shriek echoed around the yard.

I seized the remote from Jesse and shut off the water. The crowd of people turned toward Anna, who stood with water dripping down her face, the hat clenched in front of her. I held the remote along the side of my leg and covered it with my hand.

Aunt Rhonda headed straight for the side of the fountain that shot the arch of water. "What on earth?" She peered over the edge of the basin into the nozzle.

Jesse met my eyes. For half a second I thought better of it. Then I pushed the button.

～

I left the remote on the refreshment table and followed Jesse and Morgan into the house. Inside, I grabbed them both by the arms and pushed them down the hall into the narrow sunroom. The windows were partially blocked by overgrown houseplants. A small bench swing sat against the opposite wall. I shut the door behind us.

Jesse sank into the swing and cracked up. "That was awesome."

I let out a breath, laughter fighting up my throat. "It felt good."

Morgan looked at me. "Preston? You did that? Not Jesse?"

"Hey, I sprayed the first girl. She's the one Benji and Jer got earlier." Jesse hooted and slapped his knee.

Morgan's mouth curved up into a smile. "I'm actually kind of glad. She was mean at the temple."

"Ha!" Jesse pointed at me. "And you didn't want me to do it!"

The door swung open. Jesse's mouth snapped shut. Morgan and I spun around.

Mom stalked in and went straight to Jesse. "Did you do that to Rhonda?"

He lifted a hand. "No. I swear I didn't."

Mom rounded on me. "Did you?"

"I . . ." Sweat broke out in my palms. I swallowed hard and nodded.

Mom threw her head back and laughed. In the next moment she flung her arms around me. "Preston Troy, I love you."

After the reception, Mom and Alex took off in her car for a few days alone. I tried not to think the word "honeymoon," but everyone kept saying it. Josie drove the other kids and me home in the van. We reached the house in Kanab near midnight. The time at Grandpa's house had officially ended with the wedding. George would start the remodel on Monday, beginning with the basement, and now Sammy, Mom, and I would be living with Alex and the girls 24/7.

When we got inside, Edith raced circles around the living room. "Let's have a party!" She flipped over a box of flower petals. After planting herself in the center of them, she threw handfuls into the air and spun as they fell.

"Stop. It's time for bed." I reached for her arms. A handful of petals exploded in my face.

"No parents! No parents!" Edith sang as she danced away.

The puppy scurried between my legs and squeezed behind the sofa.

"Luna!" Bonnie dropped the dog carrier and ran through the petals, sending them floating in an ever-increasing radius. She pounced on the couch, pressed her cheek against the wall, and peered behind the couch.

I gathered up as many petals as I could and stuffed them into the box. Edith danced around me, flinging more petals over my head. I snagged her wrist and pulled her to me. "No more flowers."

She arched back, wriggled free, and tossed the petals over her shoulder. Singing again, she tried to grab another handful of the flowers near her feet. "You aren't the boss. You aren't the boss."

"Edith, I'm in charge while your dad and my mom are gone. It's time for bed."

She stuck her tongue out at me.

"Preston, get Luna out." Bonnie bounced down on the cushions, her face pinched with her standard frown.

"She's been in strange places with crowds or in that carrier all day. Let her be."

"She has to sleep with me!" Bonnie flew to her feet. "I wish Dad was here. You're so mean." She burst into tears.

Edith slipped out of my grasp and ran down the hallway, throwing more petals. "Everyone cheer! Dad and Natalie are married!"

Hannah wasn't in the front room at all. She should be helping. I called her name and followed Edith down the hallway.

"She went downstairs," Sammy said from where he sat at the kitchen table. The box full of tiny bottles of bubbles was open before him. We'd used them to send off Mom and Alex. Sammy had four bottles spilled in front of him, and another in his hand. He blew a puff of tiny bubbles toward me. "Can we eat ice cream for the party?"

I sighed. "We aren't having a party. We are going to bed. Put those away." I leaned down the stairs. "Hannah?"

She didn't respond.

Still crying, Bonnie followed me into the kitchen. "Why are you so mean?"

"I'm not being mean. You do need to go to bed."

"Not without Luna!"

I threw my hands up. "If she wanted to sleep with you, she wouldn't be hiding behind the couch."

Edith darted between us. I tried to snag her arm, but she shrieked with laughter and disappeared into the living room.

Bonnie landed a furious kick on my shin.

"Ow. Bonnie!" I blocked a second kick. She threw herself at me, fingers out like claws. "Whoa! Stop." I wrapped an arm around her, pinning her arms to her side and her back to my chest. My other arm locked around her legs. She screamed as I hauled her to the room she now shared with Edith on the main floor across from Alex's bedroom.

Sinking on the more sedated blue bed instead of the pink one covered in ponies, I held Bonnie until she sagged against me. Her screams faded to snot-soaked sobs. "I can't sleep without Luna. I need her. Daddy's not here, and I'm scared."

"Bonnie, you don't need to be scared," I said as softly as I could. "I'm here, aren't I? And Sam? And Hannah? You're going to be fine."

"Hannah is scared too. She always gets scared when we are alone. She doesn't tell Daddy anymore. She thinks no one notices. She's such a faker."

"Okay. Let's go get Edith reined in and then we can see if Luna is ready to come out yet." I didn't bother to hide the defeat in my voice. *And I thought getting a dog was a good idea.*

I led Bonnie to the living room.

Tiny wedding bell-shaped confetti and sparkling silver glitter glistened all over the room, along with a sea of flower petals. Sammy and Edith danced in the middle of it, tossing handfuls as they spun. Glitter sparkled from the couches to the curtains to the carpet.

"Edith! Sammy!"

Another volley of petals exploded in my face.

It took an hour to calm them down and clean up most of the mess. Sammy crashed on the longest sofa before I could vacuum off the glitter. At least the rumble of the vacuum scared the puppy out of her hiding place. Bonnie took Luna to her bedroom, and by the time I'd put away the vacuum, she and the dog were asleep. Edith passed out while still draped over my lap, her hands dangling toward the floor—after I sang ten songs and told two stories. I rotated her up and into the pink pony bed.

Then I dragged myself downstairs and tapped on the door of the smaller bedroom. "Hannah?"

"Yeah?" she said brightly.

"You okay?"

"Yeah, great!"

"I'm going to bed. The girls are asleep."

"Okay."

I stumbled up the stairs and fell face-first into the smaller sofa. After that I didn't remember anything until Bonnie woke me to a light-filled room and informed me we'd slept through the first hour of eleven o'clock church.

I went downstairs and found Hannah's room empty, the door standing open. She wasn't in the bathrooms, kitchen, laundry room, or larger bedroom recently emptied for Sammy and me. Finally, Edith found her in Alex's room, burrowed near the foot of the bed.

As she emerged from the bedding, I said, "What are you doing?"

She shrugged, her face puffier than normal. "Nothing."

It looked like she had been crying, which I didn't even know she could do. My stomach knotted. At all costs, I had to avoid Hannah crying. "Do you need ice cream or something?"

She leapt off the bed. "Sure!"

~

Jesse's dad, Brett, showed up that afternoon to help bring over Sammy's stuff and mine. He asked about us missing church, but didn't seem too surprised we'd slept in so late. We hauled the beds to his truck and tied down the mattresses. I loaded the boxes from Sammy's room into the back of my truck first. It filled the bed. Adding Sammy's bookshelves, along with his favorite bean-bag chair, his end table, and the ridiculously large stuffed bear he'd gotten for his tenth birthday, left little room for any of my stuff. Even if I did manage to get it into the truck, where would I put it at Alex's house? I left everything but clothes and shoes sitting in boxes in the middle of my room.

As it turned out, I didn't even have room for the clothes. Sammy didn't want to leave anything behind. The closet swelled around piles of his stuff. I left my clothes in boxes, rigged up some bed risers out of woodblocks, and stuffed the boxes under the bed.

Alex and Mom got home Monday evening. It took less than a day before I missed the old routine. At least with the way things were before, I could go home to my own room and space. My new bedroom had no privacy. Sammy dictated everything. Even closing the bedroom door had to happen after he fell asleep. He liked having the girls around and didn't care if they hung out in the room whenever they wanted.

Tuesday, I blockaded myself in the basement laundry room by piling laundry baskets against the door. I found Bonnie's dog sleeping in one of the baskets with the pink mouse she carried everywhere. Jesse had a twisted sense of humor, but he was ridiculously proud of having purchased Luna's favorite toy.

Apparently the dog had the same idea about privacy as I did. She climbed in my lap and went back to sleep. By the end of the week, I realized if I shut off the light, I could squeeze in a limited amount of alone time before someone started looking for me, more if I put Luna in the hallway first.

Quarterfinals for football took place the week after the wedding. We won, which meant a long drive to Weber State University the next weekend for the semifinals. I'd never been so focused on winning. If we lost, the season would be over. I wanted that one more week of football more than I'd wanted anything in a long time. We shut out the other team and rode home on a high of adrenaline.

The next weekend we went to St George for the finals. Things didn't go as well there. A loose panic set off inside me as I watched the other team's score crawl steadily out of reach. After two kids got injuries, the rest of the team turned somber and silent.

Coach Mendez pulled me to the side during halftime. "I'm putting you on offense and defense the last half."

I nodded.

He slapped my shoulder pads. "We got this. Remember, you need to make passing lanes out there when you're on offense. We can't win if we don't get a score on the board."

By the end of the game we had scored, but it didn't do us any good. Even Jesse didn't have a lot to say on the ride home.

When we reached the school, a crowd of people flooded the parking lot and gym. Mom, Alex, and the others mobbed me as I exited the bus. I didn't register anything they said. I told them I would get my truck and meet them at home. On the way out, people shouted "good season" at me, and Brett and Josie stopped me long enough to say something similar. I escaped to the truck and sat in the darkness of the cab until the parking lot emptied.

It was over. I kicked open the truck door and walked to the shadowed field. After crossing the track, I stopped in front of the bleachers where I'd watched Sammy running with Bryan and Morgan all summer. I spun away and faced the deserted grass that had been my battle ground for four years. Time was slipping through my fingers. We still had basketball tryouts, and another half a year of school, but it felt like the beginning of an ending.

A mission loomed in the back of my mind, as if waiting for answers. It used to feel like Heavenly Father would help me get through anything, but lately I couldn't quite reach Him.

An ache rose up from my stomach, tightening my chest. I'd been turning to God since I'd first realized He could help me with my anxiety. I'd only been thirteen the first time Sammy passed out while we were home alone. I had to call an ambulance but couldn't get any words out. In desperation, I'd prayed and, somehow, I'd calmed down.

Since then, I learned to turn to Him whenever the anxiety came, but prayer no longer seemed to be working for me. Now I hit a wall when I reached for God. The wall was Bryan dead.

In the Pit, there'd been nothing but red dirt, heat, the smell of leaking gas, and a bunch of kids who needed me to be strong. I'd prayed like crazy, and God told me Bryan was already dead. Everything landed on my shoulders then, but I hadn't fixed a thing that day, and in the end, I'd ended up crying. Like some broken thing God couldn't use anymore.

Now, with bruises lining my skin, my muscles throbbing, and fatigue weighing down my shoulders, I felt a lightning-sharp burst of anger and took off running—hard. My lungs burned with the effort, screaming at me to stop as the darkness reached out to envelop me. I rounded the field once before my body gave out. I fell to my knees on the track.

I'd have given anything to be able to run like Morgan then—to keep going until I stopped feeling. Instead, I waited until I caught my breath and made my way to the truck.

At the house, Mom and Alex waited in the living room. The door swung shut behind me. "Hey, nice game tonight," Alex said. "I wish it'd gone better for you."

Mom smiled. "You played well."

"Not well enough." I stopped in the archway.

They exchanged quick glances.

"You took a while getting home. Everything okay?" Alex motioned for me to come farther into the room.

"I was at the school." I couldn't believe they were going to get after me about being late—especially because they never seemed to get after Sammy and Hannah for that. I hadn't gone anywhere without telling them. Sure, I'd been late, but they'd known where I was.

Alex nodded. "Okay. Hey, why don't you come sit down for a bit? We wanted to talk to you about something."

I dragged my feet into the room until I stood in front of Mom's rocking chair we'd hauled over from the Karlon house. "I haven't showered yet."

"It won't take long." Mom pointed at the chair behind me. "Sit there. Sweat won't hurt it."

Apprehensive, I lowered myself to the edge of the seat. The chair tipped forward on the rockers.

Mom cleared her throat. "We've noticed there have been quite a few times lately when it would have been convenient—and comforting—to have been able to text or call you. We decided to get you a phone."

Alex pushed a box across the coffee table. I inched forward under their expectant gazes and slipped the phone out. It was sleek, thin, and black. It wasn't the nicest phone on the market, but was every bit as nice as Hannah's, maybe even a newer version.

I wanted it, but I also had a ballpark idea of how much it cost. I set it down.

"I've put my number and your mom's in it," Alex said. "The deal is, as long as you are responsible about it, we'll pay for it. We retain the right to read anything you text and anything you post online, and to take the phone without warning, if we feel you are misusing it." He grinned. "I have to say that. Not because I think you'll do anything like that, but because I want you to be careful and smart. Okay?"

I gave up hours at work to play football. I tried to be okay with Alex redoing our house with his own savings. The payment reminders for Sammy's hospital bills had stopped coming after the wedding. I ate food Alex made, and I lived in a house he paid rent for. But I didn't have to take that phone. I wouldn't. Every time I looked at it, I would see myself accepting handouts from him, letting him take over my family and every problem we'd ever had. And Jesse and the other kids at school would see that too.

I shook my head from side to side.

Mom frowned. "Do you have a problem with the conditions?"

"No, I'm not going to take the phone."

She and Alex stared at me. I slid out of the chair and stood. "Sorry I was late. I'll try not to let it happen again."

Halfway through the kitchen, Mom chased me down. "Hey, wait," she whisper-hissed, as if afraid of waking the other kids.

I stopped.

Her mouth pursed in a frown. "Why?"

"I don't need it."

"You do need it, and I need you to have it. I'll feel so much better knowing I have a way to get a hold of you."

"I can't, Mom. Please don't force me. Maybe I can figure out a way to get my own phone, but I don't want him to pay for it."

"Preston, Alex's care for us is more than just money-deep. Haven't you seen that by now?"

"Mom—"

"Please think about it. I know you're worried about the money, but I didn't ask him to buy the phone. It's something he wanted to do, and we talked about it a lot before we decided to get it. With everything that's happened lately, you having a phone would really give us some peace of mind."

Lately. Like Bryan dying?

I'd worked my way to the stairs. One little lie would get me the rest of the way out. "I'll think about it. I'm going to shower and go to bed. Okay?"

Mom relented. "All right. Good night."

"Night." I escaped down the stairs.

I had another nightmare about Bryan. In it I wandered through the Pit, the sound of Morgan's panicked voice coming from all around me, down the twists and turns. It was her phone call, over and over again, played on repeat as if coming out of the rocks themselves. "We need an ambulance. We need help. Please hurry."

Sixteen

Even though we had tryouts for basketball before Thanksgiving, the team couldn't officially practice for a few more weeks. That meant the basketball coach left the gym doors open so we could practice on our own. He noticed who showed up and put them on the court more often.

Basketball didn't allow the same sense of space between the players and fans that football did. Maybe it was the helmet hiding my face or something. I'd never tried hard to be a starter on the basketball team. I could play fine, but I preferred shooting hoops on the concrete pad in Jesse's back yard. It drove him crazy some days. He loved basketball the way I loved football. Maybe more.

School got out for Thanksgiving break, and we had one of those unofficial practices on Wednesday at a nearby church. I didn't want to spend the morning practicing. Morgan had gotten in Tuesday night with her parents, and I hadn't seen her yet.

When I didn't show up, Jesse called. Mom passed me her cell phone and said, "He could call *you* if you'd use that phone sitting on the counter."

Alex looked over from where he stood at the stove. Despite our ongoing conversation about me having my own phone, I'd yet to open the box again.

Jesse didn't like my plan to hang out all day with Morgan and suggested we do something with her later that afternoon.

"She's not going to be here long," I reminded him, glancing up at Mom and Alex.

"Let's go hiking up Kanab Canyon," he said. "You, me, and Morgan. Later today."

"Fine."

"But get over here and play. You're going to end up on the bench if you don't show up more."

"Fine." I hung up, tossed Mom the phone, and headed downstairs to change.

After practice, Jesse told me he'd call once he talked to Morgan. I hung around Mom for the rest of the morning, waiting for the call, but it didn't come until nearly 2:00 in the afternoon. By then I knew it would be dark before we got back from hiking. It irritated me that he'd called so late, but I wanted to see Morgan, and as long as no little kids were with us, the dark wouldn't matter as much. Jesse and I had hiked Kanab Canyon with flashlights before.

I met Sammy lurking in the stairwell when I went to get ready. He backed me into the kitchen. "I want to come."

Mom looked up from the table, where she was working on an art project with Edith, but she didn't interject.

I shook my head at Sammy. "It's getting late. It will be dark by the time we get done."

He frowned. "Bryan and I went hiking. I was out there when it was dark lots of times."

But Bryan wouldn't be with Sammy on this hike. "Not this time. If Jesse had called earlier, maybe, but not now."

"What if Hannah wanted to come? Is it bad for her to be outside in the dark?"

The irony hit me. I didn't care as much if Hannah hiked in the dark. Then again, Hannah didn't have Down syndrome. Hannah didn't have a heart condition, and Hannah wasn't my baby brother. I felt something for the girls. If Jesse tried to bully Bonnie, I'd probably flip, but not like if something hurt Sammy.

Instead of answering, I left Sammy in the kitchen and went to our room. I dug out my hiking shoes, a few layers of shirts, and a jacket from under the bed. Kanab didn't get a lot of snow, but it was a desert and the nights got cold, especially this close to winter. Not five minutes later, Bonnie shouted that Jesse and Morgan were there. I jogged upstairs. Jesse and Morgan stood in the kitchen, talking to Mom.

A bright smile lit Morgan's face. "Hey! You ready?"

"Wait for me!" Sammy shoved around me, pulling a hoodie over his head and almost tripping over his half-laced hiking boots. "I'm coming." He emerged from the neckline and shoved the hood back. "And Hannah is too. I invited her."

She came up the stairs behind me. "This will be fun," she said as I turned to see her. "I've been wanting to hike." The purple backpack hung over her shoulder, and she carried her sneakers and a jacket.

I looked to Mom again. Her brows rose a little and her lips twitched.

Jesse frowned at me. "What happened to just us and Morgan?"

Morgan whacked his arm with the back of her hand. "Don't be mean. They can come. It'll be fun."

"I didn't let Jordan or Braxton come," Jesse said. "And we won't fit in the truck."

"Jordan and Braxton are younger than Hannah and Sammy. Besides, Preston can drive. His truck has five seats." Morgan focused the challenge on me, as if waiting to see who I'd back up— her or Jesse.

I was totally on Jesse's side, but I was a sucker when Morgan looked at me like that. There were five of us. It would be tight in my truck, even if Morgan sat in the middle seat. Putting Sammy in a bucket seat would be asking for a fit, which meant folding Jesse's six-foot-five frame into the space or letting him drive while I wedged myself in there. Not happening. Mom's little car wouldn't be much better. "Maybe Josie will let us use the Suburban," I said finally.

Sammy let out a whoop. "I call the back seat!"

Mom handed some glue to Edith. "I know the car is tight with three in the back, but why not ask Alex if you can borrow the van?"

Edith tipped the glue bottle upside down and squished with both hands until the glue made a mountain over the paper, wet and still growing. Bits of glue dripped to the floor, and Luna darted under the table to lick them up. I flipped the bottle upright and freed it from Edith's hands. Driving Alex's super-expensive van made me about as comfortable as the thought of Edith and that glue.

"The Suburban will handle the roads better," I said, hoping Mom bought it. Truth was, the Suburban was one hill shy of dying. I felt it every time it groaned its way up to I-89, and that was nothing compared to the elevation gains through Kanab Canyon.

Jesse glanced at me but didn't say anything. Edith dug into a bowl of sparkling glitter and confetti and threw it over the glue in a sweeping movement. Pink and purple hearts rained over Mom's head and mine. I put the glue bottle down and sighed.

Mom laughed. "Just ask him, Preston." She stood and dusted hearts from my hair. They floated down on the table and onto my sweatshirt. I shrugged her off and brushed at my shirt, retreating from the one-person tornado of Edith before I realized the glue had stuck to my fingers. Hearts and tiny flecks of glitter peppered my hands.

Edith stood on her chair and reached for my fingers, spreading my hand open. "Wow. It's beautiful!" she said.

Jesse snorted. Edith released me and slammed her hands, palms first, into the glue-and-sparkle mountain. White oozed between her fingers. Her hands came away with a slurping sound. Strings of white dangled from her palms, mixed with hearts and glitter.

A sharp gasp escaped Mom, who caught Edith by the wrists before she touched anything. Hannah grabbed a sheet of blank paper from a stack on the end of the table and slid it under Edith's palms. Mom planted Edith's hands on the paper and pulled up, leaving glittering glue hands on the new page.

"Brilliant!" Edith beamed.

"What's brilliant?" Alex came out of the stairwell, his own fingers covered in an earthy-brown paint.

Sammy intercepted Alex before he could reach the table. "Can we use the van to go hiking with Jesse and Morgan?"

"Sure." Alex motioned to the top of the fridge. "The keys are up there." His eyes circled to me. "You driving?"

I headed to the sink. "I think the Suburban will be better." I tried to push the faucet on without touching it with my glue-caked fingers.

Alex moved to stand next to me. "I thought the Suburban was rattling itself apart. At least that's what Brett said on Sunday,"

"It'll make it, I think," Jesse put in, his voice relaying anything but confidence.

Alex passed me a towel, his expression thoughtful. I sensed he knew the truth—that I didn't want to drive his van because it was expensive, and his, and it meant I was using his stuff again. Like he was really my dad.

I dried my hands and leaned forward, rubbing at my hair until glitter floated into the sink. "I'm not worried about you taking the van," Alex told me. "I know you'll take care of it."

I stiffened. I didn't need his approval.

Jesse threw his hands up. "I'll drive the van. Let's get moving."

Alex considered him. "Will you be careful? Drive the speed limit?"

He rolled his eyes. "Yeah. I've driven before."

"Okay. I guess that works," Alex said.

Jesse walked over to the fridge and grabbed the keys. Everyone walked toward the front door. Even Luna, her white fur now sparkling with glitter, trotted down the hall. My shoulders sagged as I followed Alex out.

Hannah halted on the top step, letting everyone else part around her. She smiled at Alex. "We'll be careful."

"You have your phone?" he asked.

She patted the backpack. "Yep." She hurried down the stairs.

I slipped around Alex, dread sinking into my gut. *We could cut the hike short and try to return before dark . . .*

"Wait, Preston." Alex's voice interrupted my thoughts.

Two feet from the door I stopped, holding in a groan of frustration at another delay. Alex disappeared inside the house. Twenty seconds later he hurried back out, a worried crease across his forehead. He held out the phone he'd been trying to give me. "Will you take this? Please? Just in case."

I shook my head. "Hannah and Morgan have phones."

"It's not easy for me to put her in a vehicle with a teenager driving. I know you would be careful, but Jesse . . ." Alex's gaze traveled out to the van. Hannah sat in the passenger seat next to Jesse. Sammy and Morgan were in the back with the sliding door open. Alex let out a slow breath. "I'm overreacting. Jesse's not completely reckless, and you'll keep an eye on Hannah and Sam." Alex smiled tightly, his eyes searching my face. "I don't have to ask, really. It's the way you are."

"Yeah. Don't worry about them. I'm not going to let them get hurt."

His smile relaxed and he nodded. "Thanks."

A new load settled on my shoulders—one that wasn't just about Sammy anymore. It had Hannah all over it. I wished I'd kept my mouth shut like I normally did.

～

The trail was dusty and cold. Hannah pulled out the camera she always carried with her. Jesse tried to photobomb as many of her pictures as he could, and Sammy laughed harder than I'd heard him laugh in a long time. Morgan and I walked quietly behind them. It wasn't an uncomfortable silence, plus I was too busy watching for a good place to turn around to really think about talking. After an hour, I announced that we needed to head back. If we left now, we'd still have about thirty minutes of light by the time we got home.

Jesse tossed the stick he'd been holding. It bounced off a protruding red rock. "You can't be serious. We've hardly gone anywhere."

"It's going to get dark soon."

"Don't overthink things, Preston. Relax." Jesse moved farther up the trail.

"Let's go home and play games or something," Morgan suggested, stuffing her hands in her jacket pockets. "It'll be fun."

Sammy and Hannah agreed at once.

Hannah slung her arm over Morgan's shoulders. Morgan giggled in surprise and let her arm go around Hannah. Sammy copied Hannah, swinging his arm over Morgan from the other side. They walked back down the trail together in a zigzag, bumping into each other as their steps crossed. Jesse shrugged and jogged after them. That left me to take up the rear. By the time we reached the van, Hannah and Morgan were acting like best friends. They climbed into the middle seats, Hannah taking the spot I'd had next to Morgan on the way up.

Jesse climbed into the driver's seat. I slumped in the passenger seat, while Sammy wiggled into the back. The van pulled onto the road, but Jesse turned left instead of right.

"Hey, wrong way," I said.

He kept going. "Let's go over the top and come out on the other side. It'll be fun."

"No. It'll take longer, and we didn't tell Alex we were going to take the van up and over."

"He won't care. It's not that big of a deal. You cut the hike short anyway. We have time." Jesse glanced in the rearview mirror. "Have you guys seen all the animal-sanctuary stuff up here? We could stop and take a look."

"That sounds cool," Hannah said.

I glared at her. "No."

She deflated, turning to stare out the window. "Or not."

Jesse drove up and over the mountain, but to my relief he didn't stop. When we got to the main road that led to Kanab, I breathed easier. *There isn't much that can go wrong from here.*

"Hey, you hear about that lake on the side of the road? That one by the Montezuma's Cave that's abandoned?" Jesse's hands tapped a rhythm on the steering wheel.

"I've seen it," Hannah said.

Jesse grinned. "The lake is like thirty feet deep. They say there's Aztec gold at the bottom, and anyone who tries to get it dies. The bodies are still down there. No one can get them 'cause the gold is cursed."

Morgan shuddered. "That's creepy, Jesse."

"He's making it up," I said. "There's no bodies in the lake." I turned to see if Sammy was scared. He sat forward in the middle of the back seat, taking in every word.

"What about the gold—is that true?" Hannah asked.

"Maybe." I'd heard about the gold before, but I didn't know if it was true.

"Have people died trying to get it?" Morgan's voice came out in a squeak.

"No. No one's died." I'd heard stories of people exploring the lake and dying, but that was one lie I didn't mind telling.

I faced forward again and caught Jesse's smirk as he said, "Loads of people have died. Like forty or something."

I growled. "Shut up, Jesse. That's a lie."

"So was what you said. You were there when Brother Thomas told us about those divers."

"Just drive already."

Silence followed for about five seconds, until Jesse said, "I swam in there once."

I rolled my eyes. "You did not."

"Did. With Lauren." Half a beat passed. "Want to stop and see it?"

Exasperated, I whirled on Jesse. "No. It's private property."

"No one's ever around. I don't think the owner lives here anymore." Jesse pointed out the window. "There it is."

The small lake appeared in the growing dusk, surrounded by leafless trees and nestled under the ledge of the mountain. Jesse pulled off the road next to a padlocked gate and shut off the van.

"What are you doing?" I swiped at his arm, but he quickly opened the door and slipped out.

The back door rolled open on his side of the van. He grabbed Hannah's wrist and said, "Come look."

"Hannah, do not get out." I unbuckled my seat belt.

"Jesse, I don't think—" Morgan began.

He laughed. "Chill, you two."

Hannah leaned around Jesse, her free hand sliding to the camera on her lap. "The lighting is really nice right now," she said. "It'll only last a minute or two more."

"Yeah, so come on." Jesse handed her the car keys. "Keep those for me, will you? I might go in."

"Jesse, it's too cold for that." I kicked my door open. By the time I rounded the van, Hannah had skipped after Jesse to the gate, her camera swinging at her side. Sammy crawled out of the van and ran after them. Jesse helped him duck under the gate.

Morgan came up behind me. "What should we do?"

I groaned and stomped after the others. This was a bad idea.

⁓

I didn't know what'd gotten into Jesse, but it reminded me of the time he'd led me and three of the younger boys into the Pit near his house. That was the only time I'd seen Brett spank Jesse. We were seven years old. I hid in my closet for twelve hours until Brett came over to talk me out. After a discussion about the dangers of the Pit and going in there alone, he said he counted on me to keep Jesse out of trouble. I wasn't sure why Brett put that on me. Keeping Jesse out of trouble was a full-time job, one I wasn't so good at when things were normal, let alone the last few months after Bryan's death.

Now, on the other side of the gate, Jesse and Hannah headed to the lake, but Sammy took off toward the wooden structure braced against the cliff base. A large sign painted over the front read "Montezuma's Cave."

I hesitated before running after him. Hannah would have to watch out for herself for a minute. "Sammy!" I caught up to him and grabbed his upper arm, forcing him to a stop.

"Ow. You're hurting me," he said. My fingers loosened and he slipped free. "I want to go in the cave, Preston."

"This isn't a playground, Sammy. It's private property. It's like someone walking into our yard and going through the sheds."

He backed away from me. "I'm not going to take anything."

Footfalls sounded behind us, and Morgan jogged over. "Sammy, please listen to Preston."

"Why?" He rounded on her, fists clenched at his sides. "He always bosses me around. I'm sick of it!"

"He loves you, Sammy. He's trying to protect you."

"He's not protecting me—he's trying to lock me up."

"I'm trying to keep you alive!" My outburst brought their eyes to me. I staggered back a step, heat flushing over my face.

"I think that's the first time I've heard you really yell," Morgan said through tight lips. "It's sort of weird. Calm down, okay? It's going to be all right."

Lately, I wanted to yell all the time. And maybe I would. If I could get it past my throat more often.

"He yells at me plenty." Sammy dug his feet in, legs spread, arms crossed, accusation ringing like a kid tattling to his mom.

Morgan reached for his arm. "Sammy, stop thinking about Preston for one moment and think about how you feel, right now, about being here."

Almost reflexively, I forced my anger down as Sammy's face softened. Deep in my gut, it felt wrong to be there. That was why I had gotten so worked up.

"I have a bad feeling," Sammy breathed out.

"So do I," Morgan said. "We are going to find Hannah and Jesse and leave. Okay? Because Preston is right. Can you see that?"

Sammy stared at me, his gaze penetrating my skin. There were a million things fighting a battle inside me, and I didn't want him to see that. What if he noticed the shadow of Troy coming over me?

My brother relaxed. "Okay. But you do need to calm down, Preston. You're getting crazy lately."

I followed him and Morgan toward the lake. In the distance, Hannah stood on the pier, fighting with Jesse over her camera. He got the upper hand and held the camera high, the way he'd tease Morgan or the little boys. But Hannah, who was a good head taller than Morgan, went to her tiptoes and snatched the camera. When she came down she staggered, her feet tangled in the purple bag.

I broke into a run.

The water enveloped her with an air-ripping splash. She didn't even scream.

Morgan passed me in her full-out sprint and got to the pier first. Jesse stood there laughing. Hannah's face broke the surface of the water, her breath a gasp that echoed up the front of the overhanging cliffs. I pushed between Jesse and Morgan.

"Banana Girl! You ain't supposed to take a swim this time of year. I was joking about going in." Jesse squatted near the edge.

Hannah's desperate gaze locked on me before she slid back under the surface.

I ripped my sweatshirt over my head, kicking off my shoes.

"Relax, Superman, it's water," Jesse scoffed.

I hesitated. I'd look pretty stupid if she didn't need help.

Sammy pounded up on the pier behind us, his breaths heavy. As Hannah came up for air a second time, he pushed by me and pulled off his own sweatshirt.

"She can't swim."

Sammy's words clicked together in my head. I yanked him away from the edge. My other shirts came off in a split second and I plunged into the lake. The shock of cold shot right through my skin. My arms swept through the water, pulling me forward until I found Hannah's fingers. I snagged them and kicked upward. Her other hand looped around my arm, a terror in her grip.

We sank down into an inky blackness, with nothing but water and a long-forgotten Aztec treasure to keep us company.

Seventeen

I kicked with all my strength, and the downward momentum reversed. Finally, we broke the surface. Air rushed into my screaming lungs. I tugged Hannah's head against me, her wild hair plastered against my shoulder, her face toward the sky. My arm looped around her neck, keeping her clawing fingers away from my head. I reached for the dock with my free hand. Jesse grabbed my wrist.

Appearing above me on the pier, Sammy seized Hannah's arm. I braced myself against the wood. Jesse's hand came under my armpit. Sammy and Morgan helped Hannah out of the water, and Jesse hauled me up behind her. Morgan, her face ashen, grabbed my shirts away from the flood of water slopping over the deck.

I sucked at the air.

Jesse pounded on my back. "Are you stupid? The first rule is never jump in with someone drowning. You know that."

It had been really stupid, but in the moment, it seemed like the right thing to do. I crawled to Hannah. "Are you okay?"

Nodding and shivering, she cupped her arm against her chest.

After tugging my shoes over my sodden socks, I stood and lifted her to her feet. She staggered. I wrapped an arm around her and half carried her to the van. Morgan yanked open the sliding door before I got there. A phone sat on the seat. I tossed it to the far side and settled Hannah in its place. Freeing my hoodie from Morgan's arms, I told Hannah, "Put this on. You need to warm up."

"Is her arm hurt?" Morgan pointed to the arm Hannah clenched to her chest.

I touched Hannah's arm. She whimpered and jerked away. I stooped in front of her and asked, "Can I look at it, please?"

"I'm fine." The words slipped between her shivering lips.

I tried again, softer this time, easing her hand away from her body. The hairs of her arm stood on end, accentuating a long white scar where no hair grew, running up the entire top of her forearm. Below it was a shallow but fresh cut. Small drops of blood fell onto her lake-soaked pants.

"Sam, is that medical kit still in the back?" I said.

"I got it." He ran to the back of the van.

I unwadded the sweatshirt. "Hannah, let's get this on you."

She sucked in a long breath. "Preston?"

"Yeah?"

"Is Jesse all right?"

"Yep," Jesse answered. He had circled around to open the door on the far side, and now he leaned in. "You swallow too much water, Banana Girl?"

Hannah shook her head.

"Good." Jesse seized Hannah's wrist and examined the cut. "Yeah, you'll survive." He wagged his eyebrows at her. "That was epic. You didn't even scream. Though it might have helped if you'd mentioned you can't swim."

She yanked her arm away. "I don't like water in my ears." Her teeth were chattering.

"I found it." Sammy shoved the medical kit at my gut. "And a blanket." He unfolded a patched quilt.

"Thanks, Sam."

He grabbed the hoodie from me. "She should take off the wet shirt before she puts the sweatshirt on."

I stepped back. Sammy was calm as day, suddenly more reliable than Jesse. If only he'd be like this more often.

"I'll help her." Morgan handed over my other shirts before taking the blanket from Sammy. "You three go over there for a minute."

Following Jesse and Sammy away from the van toward the gate again, I yanked the shirts over my icy flesh and rubbed at my arms. I leaned over to drag my hands through my wet hair.

Jesse danced back from the spray of water. "Easy, we don't all need to be wet."

We stopped at the gate and gazed out toward the lake. Jesse draped his arms through the fence. "Well, that was crazy."

I didn't respond.

The sound of tires on gravel made us turn. A silver car rolled to a stop in front of the van. Jesse grinned, pounded me on the shoulder, and jogged to the car. Unease settled in my chest, like I'd forgotten an important detail.

A girl rolled down the nearest window and leaned across the seat. Her brown hair spilled around her shoulders. Melody Crawford. The girl who'd spent the last few years hinting that I should ask her out. She flashed a huge smile.

Not at me. At Jesse.

"Jesse?" My voice wafted out as facts connected in my brain in rapid succession. A long line of girls he'd dated since September. Not calling to go hiking until the afternoon was nearly over. Insisting we go over the mountain instead of taking the shorter route. His sudden determination to stop at the lake.

He yanked off his jacket and handed it to me. "You might need that, Superman. I'll catch you tomorrow, okay?"

"What?"

"Mom and Dad are worked up about me dating since they caught me makin' out with a girl from homeroom last week," Jesse explained. "They're trying to ground me from dating. So I figured Melody could meet us here and they don't have to know. I was going to have you come along, with Morgan, but you brought the other two, so it wouldn't work anyway." He motioned to Sammy, who stood behind me.

I pulled Jesse away from the car. "*She's* your newest girlfriend?"

He rolled his eyes. "You're ridiculous. You know that, right? I'm not going to marry her. She's a lot less hyper about things than Mary. Or Lauren, for that matter."

"Less hyper. As in, she's willing to kiss you."

Jesse threw my hand off. "I get that you're scared of girls, Preston. That's fine, but most guys aren't. Most guys *want* to be with girls."

Heat spread over my neck, tempered by a rush of anger. I *did* think about girls—one in particular—a lot. Morgan meant more to me than I was willing to risk by kissing her when I knew she wanted to avoid serious relationships in high school. And I wasn't about to make out with some other girl because Morgan had high standards.

Jesse's frown deepened. "Don't look at me like that. You're worse than my dad."

"Hannah almost drowned and you're taking off with Melody because you want to kiss her?"

Jesse shook his head. "No. Because I'm sick of all the stupid rules. I want to be normal. I want to go out with my girlfriend without some paranoid system to make me feel I'm sinning every time I look at a girl. And you're really lame if you honestly think this is only about kissing."

My mind spiraled to places I didn't want to go. Jesse might take things farther than making out. Maybe he had already.

He grinned as if he could read my thoughts. "Hannah's all right. Take Morgan to your place for an hour or so. Buy me some time."

"There's no way we can coordinate this perfectly, even if I wanted to help you," I said. "And I don't." Jesse's jacket slid down my arm, hanging in the dust.

"I don't really care, Preston. I just want a bit of time before Dad comes after me. 'Cause knowing him, he'll try to crash this date the second he finds out." Jesse slid into Melody's car. "'Course he'll have to track me down first." He slammed the door. As the car pulled out onto the highway, a sick lump settled in my stomach.

"Preston," Hannah called out into the unfolding darkness. "Did he leave? Where did that car go? Preston!"

Morgan hurried to Hannah's side and said, "No, he's still here. Jesse left."

Sammy trailed me. "What does he mean by more than kissing?"

"I'll explain later, Sam."

"What is he thinking?" Morgan pressed a hand to her mouth. Tears splashed onto her checks and she spun away from me.

It shook me out of my stupor. I wrapped one arm around her and pulled her to my side. She sagged against me. "It's 'cause of Bryan, isn't it?" she said. "There's this tension between Jesse and everyone else. I didn't want it to be true. But he and Uncle Brett—it's like they're trying to stare each other down all the time." She rubbed at her tears. "What should we do? I don't know what to do!"

I forced a smile and squeezed her once before letting her go. "Let's get home, okay? We can figure things out there."

Biting on her lower lip, Morgan nodded. "Okay."

I opened the driver's door. "Everyone get in the van." Out of habit, my hand went to my jean pocket for the keys. Empty.

I jogged to Jesse's jacket lying in the dirt and dug through it. Nothing. "Where did he put the keys?"

Morgan took in a sudden breath. "He gave them to Hannah. They are in her backpack! I think it fell in the lake." Morgan paused. "Oh no. Her phone and camera are probably in there, too."

Wordless, Sammy, Morgan, and I stood for several long moments in a semicircle in front of a shivering Hannah. Then Sammy moved in and draped the blanket around Hannah.

"I could call Brett." There was regret in Morgan's voice. She climbed over Hannah, back into the van.

Morgan's reluctance reflected my own. As mad as I was at Jesse, he would never rat on me. It had been an unwritten code between us since we'd almost set a shed on fire when we were ten years old. We didn't tell on each other.

Bundled under the blanket, a pale Hannah gazed through me.

When I said her name, her eyes refocused and she smiled. "Okay." She kept smiling, eerily calm, as if she didn't know what was happening. Her knee bounced under the blanket, her finger tapping on the seat. I stepped closer and squatted in the doorway to get a better look at her face. A soft wheeze hissed out her lips—rapid, short breaths.

"Sammy, can you see my phone?" Morgan asked, digging around on the floor. Sammy circled around the van to help.

"I saw it before I put Hannah in," I said. "I tossed it on your seat." I cupped Hannah's head in my hands. "Hannah?"

She blinked at me. "Yeah?"

"Are you okay?"

"Yeah."

"You're breathing really fast."

She let out a little laugh. "Stupid, I know. I do that sometimes." She took a deep breath and then another. "It's freaky not being able to see right now. It's getting dark. It's better with my glasses."

Relieved, I let Hannah go. But all at once she seized my arms. "Don't leave me. I know I should have listened. I'm sorry I didn't stay in the car. Please, please don't leave me." Tears welled up in her eyes.

My mouth dropped. I'd never seen her cry.

Hannah blinked over the tears, took in a long and slow breath, and released my arms. Another strained smile danced over her lips. "It's okay. I'm fine."

"Did you find it?" I asked Morgan and Sammy.

Morgan stood up on the opposite side of the car, her hands at her sides. "He took it, didn't he?" she said slowly.

"What?"

"Jesse. He took my phone. That's why he came over to this side of the car. He wasn't checking on Hannah—he was taking my phone because he didn't want us to call anyone."

"What good would that do? Hannah had a phone too. He didn't know it was gone . . ."

Jesse knew. He knew from the moment we pulled Hannah out of the lake that her phone and bag were gone. Which meant he knew the van keys were gone.

He left us stranded here on purpose.

⁓

Sammy and I found a flashlight and walked down to the now-dark lake. The water on my skin dampened my shirts, and the hairs on my arms prickled under the cold. I took the flashlight from Sammy.

The icy water lay shadowed and still. I crouched on the edge of the pier and moved the beam of light around the wooden supports below. A cold breeze skirted over my skin and my body shivered.

Sammy knelt beside me. "There." He pointed.

I shined the light in that direction. The straps of the bag, murky shapes through the semi-clear water, were snagged on a jutting piece of rebar coming up from the muddy ledge just before the drop-off where Hannah fell.

"Are you going to go in and get it?" Sammy asked me.

"Maybe. Let's look for a long stick first."

Thin willows surrounded the lake, so we headed for the shoreline. Finding a sturdy and long-enough branch not still connected to the ground or a tree turned out to be harder than I expected.

"Preston?" Morgan called down from the van.

"Yeah?"

She stood in the light from the open door, one hand on Hannah's back. "She's asking where you went. She thinks you are going to leave her here. I'm worried about her."

I jogged to the van. Hannah had curled up under the blanket, her knees to her chest. Her fingers peeked out from the cloth. I touched her shoulder. "Hey, are you breathing?"

"Yeah. I'm fine. I'm sorry." Her voice had returned to its normal cheerful tone. "Did you find it?"

"Yeah. I'm trying to figure out how to get it out."

Hannah flinched, then lifted her head. "Hurry. Please."

"I'll be five minutes, all right?"

Hannah nodded.

Back at the lake, I handed Sammy the flashlight. "Point it toward the bag, Sam."

"You're going in?"

"Yeah. We need to hurry." I pulled my shirts over my head again. The damp sleeves stuck to my skin. I yanked hard, wriggling my arms out, and dropped the shirts on the deck. They were just dry enough it might be worth saving them for after. I tugged my shoes off.

"You ready?" I glanced at Sammy.

He nodded, training the flashlight on the submerged bag.

I took a lungful of air and jumped out, past the rebar into the deeper water. The lake embraced me and my legs kicked hard, propelling me up. I surfaced with a gasp. The cold gripped at my skin in a renewed effort to freeze me solid. Without Hannah's almost drowning to distract me, the water felt even colder. I swam toward the light Sammy held pinned on the water's surface.

Diving down, I kicked hard and reached out. The bag caught on my fingers. I tugged it up with me. The flashlight danced over my face. I swam to the pier, where Sammy gave me a hand up. I sat down on the edge of the dock, shivering as I passed the bag to him.

He ran the light around the lake. "Did you see her camera?"

"I'm not going back in there for a camera."

Sammy kept searching the water with the flashlight beam. "She loves her camera."

I got my feet under me and stood, brushing beads of water off my icy skin. "Even if I could find it and get it out, it's ruined now."

"Maybe. There's stuff you can do to get photos off some electronics that get wet."

"Sam." I sighed over his name, wishing I could put all my reasons for not going back in that lake in his head all at once and be done. I leaned over and pressed my hands along my head. Water splashed onto the wooden boards. I had to warm up. Maybe it was a good thing Jesse left his jacket after all. I grabbed my shoes.

"I'll go." Sammy lifted the edge of his shirt.

I caught his arm. "No, you're not going in there too. I've got enough to worry about with Hannah soaking wet."

"I can swim."

I waved my shoes toward the water. "Can you see it in there?"

He shook off my hand. "You didn't look. I'm going to look."

I reached for him again. "Hannah's close to having a panic attack. We need to get her home."

"There!" Sammy pointed. "It might be there."

I groaned and followed the beam of light into the water below us. "That's a rock."

He shoved the flashlight at me. "It could be her camera. I'll go in and see. You go check on Hannah and tell her."

"You're not going to jump in that water while I'm at the van!"

"I don't need you to babysit me!" He flopped down and tugged at his shoes.

"Sam. You're so frustrating sometimes." I dropped my own shoes. "Where? Show me again."

He glared at me but released the grip on his shoes to grab the flashlight and point it. "There."

"Okay. I'll go in. Two minutes. That's all. If I can't find it in two minutes, we go home."

Sammy hesitated, but finally nodded.

I jumped back in the water. The cold wasn't as shocking this time. In fact, it was almost warm compared to the cold air on the dock. I swam toward the beam of light and dove down. I brought Sammy five rocks from several sides of the deck before I convinced him the two minutes were long since up. While he stood watching, I hauled myself out and yanked on my shoes and clothes. Slinging the bag over my shoulder, I motioned for Sammy to lead the way to the van.

On the deck he stacked the rocks I'd pulled out for him. He'd been certain each rock was the camera. When he straightened, his face pinched up as if he'd been socked in the gut.

"Sammy." I slid my arm over his shoulders. "I'm sorry, okay? I'd swim that whole lake top to bottom to find that camera for you if I had the time and ability. I really would."

He shrugged my arm off. "You're getting me wet. And the camera isn't for me. It's for Hannah." He stomped toward the van and left me alone on the dock.

I blew out a breath as shivering took over my body. My stiff jeans stuck to my trembling legs, water running off them into my shoes. The cold leached inward.

We had the keys, but I still had to get us home. I walked up to the van in the dark.

Hannah sat with her eyes closed, her lips whispering. Her eyes popped open. "Sammy." She jerked around. "Preston. That took forever."

Swinging the bag around, I found myself faced with a multitude of pockets and zippers, all dripping lake water on my feet. "Which pocket did you put the keys in?"

Her hand slipped out of her blanket, and I passed the bag to her. She dug out the keys, frowning at the sodden contents in the bag.

"I tried to find your camera," Sammy told her. "Preston wouldn't keep looking."

Hannah patted his hand. "It's okay. I want to go home now."

Sammy sighed and climbed into the seat next to her.

Morgan lifted Jesse's jacket to my shoulders. "You're shaking really bad."

"Yeah." I threaded my arms through the sleeves and zipped it closed.

Morgan and I got in the front seats. I inserted the cold, damp key into the ignition. The second the van purred to life, Morgan flipped the heat to its highest settings. I checked the mirrors and pulled the van out on the road. Behind me, Hannah's breath picked up speed.

My fingers tightened on the wheel. When I saw Jesse again, I'd give him two black eyes.

Eighteen

The lights of oncoming cars flashed against the windows as we wound into Kanab. Morgan cycled between sounding calm and breaking into silent tears. I wanted to tell her everyone would be okay. That Jesse would be back to normal by tomorrow. But my telling her that would not make it true. She had been the safe place for a week and a half after Bryan died. It felt as if we would survive just fine with her around. But when she left, real life hit. I wished she wasn't seeing it. I wished I could put one of Alex's idyllic landscapes in front of her and tell her that was how we were all going to end up.

In the back seat, Hannah's breath got harsher with every swish of a passing car.

Kanab appeared, the city lights a beacon below us. I tried to breathe deeper myself, to calm down, but I didn't want to face Alex. I was pretty sure I'd broken Hannah. *I don't know what to do. Heavenly Father, please help me fix this.* Worry, fear, and anger writhed inside me. Desperate, I willed myself to push past the emotions to find a trace of God.

A semitruck roared by us, and Hannah let out a full-blown scream right behind my head. I jerked and the van swerved. I brought the van back to the center of the lane and forced myself to tune out the screaming.

Morgan's hand dug into my bicep. "Preston, don't get in an accident, please."

"It's okay. We're all right," I said, as much for myself as her.

Hannah's scream died, replaced by a harsh whimper that morphed into words. "Daddy. Please, Daddy."

Alex is going to kill me.

Sammy shifted behind us. In the rearview mirror, I saw him take Hannah's hands. "Breathe with me," he told her. "I'll count." Calmness radiated off my brother.

Hannah cried for Alex until we reached the house. Mom's car was gone, and the house lights were off. I got out and opened Hannah's door.

Sammy emerged from the other side of the van. "Where are they?"

"I don't know." I slid my hand onto Hannah's shoulder.

"How will we call them? Alex doesn't have a landline." Sammy frowned toward Hannah. "We need to find Alex."

My mind had gone blank, but suddenly I remembered. "There's a phone in the kitchen. It might still be in a box. I think Alex put his number in it. Use that."

Sammy headed inside the house. Morgan hesitated and then followed. I unbuckled Hannah's seat belt. Her face was soaking wet, red, and swollen. I swung her feet out the door and bent over her.

"Hannah?"

She opened her eyes, but blinked at me like she couldn't get me in focus.

"I can't see." She grasped at me and slammed her face into my chest.

My arms inched around her. I'd never hugged her, never seen her cry until tonight. She was not supposed to freak out on me. "Mom and Alex aren't here," I told her. "I thought they would be."

She lifted her face and scrubbed at her tears. Awareness flickered in her eyes. "I'm having a panic attack."

"I figured that out."

"Where are Sammy and Morgan?" she asked as I started leading her around the van.

"They're inside, calling for help."

"Are they hurt?"

"No. They're trying to get a hold of your dad so we can figure out what to do about you screaming bloody murder for him for the last ten minutes."

"I'm sorry," Hannah mumbled. "I was trying not to."

We went into the kitchen. Sammy stood at the counter, pouring milk in a cup. Pressed against Morgan's ear was the phone Alex had tried to give me. I listened long enough to be certain she was talking to Alex. My stomach clenched like I'd taken a punch to the gut.

I put Hannah on a chair, pulled out another one, and sat in front of her. The red of her eyes and nose created a drastic contrast with her gray coloring.

Sammy handed her a cup of milk. "I was going to get you water, but I thought it might remind you of the lake."

She giggled. The centers of her cheeks turned a splotchy red to match her eyes and nose.

Morgan handed me the phone. "He wants to talk to you."

Dread flowed through me in a downward rush that went clear to my feet. "Hello?"

"Preston, how are you hanging in there?" Alex said. "You okay?"

"Fine. Hannah is . . . ." I trailed off, not sure how to explain.

"It sounds like she had a panic attack."

"Yeah."

"The lake reminded her of the accident," Alex explained. "She won't want you to worry about her, but she's not okay. She needs to have someone with her when she gets like this. Talking it out helps, but I don't know if you'll be able to get her to tell you anything. Anyway, stay with her if you can. Okay?"

"Okay."

"We'll talk more when I get there."

I wasn't sure what he meant by that. He'd probably chew me out or hand down some kind of punishment. The phone slid from my hand to the table. "They're on their way," I told the others.

Sammy pulled up a chair next to Hannah and took off talking.

"You've got to slow down, Sammy," I said. "We can't understand you." I unzipped Jesse's soaked jacket, wishing I dared go downstairs

179

for some dry clothes. The last time I'd been this cold, I'd been camping in the snow. But Alex had said not to leave Hannah.

Before Sammy could restart his sentence, Hannah stopped him. "It's okay. I understood. Thank you for doing that, and sorry about your shirt getting my tears on it. I was having flashbacks to my accident. I think I was comparing you to Edith."

Sammy's lips pouted. "I'm not like Edith."

"I know." Hannah put her hand on his arm.

I got up and paced along the wall near the hallway.

"You don't have to treat me like I'm a baby," Sammy said. "I know about accidents. I stayed with Bryan that day. When he died. I held his hand until Jesse and Preston got there. I was scared, but then I prayed. I knew Bryan was okay, even though he wasn't alive anymore."

Sammy always threw everything out in the open in such a raw, unfiltered way. I hated it. My pace quickened, but no matter how many times I passed by the hallway, the front door stayed closed.

Morgan moved to sit on the other side of Hannah. "We all know what it's like to be scared, Hannah."

Hannah clutched the cup of milk with both hands. "I feel silly now. I didn't want you to know I was having such a hard time. A lot of stuff reminded me of the accident, but I knew you were all trying to help and that I should have listened to Preston. I felt stupid."

"It's okay." Sammy patted her knee.

"Is my dad here yet?" Hannah asked.

Morgan shook her head. "No. They were at the Powells' house. Ironic, considering. But I'm not sure I really care if Jesse gets in trouble for this. I wish we were staying somewhere else tonight, though. I don't want to be around when Jesse gets back."

I should have realized Mom and Alex and Edith and Bonnie would be at Jesse's parents' house. Josie and Brett always had Mom over to play games the night before Thanksgiving.

Silence settled around Hannah and Sammy and me. The lights in the kitchen and hallway were a muted orange that didn't reach the rest of the darkened house.

After a few minutes, Hannah balled up her hands inside the sleeves of my sweatshirt she wore. "The night of the accident, Dad pulled me out the side window," she said quietly. "My arm was all cut up. It was pitch black and snowing, and the van had landed in the river." She cut off, leaving us all hanging.

I stopped pacing. I didn't want her to tell me this. Even though Alex told me Hannah really needed to talk, I never planned on hearing this.

Sammy scooted closer to her. "I think it helps to talk about it, Hannah. I talk about Bryan to you and Mom a lot. And to Brett. He said it's good. It doesn't bother him, but Jesse won't talk about Bryan. Preston either. I think they need to."

"Just 'cause I don't talk doesn't mean I need to. Talking isn't my thing," I mumbled. With Sammy, I always ended up being the bad guy.

"My dad stopped talking—my mom did too—about my uncle who died," Morgan said, keeping her head down. "It was easier for them. It wasn't good for us. I know what Sammy's talking about, Preston. I see you and Jesse doing that same thing. It scares me."

"It's not like that." Talking wouldn't change anything. Bryan would still be dead.

Hannah took a deep breath. "It's the waiting I hate. Dad led me over to this ledge. We'd rolled off the interstate, and all these cars were zooming by above us. He put Edith in my lap and told me to keep her warm. Then he left me."

She was going to keep talking, no matter how much I wished she'd shut up and wait for Alex.

Sammy took her hand. Hannah studied him. All at once I realized she wasn't telling any of this to me. She was telling him.

"I was so scared. I thought he'd never come back. Now I know he was trying to get everyone else out. I really was lucky. Bonnie was trapped between Karen and Andrew in the back seat. They were already dead. She still can't see blood without fainting. I had to sit in the dark and the cold for a while. My arm got cut. That's it. And I had Eddie even though she was a tiny baby. Still, when I get scared now,

I can't be alone. It makes it worse, you know? Even though it's been four years. Some stuff triggers it. The lake did. And the dark. And the cars." Hannah leaned forward. "I really wish Dad was here."

Sammy wrapped his arm around her. "I'll stay with you. I won't leave you."

The sound of vehicles came from the driveway. I walked to the front door, fighting off the images of Bryan that surged up because of Hannah. Mom's car pulled into the drive, and Brett's truck lumbered up behind it.

I didn't want to deal with Brett right now. I was mad at Jesse, but I didn't know what to do about him yet. Mom and Alex got out of her car, just the two of them. They probably left the younger girls with Josie. Brett's truck door banged shut, and he followed Alex and Mom inside.

Alex strode right by me to Hannah. He smoothed down her hair, then tipped her head. "Are you okay?"

She shrugged, back to her calm self.

With her story in my brain, Alex's earlier concern weighed on me. He hadn't sent her with me lightly. And I'd almost let her drown.

Brett stopped in front of me, a tense fury running along his brow. "Where's Jesse?"

I glanced around for Mom. She stood with an arm around Sammy, listening to his rapid-fire explanation of the night. I couldn't understand half of it, and I had been there. Morgan moved to the background behind Sammy and Mom. Smart.

Brett caught my upper arm, his fingers digging into my muscles. His eyes bored into me. "I swear if you know where he is and you're trying to protect him again . . ."

Perspiration sprang up over my skin, creating a paradox of heat and chill that crawled across my lake-soaked body. "He took off."

"With who?" Brett dragged me toward him until his face and mine were inches apart. "This isn't a game. You know you aren't supposed to be trespassing up at the lake. What were you thinking, taking those three there?" He pointed to Sammy, Hannah, and Morgan.

"Brett, calm down." Mom stepped toward me. Sammy moaned a little, rocking in response to the rising tension. Mom stopped and glanced at me as she steered Hannah and Sammy toward the basement. Hannah grabbed Sammy's hand and pulled him onto the stairs.

Appearing beside Brett, Alex said, "I don't think Preston meant for any of this to happen."

Brett faced Alex. "Of course he didn't. But it happened." He rounded on me. "After everything this summer, how can you two still be so reckless?"

My stomach back-flipped and landed at my feet.

"All right, Brett, let him go." Alex worked his way between Brett and me.

Brett relinquished his vice-like grip on my arm. He stormed across the kitchen, clamping his hands around the back of his neck. "What am I supposed to do? I already lost one son!"

Mom closed the door to the basement. "I know you're worried about Jesse, but please don't take it out on Preston."

Brett shook his head. "I just want to know where my son is and how he ended up almost drowning a girl while trespassing on private property." His eyes focused on Morgan. "I take it you're not going to tell me where he is, either?"

"I didn't want this to happen," she said. "I didn't want you all to fight." Tears ran down her face.

Brett sagged. "Morgan, don't cry." He and Mom moved to calm her down.

Still in front of me, Alex said, "Brett is scared. That's why he yelled at you. Not knowing where Jesse is brings what happened with Bryan all back to him. You know that can be the worst thing possible."

A plea crossed Alex's expression, like the way he'd looked at me before asking me to watch out for Hannah. A shadow of the worry that came when I couldn't find Sammy limped up, worn and tired inside me. I didn't wish that sort of torture on anyone.

"He went with Melody Crawford," I said. "She pulled up by the side of van like it was all planned out, and Jesse got in." The words came out strong, carried by the anger still running through me.

Brett, Morgan, and Mom stopped talking. *There. Brett knows. I told him.* But when I looked at Alex, I realized there were more things I wanted him to know.

"Jesse pulled up by the lake and kept telling Sam and Hannah it was okay to be there," I continued. "I couldn't keep them in the van. They wouldn't listen. While Morgan and I were trying to get Sammy, Jesse was messing with Hannah's camera by the lake. She tried to get it back and fell in. I don't think he meant for that to happen. But after, I'm pretty sure he knew the car keys and her phone were in the lake. He took Morgan's cell phone. He knew we were stranded." I sank against the wall. "He knew."

I slid to the floor, wishing I could pull the words back, yet relieved to let them go. "I had to go in the lake to get the keys. Then Sam wouldn't leave until I looked for the camera. I couldn't find it." Shivers ran up and down me, my wet clothes tugging at my skin in new places now that I'd sat. "I didn't know Hannah couldn't swim."

Alex crouched in front of me. "What happened wasn't your fault. You don't need to feel responsible."

I shook my head at him.

He squeezed my shoulder and left his hand resting there. "Why don't you head downstairs and get warmed up? Your clothes are like ice." He stood and helped me up.

A weight lifted off my chest and gave me room to breathe. I wanted nothing more than to get out of that kitchen. Striding to the stairs, I passed the new phone resting on the table. My shaking hand swept out and grabbed it. With my heart pounding against my ribs, I looked at Alex.

He met my eyes and his expression didn't even flicker.

I took the phone downstairs with me.

nineteen

Alex left to get the little girls from the Powells' house. After dropping them off, he went to help Brett look for Jesse. When Alex got back, he stopped by our room to let Sammy and me know Jesse had been found up by the dam behind Kanab. Alex told us everything was fine and headed into Hannah's room.

I memorized Alex's number on my phone before I fell asleep. I dreamed about the lake, and Hannah yelling for Alex. Around 1:00 AM, I woke to an actual scream. My body bolted upright. I waited, but no other sound followed. *I better check on Hannah.* My feet inched to the floor.

Footsteps creaked down the stairs. I froze, waiting as they descended. The door to Hannah's room squeaked open and then closed with a click. Alex's voice drifted out, followed by Hannah's. Several seconds of silence passed before he began singing in a hushed tone. I relaxed and climbed back into bed. Alex knew what he was doing. I rolled over and fell asleep.

The next day, Thanksgiving, we were all supposed to be at the Powells' home by noon. I hadn't been there since summer. Between the memories of Bryan and the dread of facing Jesse again, I thought I might be sick. After breakfast I turned on Sammy's latest video game and played through the food prep. At 11:30, Mom realized what I was doing and sent me to shower.

"Just go without me," I shouted through the bathroom door.

She thumped the door in response.

Soon the warm water ran out. I stood there anyway, my skin prickling and then growing numb.

Finally, Sammy pounded on the door. "We are a minute late!"

I grabbed the shampoo and washed my hair again.

A second knock sounded.

"I'm coming!" Instead of shutting off the water, I stood under the cold stream and let it run over my face.

Alex called, "Sammy's pacing with that watch of his counting seconds out loud. Please have pity on the rest of us."

I turned off the water.

~

All of us, including Bonnie's dog, piled through the Powells' door and tripped over the shoes in the narrow entryway. Everyone else took off, but I stayed in the entry with Bonnie, staring down the hall like it was some sort of line I shouldn't cross.

She shifted the dog carrier in her arms. "I don't like Jordan. He's a jerk."

"I won't let him bother you."

Bonnie gave me a tiny smile. "Okay."

We walked to the kitchen. Josie circled the table faster than a woman her size should move, and snagged me in a stifling hug. My arms came around her, wrapping farther than they had before, as if she was shrinking. Even though losing weight was probably good for her health, I didn't like it.

She pulled my head close and whispered in her most serious voice, "You have been away too long. I don't care how hard it is for you to be here without Bryan, it's twice as hard for me when you don't come. So you had better get your butt over here at least twice a week from now until you leave for your mission, or I'm going to sell this place and move us all somewhere you will come. I can't stand it, you hear me?" She blinked back the moisture in her eyes. My head nodded an agreement and she released me.

The kitchen swam with people, too close and narrow to get a lungful of air. I maneuvered my way through the chaos, aiming for the back yard. Morgan's parents stood on the other side of the counter. I nodded at them as I passed.

Morgan popped up behind them, her hands full of wet potatoes, and smiled. "Hey, Preston."

"Hey."

Brett wrapped his arm around my shoulders. "I need some help outside, okay?" I let him steer me through the back door. Bonnie trailed us. He stopped at the foot of the narrow porch stairs and said, "Hey, I'm sorry about last night."

I studied my gray shoes. "It's fine. How's Jesse?"

Brett sighed. "Angry." His arm slid off my shoulder.

"That's an understatement." Jordan stomped onto the porch with a roll he'd pilfered from the kitchen.

Bonnie slipped around me, squishing herself between Brett and me. The dog carrier hit my knee. I shifted so she was out of Jordan's direct view. She grabbed my hand. Brett raised his brows at me.

"Dad and Jesse have had lots of fights lately, but last night . . . Wow." Jordan tugged on his too-short shirt and took a bite of roll, talking around it. "He's been cursing you a bunch too, for ratting him out."

"Jordan." Brett motioned him down the stairs. "Go get Braxton to help you pull those tables and chairs out of the shed."

Jordan stuffed the rest of the roll in his mouth. "Okay." Crumbs sprayed out with the reply. He strolled off across the yard to the shed behind the concrete pad where we played basketball.

Brett forced a smile. "Don't worry about Jesse. Try to enjoy the day. He's upstairs—didn't want to leave his room. Josie told him he has to come down for dinner, but I don't think he'll stick around after. Anyway, I'm sorry about last night. You all right?"

My head bobbed once.

"Hmm." He patted my shoulder. "Let's go help them. Looks like Jordan's delegating everything to Braxton."

~

We were all outside, the food steaming on the table, when Brett headed inside the house. A few minutes later he emerged with Jesse. Only one chair remained open, two down from me on the right. Jesse stalked to the chair, yanked it out, and sat. Bonnie was the only thing between us.

My foot bumped something and I looked down to find Luna under the table, her leash looped around the leg of Bonnie's chair. Bonnie shook her head a fraction and put a finger to her lips. I winked at her and she smiled.

Brett welcomed everyone, a renewed tension lining his words. His gaze drifted to Jesse before shifting away again. When everyone got quiet, Brett bent his head and offered a prayer on the food. After the usual prayer of thanks for the holiday, Brett continued, mentioning the Savior's Atonement and Resurrection. A nervous itch crept up my back. Brett's voice broke over Bryan's name as he thanked God that we would see Bryan again.

When the prayer finally ended, everyone started talking and passing food. Bonnie fidgeted with her napkin. The blue cloth spilled open, and her silverware clattered to the ground under Jesse's chair. Her foot shot out, blocking Luna's race for the fallen objects.

With a fluid swipe, Jesse swept up the utensils in one hand. He held them over Bonnie's head. She stretched upward, but he moved them an inch or two higher and laughed.

"Give them back," she demanded. When Jesse ignored her, she dropped her hand and whipped toward me in an appeal for help.

I leaned around Bonnie. "Jesse."

He scowled at me, his eyes glinting with an anger that mirrored mine. "What? You going to tattle on me?"

My fingers curled into fists as something pounded hard in my ears. "Don't. You have no right to blame me for any of that. Give her silverware back."

"I have stuff I can tell on you," Jesse replied. "You aren't everyone's perfect boy, you know."

I clamped a hand around his wrist, yanked the silverware free, and gave it to Bonnie.

The conversations around us went silent.

"Jesse." Brett's clipped warning rang out from the other end of the table.

Jesse reached out and flicked Bonnie's ear. "I was just messin' with her."

She grabbed the side of her head. "Ow."

I sprang upright, red anger exploding through me. My fist flew hard into Jesse's face.

Our chairs crashed behind us with the rattle of metal. Bonnie ducked under the table. Jesse stumbled over his fallen chair, gained his footing, and sprinted straight at me. Wind whistled by in a rush as his fist missed my ear by a fraction of an inch. He pounced and took me to the grass in a head lock, his bony knee riding up into my gut with a stab. I worked my arms free and twisted around to pin him under me, then swung another punch at his face. It connected with the palm of his hand. His shoes scratched up my leg before his feet slammed into my chest with a breath-stealing thrust. I catapulted upright and landed on my butt in the grass near the edge of the lawn.

Shouts came from people at the table. A single breath made it into my lungs. Jesse landed on top of me, hands at my shoulders, shoving me down. Dirt bit into my elbows and back. I swung my legs up, wrapped Jesse's torso and rolled. He spilled onto the red dirt at the edge of the lawn. I swung another punch. A hand from above caught my wrist. Triumph glinted in his eyes. He threw his own punch. A second hand looped under my left arm, hauling me up and out of his reach. The hands dragged me onto the grass. I threw my shoulders from side to side, trying to free myself. Both hands locked tight around my biceps. I stopped moving.

Jesse scrambled up, taking advantage of my restrainer to rush me again. Brett stepped between us midcharge. He let out a grunt as Jesse, staggering toward me, connected with his chest. My unseen captor dragged me out of the way.

Brett got his footing and seized Jesse in a full-armed hold, forcing a few more feet between us. The pounding in my head and chest eased off a beat at a time. The wound-up tension I'd been carrying since last night was gone, spilled out on the lawn. Jesse struggled against Brett for a few more seconds before giving up.

Josie stomped toward us, her finger pointed at Jesse's chest. "This is not how we handle things in our house." Her head swiveled between her son and me. "If you have a problem, talk it out. We don't use fists. You both know that. Now get in your chairs and behave. It's Thanksgiving, not a WWE tournament."

My arms unflexed as reality settled in. An ash-pale Morgan stood beside her chair, her arms wrapped around herself. Bonnie peered out from under the table, Luna in her arms. Half out of or standing on their own chairs, the other kids gaped with mouths hanging open. Behind Josie, Mom held her hand over the lower part of her face, her eyes flicking between me and the person behind me.

Something dawned on me. I pulled against the hands wrapped around my biceps. They released me and I turned. I'd never taken Alex for the working-out type, but seriously, the guy was strong. I rubbed at my biceps as a flush ran over my neck.

As he crossed behind me, his hand slid across my shoulders and turned to an unexpected pat of encouragement before he headed toward Mom. He looped his hand through her arm to lead her to the table.

Not knowing what else to do, I walked to the table, righted my chair, and sat. Jesse did the same. The parents returned to their seats at the other end of the two tables butted next to each other, and the food was passed in uneasy silence. Eventually the adults started talking and the hush around the rest of us cracked.

Morgan leaned across the table and glared at Jesse. "What's wrong with you?"

"I'm not the one who threw the first punch," he grumbled into his plate. He piled on some mashed potatoes, passed the bowl to Braxton, and fingered his swelling eye with a grimace.

I helped Bonnie with the gravy before I realized it wasn't hot anymore. Between waiting for Jesse to get to the table, the long prayer, and the fight, a good amount of time had passed. The rest of the food appeared to be in a similar state.

Morgan took the potatoes from Braxton across the table and frowned at Jesse before serving herself and passing the bowl to Hannah.

Jesse glanced around at everyone as if searching for support. "You all saw it. He threw the punch." He pointed his fork at me.

Bonnie scooted her chair closer to mine.

"He's just worked up about Hannah takin' a plunge last night." Jesse zeroed in on her and grinned. "He's totally overreacting. It wasn't that bad, was it, Banana Girl?

With stormy eyes she studied him over the bowl of mashed potatoes. She lifted a scoop of potatoes from the bowl and frowned at it. "Jesse."

"What?" he said around a mouthful of food.

"It *was* that bad." She bent the spoon back and let the potatoes fly. They splatted against the side of his face. "You were a jerk last night and you know it. So get over yourself."

I dropped my spoon as the stunned expression on Jesse's face morphed into a scheming grin. He dragged his hand along his cheek and held the mashed potatoes like a baseball.

Down the table, the parents continued talking, oblivious to what was happening.

Jesse chucked the potatoes back at Hannah. They hit her chest. Braxton gasped and jerked away from the flying food.

Edith stood up in her chair. She pointed her finger at Jesse, the other hand on her hip. "Stop picking on my brother and sister."

Jesse laughed.

Oh boy.

Edith scooped up a pile of stuffing and chucked it at Jesse. She pegged Jordan on my left.

He jerked in surprise. "Hey! What's the idea?" He threw the stuffing back at Edith.

Bonnie darted behind me, yanked on the neck of Jordan's shirt, and dumped corn down his back. "Leave. My. Sister. Alone. You fat jerk."

Jordan shrieked. I snagged Bonnie around the waist and pulled her out of the way. Jordan's spoon of JELL-O splattered over my chest. Edith jumped up and down in her seat. She seized an armful

JoLyn Brown

of rolls from the basket in front of her and chucked them at Jordan as fast as her arms could go.

Everything dissolved into shouting and chaos.

Somewhere on the other side of the table, the adults shouted over the din. A lump of sweet potatoes hit my arm. I jerked around. Jesse stood grinning at me, with the evidence all over his spoon. I grabbed a serving spoon and sent a pile of sweet potatoes soaring. They pegged him in the forehead.

He laughed and threw a handful of salad at Morgan. "Heads up, Crazy Girl."

She blocked it with a plate.

"Ha! Nice block." Jesse grabbed a plate too.

A smile flickered on Morgan's lips.

Sammy broke into hysterical screams. The little kids didn't even notice, but Jesse, Morgan, and Hannah lowered their food ammo. Brett shouted over the remaining noise, the deep-throated sound ringing out like a clap of thunder, and everyone froze.

Sammy kept screaming.

"That's enough!" Brett shouted. "The next person who throws something will deal with me. Am I clear?"

Aside from Sammy, silence met his words.

A perfectly arched ball of wriggling JELL-O shot through the air, soared down the table, and splashed across Brett's shoulder.

Jesse snorted behind me. "Okay. I threw something."

Several quick breaths sounded near me. My stomach lurched. Brett stalked toward Jesse, his arms swinging free. He circled right around the end of the table until he stood inches from Jesse. Still, Jesse didn't move, but met him face on, a cocky smile on his lips.

Brett picked up the bowl of gravy and dumped it over Jesse's head. Jesse's youngest brother, Benji, burst into laughter, and the chaos erupted around me again.

Several pieces of turkey and a wad of green beans hit me as I weaved between the chairs and kids. Sammy continued to scream.

I reached the other side of the tables. Mom knelt on the grass by Sammy, talking and rubbing his back. I crouched in front of them.

He stopped screaming and squinting around. Mom lifted a spoon of potatoes. "See. It's a game. Nothing to worry about." She catapulted the potatoes at me. They hit my nose straight on.

Sammy cracked up. I scrapped the potatoes off, snorting out white chunks into my palm. I wiped my hand on my jeans, then seized the closest plate and spoon. I scooped up a potato-and-gravy mixture and lobbed it back at Mom. She laughed and ducked behind Sammy.

The every-man-for-himself battle morphed into a war between the parents and the rest of us. They barricaded themselves behind an overturned table with most of the food dishes, pelting anyone who tried to get close. Jesse and I set up the other table, and the older kids all catapulted food from behind it. The littler kids ran back and forth, too excited to decide if they wanted to hide or get close enough to the Parent Zone to be hit with food again. Luna was the only one who ate anything. Twice I pulled her out of the pan of sweet potatoes, but she really had a thing for the sugary marshmallows melted over the top.

When they ran out of food, the parents declared a ceasefire and went indoors. It took a few minutes, but the energy faded out of things. Jesse, Morgan, Hannah, and I settled down with our backs to one of the tables, and Sammy and Jordan sprawled on the lawn. The other kids took off to play on the concrete pad under the basketball hoop. Luna loped after them, barking at their shouts.

Next to me, Morgan brushed flecks of food off her jeans. "Well, I've never had a Thanksgiving meal like this."

Jesse laughed. "I try to keep things from getting boring."

"I'm pretty sure Hannah started the food fight," Morgan said, her arm brushing mine.

"Well, I got things rolling before that." Jesse thumped his hand against his chest.

Morgan grinned. "Didn't you say Preston started it? You've got the black eye to prove it."

Jesse scoffed. "Well, if Alex hadn't saved him, he'd have a black eye too."

Morgan leaned around me and told Jesse, "If Alex hadn't pulled Preston off you, you would have two black eyes."

He shook his head. "Whatever."

Jordan sat up. "Why'd you let him pull you off anyway, Preston? You were winning."

"I didn't let him. He just did."

"Fancy Clothes?" Jesse snorted. "He ain't that strong."

"Yes, he is," Hannah said.

"Nah. You can tell. He's not the athletic type. Preston's just jumpy around him."

Hannah shook her head. "He has weights in his room and he goes running every morning."

"He does?" *Why didn't I know that?*

Hannah shrugged. "He started after the accident."

Jesse tensed at once. "What accident?"

"The one that killed my mom and my older brother and sister. We fell off the interstate and rolled into a river."

Jesse paused. "A river?"

"Not a deep one. There was a little bit of water inside the car, enough to cover one side of my face and get in my ear."

Jesse stilled, his fidgeting hands dropping the crumbles of a roll to the ground. "How'd you get out?"

"Dad talked me through climbing out the window to him. I think he blamed himself for not being strong enough to lift me out. I was only eleven, and I was begging him to help me. I didn't understand that he couldn't. He got Edith out after that."

Jesse scrambled to his feet and paced in front of the table. Hannah watched his movements. I willed her to stop talking. Instead, she straightened her shoulders and continued, "He tried to help the others, but he couldn't even get Bonnie out. The thing is, I doubt he'd have been able to anyway, because parts of the van were crushed on them, but ever since, he's been exercising and lifting weights."

Jesse's pacing increased.

"That's why I said things were that bad last night," Hannah explained. "Everything triggered that."

Jesse halted right in front of her. He stood over her, his jaw clenched. "I didn't mean for you to go in."

"I know. But then you left us stranded. On purpose."

"Whatever." Jesse took a long step around her and stalked off across the yard. At the back steps he stopped, returned to Hannah, and crouched. "Are you okay?"

She almost smiled at him. "Is that your way of apologizing?"

"No. Are you okay?"

"I'm doing better now."

"Is your dad mad at me?"

"For a second I thought he was going to let Preston punch you again."

"Figures." Jesse tugged on one of Hannah's wild blond curls. "I'm sorry." He stood up, glancing at me for half a second before he disappeared inside the house.

Morgan whispered my name.

"Yeah?" I dragged my attention to her.

"You're hurting my hand."

I dropped my gaze to where my fingers were clenching hers, which were turning white. My grip loosened at once.

When had I grabbed her hand?

Twenty

Alex bought Hannah a new phone on Friday. We spent the rest of the weekend working on the Karlon house. Mom wanted to move the extra stuff in the house to the metal shed to make room for the upstairs renovations. While the others sorted through things left in the house, I worked with Alex outside, hauling everything I'd been avoiding to the truck. He tried to get me to go through the boxes, but I didn't listen. After a while he fell silent.

True to my promise to Josie, I forced myself to drive over to the Powell house Sunday afternoon. It wasn't a huge sacrifice. Morgan was leaving in a few hours, and I wanted to say goodbye. Sammy and Hannah came with me. As soon as we pulled up, they took off around the side of the house where Jesse, Jordan, and Braxton were shooting hoops. I joined them for a while, but when Morgan came outside and sat on the back steps, I jogged over to her and sat down. "Hey."

She nudged me with her shoulder. "Hey. I was hoping you'd come by. I need your number now that you have a phone." When I grimaced she said, "What? Hannah mentioned that Alex and your mom have been trying to get you to carry a phone for a while. I swear I saw you grab the one on the table Wednesday night."

"Hannah talks too much." I smiled a little and held out a hand. "Here, I'll put my number in for you. I left it in the truck."

Morgan pulled out her phone and passed it to me. "Most people carry their cell with them, you know." She leaned back on the stairs and kicked out her feet. "But don't be so grumpy about Hannah. That's what sisters are supposed to be like."

"I wouldn't know. I've spent all of my life around the Powell boys."

Morgan flicked her gaze to Jesse.

"You okay?" I asked, handing her phone back. "Is Jesse still being stupid?"

"No, but I think it shook him—you punching him, and Hannah's little story. He went to church today and didn't fight with Brett about it. I guess that's been a battle between them every Sunday since the end of August."

"Yeah. Well, he's been coming to sacrament meeting. When I saw he stayed for priesthood and Sunday school, I figured Brett finally got the right leverage on him."

"They didn't fight," Morgan said. "Jesse just stayed."

"Huh."

"Apparently today is the first time he's let Jordan or Braxton shoot hoops with him since August, too. That's the only reason Brett is letting them play on Sunday, I think. He and Josie are just relieved Jesse's doing stuff with the boys again. He's been coming out most evenings, pounding the ball against that hoop until way past dark."

Uncle Brett dragged him in at least twice while I've been here. But Thursday night, Jesse sat out there in the center of the concrete pad and didn't shoot at all."

I didn't know what to say. Maybe Jesse was finally snapping—or getting better.

Morgan turned toward me. "Preston?"

"Yeah?"

"Do you have someone you can talk to? About what happened with Bryan? About your dad?"

I leaned my elbows on my knees. "I don't need to talk. I handle stuff differently than you."

She grabbed my wrist and tugged me around until I looked at her. "Jesse's been saying that same thing to me. Since August. Then he does stuff like he did Wednesday."

"I'm not Jesse, either. I wouldn't have taken off like that and left you guys stranded."

"No, but Sammy said—"

I huffed. "Really? You're bringing up Sammy? He's the one that won't listen to me anymore."

"Jesse said it too, that you've been way crazy about Sammy. That you freak out when you don't know where he is."

"Yeah, well, that's Jesse, ain't it? He was probably trying to get you to stop bugging him by putting your attention on me."

Morgan's face fell. "I'm not trying to bug you, Preston. I'm trying to help."

"That's not what I meant."

Taking a deep breath, she frowned at the brown grass. "Okay. I know it's not. The thing is, Jesse told me that yesterday. So he was probably trying to get me to stop bugging him before, but yesterday he was worried about you. He said you've had a hard time talking in class, too."

Great. What else did Jesse tell her? She's probably decided I'm turning into Troy after all.

"Jesse's mad at me for telling Brett about Melody," I didn't mean to sound desperate, but that's how it came out. I really couldn't lose Morgan right now. I needed her to remind me I could be normal.

She shook her head. "I don't think Jesse's mad about that anymore. The thing is—and you can't tell him you know—Thursday night, when Brett went out there to get him inside, Jesse broke down. He cried. Brett stayed out there with him a long time. Since then . . . well, they're rearranging the rooms upstairs, finally going through Bryan's stuff. Jesse wouldn't let them before.

"When Jesse told me about you on Saturday, Preston, he said you needed help, but he didn't know if there was anyone you'd let help you. He said, 'I have my dad, but Preston doesn't have anyone. He won't talk to his mom 'cause he feels like he has to protect her.' I think Jesse wanted me to talk to you."

My mouth opened and closed on nothing but the cooling evening air. Every part of me wanted to get up and walk away. It'd been a long time since I'd felt this uncomfortable around Morgan.

She put her hand on my knee. I flinched.

"I don't think you can tell me all of that either," she said after a pause. "Maybe some stuff. Jesse said you'd never told him about your dad before, and the only reason you did was because I was there. But I think there is stuff you won't tell me because you protect me too."

I sat there, my tongue stuck to the roof of my mouth.

"But I think you do have someone you'd talk to," Morgan went on. "Alex."

Panic shot through me. I started to rise.

"Wait. Please." She clutched my hand. "I know you don't want to hear that, but I'm trying to help you." Her voice wavered.

I sank beside her. "Don't cry. I won't run off."

Morgan gave a small smile of relief and blinked back tears. "Think about it, okay? Because you told me yourself that Alex had changed your mind about art before your mom started dating him—that you liked him. Then, at the wedding, you told him about Rhonda, and it was sort of like he just *got* you when we were out in the hall. At first, I thought I'd have to defend you, but he didn't even need an explanation. He gave you that notebook and you started talking to us."

I shook my head, ready to dispute her, but Morgan plunged on before I could get the words out.

"And Wednesday you were a mess, so worried about Alex being mad at you, you couldn't stop pacing. He got you to rat out Jesse. I don't think anyone else has ever gotten you to do that."

I breathed a sigh. When she put it that way, it sounded like I'd been sucking up to Alex.

"Can you really, truly tell me that you are fine?" Morgan asked. "Because I'll stop. I'll let you be. But only if you're honest."

I hadn't slept well since football ended. The feeling of unsettled anxiety was so constant I almost couldn't remember what it was like not to have worry squeezing my insides. But I couldn't talk to Alex. Jesse opening up to Brett—that was different. Alex wasn't my dad. He had no reason to listen to me, no reason to even care.

"Preston?"

"I know I haven't been my usual self, Morgan, but there's been a lot happening. It'll pass. I just need time."

She raised a brow. "Can you talk about Bryan—about what happened? Can you even *think* about that day? Until you can, you aren't going to heal. It won't just go away. Not in a few months, not in ten years. You have to deal with it eventually. So whatever way you need to deal, you've got to at least start trying. Maybe you need to write it out, find a quiet place and give yourself permission to think about it, or get a priesthood blessing. I don't know. I do know that you aren't dealing. You're avoiding. Based on what you've told me, that's what your father does. You aren't like that. You don't have to be like him."

"I'm not Troy!" The words exploded out of me. I came to my feet in a rush, my hands trembling at my sides.

Morgan stood up as well, grabbed both my arms, and moved to the second step of the porch so she was almost face to face with me. "No? Prove it. Talk to Alex."

My chest rose and fell with each sharp breath. Morgan's hands slid up my arms and came to rest on my shoulders. She didn't speak, just waited.

"Maybe I will," I said in a strangled voice.

"It doesn't sound like you will."

"I said I will."

A smile flickered on her lips and danced up to her eyes, breaking through the challenge that had hardened her gaze. "Good."

She remained standing there, so close I could smell something citrusy on her hair and skin. Her fingers on my shoulders and the lean of her body toward my own sent a wild, hot rush through me. My anger and discomfort burned away. Thoughts of Troy retreated. I could only think of Morgan's hands resting on my shoulders, the steady comfort of her presence, the unmistakable pull of my body toward hers. Then all else was replaced by a rush of madness.

I wanted to kiss her.

Her parted lips seemed to draw closer at the thought. Fear tangled through the desire, and our eyes met. Her smile faded as she considered me. She pulled away and inched along the step.

I stood stock still, the heat of the moment turning on me until the shock of my own stupidity hit me. She'd seen that I'd wanted to kiss her—that I almost had.

Morgan wrapped her arms around herself and took a deep breath. "After this summer, I made a promise to myself that I wouldn't let anything between me and a boy get that serious again, not while in high school. You make it really hard to keep that promise."

My mouth dropped slack.

"Maybe it's a good thing we don't see each other more often." Her pink face deepened to a rosy red. She retreated up the stairs but stopped in the doorway. With the screen door propped open against her hip, she said, "Hey, you better respond when I text you."

"I . . . Okay."

"And don't forget you promised to talk to Alex," Morgan said just before the door swung shut behind her.

Twenty-One

I lay awake long after Sammy fell asleep, my thoughts racing. I didn't want to sleep. If I slept, I dreamed. Whether a replay of Bryan's death, or a twisted new version that included Sammy or one of the girls dying instead, I dreaded the moment I could no longer keep my eyes open.

I kicked off the covers and paced around my bed to the closet. My feet made the loop a second time and a third. Troy, Jesse, Alex, Bryan, and even the almost kiss—Morgan hadn't left anything untouched. She'd almost kissed me too. I was sure of that. Still, if we never spoke about it again until we were both in college, what more could I offer her when I couldn't figure myself out?

I rounded the edge of the space before the closet for about the millionth time and caught the red numbers of Sam's alarm clock— 4:34. My feet stopped midstep. This wasn't the first time since the wedding that I'd been up all night.

I might as well still be in the lake, drowning with Hannah. No matter how hard I fought, I couldn't quite get to air.

I need help.

I sank to the bed. Would talking to someone help me, or did I need professional help? My dad took medication—I knew that much. Maybe the doctors would say I needed medication too. Maybe I'd have to take it for the rest of my life. If I never got better, how could I get married, have children, keep a job?

Uneven breaths snagged up my chest and throat, the fear rising like some newly woken dragon. I curled up on myself. In the quiet of the sleeping house, a full and silent panic attack seized my body.

I couldn't get it to stop. My thoughts reached for God, straining to find a thread of the comfort I'd learned to depend on in the past. He'd always been there, but I couldn't find Him anymore.

Please, help me.

At 5:30, I dragged myself to the shower. Raw and drained, I stood under the spray until the water turned cold.

I didn't know what to do.

I could tell Mom.

But Jesse was right. Even considering telling Mom what a mess I'd become pulled me up short. She'd been hurt so much by Troy. Knowing how bad things were getting for me would only hurt her again. The only one who could fully understand what was happening to me was Troy, and unless I drove myself to Arizona and forced him to talk to me, there was no help there.

I got dressed, then slid down the wall to stare at the door across from me.

Talk to Alex. The thought came to me in Morgan's voice, but something more pierced through my chest, a soft warmth I'd once connected with a prompting from Heavenly Father. It stilled a bit of the frantic pulse shaking my body.

Alex didn't flinch when he found me in the hallway at the wedding. He didn't tell Mom about Aunt Rhonda, and he didn't blame me for Hannah's accident. He rarely gets angry, rarely jumps to conclusions.

I was halfway up the stairs before the sound of the other kids waking stopped me. I couldn't talk to Alex now. It would be too crazy with everyone getting ready. Maybe after school.

⁓

Jesse sat on a bench in one of the quieter halls, holding his basketball. I stopped in front of him and nudged his foot. "Hey."

"Oh, hi." He lifted the ball. "You staying after for open gym?"

I'd forgotten about that. I didn't want to stay, but if talking to Alex didn't work, playing hard again, like I'd done with football, might. Which meant I needed to convince the basketball coach to make me a starter. I'd never get the kind of workout I needed if I was warming the bench.

"Yeah, I'll stay." I turned to leave.

"Where you goin'?"

"I've got to tell Hannah to have Alex pick her and Sam up."

"I thought you had your own phone now," Jesse said.

Did *everyone* know? "It's in the truck." I strode off.

When I stopped by Hannah at her locker, she jerked in surprise and dropped her backpack. After glancing around, she whispered, "Are you sure it's safe to talk to me? You might be seen."

I rolled my eyes. "What are you talking about?"

She laughed. "You never talk to me at school. How am I supposed to act?" She bent to scoop up her bag.

"Normal."

"Because this is normal how?" She shouldered the bag and slammed her locker, her smile fading. "Did you get in a fight with Jesse again or something?"

"No. I want you to text Alex to come get you guys after school. I'm staying for basketball."

"What happened to your phone?"

"Seriously? What is up with everyone and that phone?" I spun around and stomped off.

She called after me, "You do know how to text, don't you?"

Pretending I didn't hear her, I rounded the corner of the hallway and made a straight line for my class. If I got there early enough the room would be empty, and if I pulled out my drawing pad, there was a good chance I wouldn't have to talk to anyone else this morning.

After school I met Jesse in the gym to shoot hoops. I'd only made one basket when Sammy shouted across the room. "Preston!" He stood in the double doors, Hannah behind him.

I jogged over. "What are you doing? Where's Alex?"

Hannah's smile stretched into a guilty grimace. "I sort of forgot to text him. He's doing the grocery shopping."

"How long will he be?"

She lifted her phone so I could see the text message. *We just got to the store. I don't want to have to make two trips. I'll be about forty minutes.*

Sammy yanked on my arm. "Take us to him. I don't want to wait. I've got something I want to talk to him about."

"I'm not skipping basketball to drive you to the grocery store. By the time I got you two inside, found Alex, and drove back, practice would be pretty much over."

"It's not a real practice," Sammy said. "You only play because Jesse makes you. You don't even like it. This is important."

Sammy would be nothing but a distraction if he stayed. I should take them to Alex, but that thought clashed with the need to drain myself like I'd been doing with football. I had to get some sleep tonight. I glared at Hannah and my brother.

"We could walk," she said.

"No way am I letting you walk along the busiest street to the grocery store." I paused. "I'll leave early—give me twenty minutes." I pointed to the bleachers. "Sit over there. And don't wander off."

Sammy protested, but Hannah headed to the bleachers and motioned for him to follow. He stomped after her, his footfalls echoing through the gym. The other guys turned to see what was going on.

I headed to the hoop. We shot free throws and moved on to layups. Jesse sank his first one and passed me the ball. It slipped right through my fingers, spinning free and bouncing off toward the wall.

He groaned. "What's with you? You're missing everything."

I ran after the ball, glancing over to check on Sammy and Hannah. The bleachers where they'd been pouting were empty. I slid to a stop and scanned the room. "Jess, you see Sam or Hannah anywhere?"

"You've got to stop worrying so much about him," Jesse said after chasing down the ball for me. "He's going to hate you if you keep that up."

"Well, if he'd stop running off, I wouldn't have to worry."

Jesse shoved my shoulder. "Chill. Maybe they went in the hall." I headed toward the hallway. "Okay, I take it we're checking," Jesse said, striding after me.

Sammy wasn't in the hallway. I walked up to the adjoining one to be sure before heading back to the gym. Jesse had stopped in the doorway, his brow furrowed, staring at something on the bleachers.

"You leave your bag like that?"

All my stuff hung out the open top of my bag. I jogged over and grabbed my jeans off the bench. "Weird." I shoved them back in. There wasn't much worth stealing. The cell phone still hadn't made it out of the truck.

Jesse joined me. "What would someone want with your bag? Are your truck keys in there? I guess if someone was desperate to get a car or something . . . though I wouldn't have chosen Blue."

Ice raced up my spine. I jerked open the bag's zipper, dragged my pants out, and searched one pocket after another. Nothing. "My keys are gone!" I shoved the pants in again, shouldered the bag, and bolted for the door.

Jesse followed me out into the blazing light of the parking lot, putting his own bag over his shoulder as he jogged along. "You know, I really don't think you're going to let me practice today, are you?"

My parking spot sat empty. I spun around to search the rest of the lot. Jesse grabbed my arm and pointed to the road along the front of the school. My truck moved out onto it, then turned left and headed for the main road. I raced after it, gaining only enough to see that some random kid wasn't stealing my truck.

It was Sammy. He was driving my truck with Hannah in the passenger seat beside him.

I swore.

Behind me, Jesse let out a hoot. "Is that Sammy driving? What do you know?"

I whirled around.

"I didn't know he could drive," Jesse said, grinning.

"He can't! Where are your keys?"

"What?"

"Jesse, he can't drive! He's going to get them both killed!" A mad pounding thundered through my head. I could smell gasoline again, hot and sticky. I seized Jesse's bag.

"Whoa." He yanked it out of my hands. "You need to calm down." He pulled out his own jeans and dug through them, one pocket at a time.

I grabbed the pants and shook them. Jesse's keys clattered to the blacktop. My fingers wrapped around them a second before his.

"What are you going to do?" He ran after me toward his black-and-red truck.

I yanked open the door and climbed behind the wheel. "Are you coming?" I slammed the door shut before he could answer.

By the time I got the truck running, he had climbed in the other side. "You do know this is my truck, right?"

I shifted into gear and screeched out of the parking lot. For the first time in all the times we'd ridden together, Jesse scrambled to put on his seatbelt without any prompting. "Well, yes," he muttered under his breath, "you can borrow my truck. Thanks for asking."

The wheels squealed as I shot onto the road, too close to an oncoming car. A horn blared. I accelerated, furious that Hannah had let Sammy drive. I turned onto Main Street and shot past the Junction.

"Just so you know, if you get pulled over I'm telling the cops you stole my truck." Jesse leaned hard into the door as I switched lanes to pass another truck.

Up ahead, Blue came into view, bouncing along like nothing was wrong. "Well, he's good at driving, for someone who doesn't know how," Jesse said.

I swore again and pressed on the gas.

Jesse let out a strained sigh. "Preston, you're freaking out about nothing. Sammy's fine. Plus you never swear. It's kind of weirding me out."

Weirding him *out? Sammy is driving! Hannah* let *him drive. If they die—*

I didn't let myself finish the thought.

We caught up to Blue right before the grocery store. I sidled up, turning Jesse's truck toward them and forcing Sammy into the parking lot. He swerved to a stop, straddling the lines at the back of the lot. I parked Jesse's truck right behind mine. Blue stalled with a shudder.

"What are you tryin' to do? Kill us all?" Jesse had braced himself against the dashboard with both hands.

I reached Sammy before he got all the way out of my truck. I caught him by the shoulders and shook him. "What's wrong with you?" My voice echoed around us. The rattle of a lady's shopping cart cut off as she stopped to gape.

"Let me go." Sammy flung me back. "You. Aren't. My. Boss." His hands slammed into my chest with each word.

The roar of something torrential I'd been trying to hold back exploded inside me. In three seconds I wrestled him to the ground, pinned him under me, and yanked the keys from his hand. He shoved me aside, tears on his face, screaming wordlessly.

"Shut up, Sammy!" On my knees, I leaned toward him and shouted over his screams. "You could have gotten yourself killed. You could've killed Hannah."

Jesse strolled up beside me and called over Sammy's screams, "I might be wrong, but I don't think that's the best way to handle this."

"What do you know about it?" I shoved my keys in my pocket and stood up. "You haven't helped at all."

"You're the one acting crazy," Jesse said.

"I'm crazy? Because I don't want my brother with Down syndrome to drive a truck?"

Jesse threw his hands up. "I'm trying to help."

"Well, don't."

Hannah came around the front of the truck and knelt by Sammy, reaching for his hand.

All my anger and fears wadded up in my chest, but instead of clogging my throat like they usually did, some overwhelming force broke through the ball of emotion. It was like dynamite. I seized Hannah by the arms, hauled her upright, and slammed her against the truck.

Fear rushed over her face, stark and real. Good. If she didn't stop putting ideas in Sammy's head, sooner or later it would be too late. In the background, I was vaguely aware of someone running across the parking lot toward us.

"What were you thinking? He can't drive." I shook Hannah as I spoke.

"I didn't—"

"No. You never think. You take him anywhere that might hurt him. Anything that looks remotely dangerous and you're like 'Hey, let's take the kid with Down syndrome there.'"

"You're hurting my arms." Her quivering voice snaked through my anger, piercing it like a sudden pop of a balloon. I blinked down at her, not sure what I was doing, or how I'd gotten her pinned against the truck, terrified of me.

It was wrong. So wrong. My own fear hit me between the eyes. I didn't understand the anger in me, the crazy voice that told me to hurt her, or the part of me that listened.

"Preston. Let go of her. Now."

The words were hard, so furious that I jerked my hands back and stepped away from Hannah. She crossed her arms at once, rubbing at the two points where I'd grabbed her.

"What is going on?" Alex forced me farther away from Hannah with the flat of his hand against my chest. There was none of his usual control, no restraint in the fury in his voice. I retreated another step.

Sammy's screams stopped. He sat up and Jesse helped him stand. "Preston forced us off the road. He tried to kill us."

My jaw dropped. "You were the one trying to get yourselves killed. I stopped you."

Sammy barreled at me. "I hate you!"

Alex caught him, bringing him to a stop before he hit me. But I didn't care if Sammy hated me or even if he hit me, as long as he was alive.

Alex took a deep breath. "I want everyone in the van, now."

Hannah headed off, cool and unconcerned, like she didn't do a thing wrong. With my luck, Alex would let her get away with it again.

I pulled out my keys and opened the door of my truck.

Alex's hand came between me and the door, pushing it shut. "I want the keys, Preston."

"What?"

"You heard me. Give me the keys and get in the van."

"No. I'm not leaving my truck here." The door opened a fraction before Alex slammed it shut again. I'd forgotten he was stronger than he looked.

"The keys, Preston." He stood behind me, trapping me against the truck, his other hand keeping the door closed.

I slammed my palms against his shoulders, desperate to get more space around me. "You have no right to tell me what to do with my truck." My words spilled out on another wave of anger. When Alex stood his ground, I shoved again, harder.

He swayed and one foot slid a fraction, but not far enough for me to open the door again. "I have every right," he said firmly. "Driving is a privilege. And that privilege has been revoked for all children who are living in my household." Here he glanced at Jesse, who sprang into action.

"Right then. I'm off." Jesse looked at me. "See you around." He headed for his truck, got halfway there, and turned back. "Alex, Preston's still got my keys. In the right pocket of his shorts. He put them there before he took Sam down."

Alex met my eyes. "You took Sam down? Why would you do that?" His hand fell from the door, freeing up the space around me.

Instead of trying to get in the truck again, I recoiled two steps. Why *had* I done that?

Holding out a hand, Alex said, "Give me Jesse's keys."

I let them fall into his palm. He tossed them to Jesse. Jesse yanked my backpack out of his cab, opened the passenger door of my truck, and tossed the bag onto the seat. As his truck moved onto the road, Alex held his hand out again.

"Now the other set. It's not a choice. You are not driving anymore. Not until I'm absolutely certain you will never do what you did today again. It was dangerous and you hurt Sam and Hannah. You are too close to this. You need to let me and your mom handle it."

"Sam was driving! What part of 'the kid with Down syndrome was driving' do you not get?" My voice rose again, ending on a shout that didn't even begin to cover the storm inside me. "You never tell him to stop. You never get mad at Hannah. She let him drive! It's just like when you let them go bike riding. They were forty-five minutes late getting home and you didn't do a thing!"

Sammy shoved his way between us, pushing me away from Alex. "Stop blaming Hannah! She didn't let me drive! I decided to drive on my own. She told me to stop. And it wasn't her fault before, either. She helped me that day we rode bikes. I was sad. I missed Bryan and she let me talk about him. We lost track of time. You never let me talk about Bryan. But she does."

I didn't want to look at Alex, but my eyes darted to him. He already knew what Sammy had just told me. It was all over his face. My anger dwindled, lost on the idea of Hannah comforting Sammy. He should be talking to *me* about Bryan.

But I couldn't even say Bryan's name.

"Hannah let Sam drive," I mumbled, the conviction leaving me.

Still tense with anger, Alex shook his head at me. "Do you really think after losing half her family to a car accident she takes anything with a vehicle lightly? Do you think it was an easy choice for her, when she realized Sammy was going to take off with that truck with or without her, to get inside it with him?

"No, I'm not going to be punishing Hannah. You were the one who shoved her into the side of that truck, Preston. I watched it. That is not okay. It's also not okay to hurt your brother. If anyone else did that to Sam, you'd have given them a black eye."

Sammy's chin lifted. "See! It's your fault."

Alex turned from me. "Sam, you were at fault too. You do not have a license. You should never have been driving."

"He wouldn't take me!" Sammy jabbed his finger at me, then turned to Alex. "I needed to talk to you. I wanted to know." My brother's eyes refilled with tears. They rolled over his cheeks and he took a wet breath.

I'd hardly ever seen Sammy cry without screaming. I reached for the edge of the truck, steadying myself against it.

Alex wrapped an arm around Sammy. "You couldn't talk to me on the phone? What you did was *so* dangerous. When I got the text from Hannah that you were driving, do you know how scared I was?"

Sammy pulled away. "I didn't want to ask on the phone. I waited all day. Preston won't listen to me anymore. He wouldn't bring me to you. I was fine driving until he tried to run into me."

The rush of adrenaline had evaporated, and a sickeningly clear realization hit. What if Sammy had run into something, or swerved into a car when I pushed him off the road? What if I had hit him?

"I will deal with Preston," Alex told Sammy. "I want you to head over to the van. Your mom will be here soon. I called her after I got Hannah's text."

I slid along the back of the truck and had just reached the open tailgate before I sank down. I leaned over, hands braced at my sides, and counted breaths as the urge to vomit increased. The truck sank a little from the weight as Alex joined me.

"Preston, what happened? None of this is like you."

I didn't know what was going on—why my brain and body didn't seem to be listening to logic anymore.

Talk to Alex.

He stood and paced in front of me. "Maybe we better wait for your mom. Would you give her the keys and ride home with her? Is that easier for you?" Alex looked over me to the front of the truck. "Sam, what are you doing up there? I want you to get in the van." He circled around the side of the truck.

If I didn't speak now, I might never get the courage. I had to get help. Before I did something like this again. Before I actually killed someone. "Alex."

"Yeah?"

In the second it took him to rotate toward me, my lips stuck to each other with a dryness that spread into my mouth. *I need help. I need help.* The words relayed themselves through my brain. He returned to the tail gate and stopped near my knees.

I could do this. I'd promised Morgan. My mouth peeled open.

"Alex, I wanted to talk to you." Sammy beat me to the words I needed to say. Joining us behind the truck, he wiped snot on his arm and held out a manila-colored envelope.

"I found this on Saturday. I didn't understand it. So I took it to Mrs. Harper to help me read it. She explained it to me and said I should talk to you or Mom."

Alex frowned. "Sam, where did you get that?"

A scrawling scrip covered the front of the envelope—handwriting I knew, on an envelope I'd seen three months ago.

"It was in Mom's old bedroom," Sammy said. "It's from my real dad. He always writes letters that make her cry. I hate that mailbox. I tried to get rid of it so he couldn't send more letters, but Preston keeps fixing it." My brother sent me an accusatory glare.

Alex reached for the letter. "You shouldn't read other people's mail."

Sammy stepped back. "No one tells me stuff if I don't. I want to know, are you going to adopt us, like Troy said to?"

I whipped the letter away from Sammy and unfolded the top. My hand trembled as I reached in.

Alex stopped me. "Preston, I think you'd better give—"

Sammy wedged himself between us. "Are you going to adopt me and Preston?"

I pulled out a thick stack of papers and flipped them over to find a form for a signing away parental rights, and another for applying for legal adoption. Troy had filled out all his information and signed it. "Mom asked him to give us up?"

Alex grasped Sammy's shoulders and moved him to the side, opening the space between us. "No. She didn't ask him for that. He just did it. But I think we better wait for her before we talk about this anymore. Let's go home first."

"No. I want to know now." Sammy stomped a foot. "Why won't you answer me?"

After a reluctant pause, Alex said, "I'll adopt you if that's what you want."

My fingers dug into the papers. Alex's hand found my shoulder, but I shrugged him off and took several steps away.

He breathed out a sigh as Mom's car drove into the parking lot. "There she is."

"I want you to adopt us. Then the girls will really be our sisters." Sammy's voice rose in excitement. "I think I'll call you Dad now. I didn't before, because it wasn't real, you know, but now it can be."

"No," I whispered.

"No, what?" Sammy demanded.

"No, he's not going to adopt us."

Sammy shoved me. "You are not in charge of me!"

Alex seized him at once, drawing him back. "Calm down, Sammy. It's okay. You both have a choice. You can decide for yourself."

Mom pulled up next to us and scrambled out of the car. "What's going on? Sammy, did you really drive the truck?"

As Alex and Sammy went to meet Mom, I shuffled through the papers and found a letter written by Troy at the bottom of the stack. I couldn't focus on the words.

Was this why Alex had been nice to Sammy and me? Had it all been an obligation he felt because he knew Troy didn't want us? I should have known Troy would drop us the second he found a way to do it. He'd never taken responsibly for anything. Instead, Alex had taken responsibility for everything Troy had left behind.

The sensation of falling had me reaching for the side of the truck again. I'd almost dumped all my own problems on Alex. Just like Troy had tried to do.

Mom reached me, her expression a mix of concern and fury. "Preston Troy Bensen, what on earth were you thinking? Give me your keys and get in my car. Now."

"What about this?" I lifted the papers. "When were you going to tell us?"

Her shoulders sagged as she frowned at the letter. "I didn't want you to find out like this. But I'm not going to let you use that as a distraction from what *you* have done today. We will talk about Troy after we talk about you."

I didn't want to think about what I'd done, so I plunged on. "Were you going to make Alex adopt us? Put *all* of our baggage on him? It wasn't enough that he's paying our bills and fixing our house?"

My stomach plummeted at the pain on Mom's face. The words burned in my throat. I hadn't wanted to say them, or to hurt her. The blame belonged to Troy, but he'd never be around to take it.

"Do not speak to your mother like that," Alex said, putting a protective hand on her shoulder. The flash of anger from earlier pulsed off him, clenching his jaw as he drew his body up to its full height. "No one has made me do anything I didn't want to do, Preston, and you know that."

A cold sweat broke over my skin. The guilt seized me like a choke collar, wedging tight around my windpipe. Only minutes ago, I'd thought I could talk to Alex about Bryan. Now I'd be lucky to even get my breath out. I shook my head, trying to dislodge the beginnings of another panic attack.

Mom stepped closer, taking in my shaking, the ragged sound of my too-fast breath. But instead of her expression softening, a firmness stole over it. "Give me the keys, Preston. Now. And I'm going to want the three-wheeler keys too, when we get home. I'm done. I'm not going to keep letting this control our lives."

This?

My panic attacks. The anxiety disorder. Draining us, our lives, me. Taking everything I wanted to be away from me. Mom was done. She knew it was swallowing me whole, and she was done.

I didn't blame her. I'd almost killed Sammy.

The thought unleashed inside me, whipping free and colliding with the news of Troy. If I stayed I would hurt her again. If I talked to Alex, I'd be like Troy. But if I didn't do something, I might snap again. I might actually cause something I was desperately trying to prevent.

Troy is the only one who can help me. He knows what's happening to me. The thought emerged from the tangle of panic inside me, standing out stark. Troy lived what I was experiencing every day.

But he would never help me on his own. I'd have to go to him.

My fingers tightened around the keys in my pocket, pulling them free. I turned away from Alex and Mom, yanked open the door of my truck, and climbed inside.

They shouted at me through the window. I pressed down the lock and started the engine. The papers fluttered to the seat beside me, the envelope on top, the address across the corner.

Troy's address, in Arizona.

I could be there before dark.

Twenty-Two

The clarity drove me through Kanab and almost to Karlon. I slowed a little near the turnoff. In the rearview mirror, the cliffs above Kanab spilled out into the valley, fingers crawling outward as if reaching into the open expanse of flatter land before it. They'd always seemed to be pulling me back to Kanab. Now it was like they'd been marking an ending.

Everything I knew was right there, cradled in the canyons, encircled by cliffs. But my truck faced a brown-gray desert, and a long road winding south. I'd been in a place like this in my head for a long time—since Bryan died—trapped between what I'd always known and what had to come.

I couldn't stay trapped any longer. I had to get answers, and the only one who could really understand me was Troy.

I accelerated. My phone rang in the glove compartment three times before I yanked it out and switched it to silent. I stopped again for gas at Lake Powell. Three hours later when Old Blue bounced into Flagstaff, the sun had set.

I followed the address on the envelope, using the GPS on the phone and ignoring the red missed calls and text notifications. Once I reached the right road, I didn't need the address anymore.

Aunt Jaclynn's house stood three lots down with dirty white siding, a patched gray front door, and a treeless yard of yellowed grass. I parked in the driveway and killed the engine.

My hands gripped the wheel so tight my arms ached. The last twenty-four hours jumbled in my head, spinning in a tangled mass. The fact that I sat outside my dad's house hit me in the center of my chest. *What if I can't make it to the door, can't even knock? What if Troy won't let me in?*

But I hadn't come all this way to sit in my truck and panic. I steeled myself. I would do this. It was a long shot, a gamble. But if I asked the right questions, I might get what I needed. Troy had hurt Mom and Sammy, had messed up our lives and left us to scramble on our own. I hated Troy. I hated that I was becoming him, but he wasn't going to run anymore. Neither was I.

The anger got me out of the truck and up to the front door. I knocked. Footsteps sounded and a TV shut off. The door opened.

Aunt Jaclynn stood there. Her build was thin, her light-brown hair cut short. A tense strain circled her eyes. Frowning, she held the door against her side. "Preston. What are you doing here?"

"I want to see him," I told her.

"He won't see you." She looked past me. "Go home." She backed into the house and began to inch the door closed.

I stopped the door with my hand. "He's my dad. He owes me that much."

Jaclynn's eyes focused on my hand before traveling to my face. "Does Natalie know where you are?"

My aunt might as well have slapped me. I recoiled from the door, releasing it. She closed it at once.

The rage snapped in me, the fire of all I'd been holding back for so long erupting like an inferno. I pounded on the door with my fist. "Troy! I want to talk to you." Images flashed through my head—a much younger me, pounding on his door, begging Troy to open it.

"Let me in or call the cops," I yelled now, "because I'm not leaving this step until you talk to me."

Aunt Jaclynn opened the door again. I stumbled back, my fist raised to pound. "If you keep that up, I won't have to call the cops," she said. "The neighbors will. What happened? Why are you here?"

"I have to see him." My chest heaved with resentment. I shouldn't have to beg like this.

Jaclynn rubbed a hand over her hair, her lips pressed in a tense line. We stood there for several long seconds.

"I need his help." Faltering, I focused on the concrete under my feet. "I can't. My anxiety—it's getting worse."

My aunt let out a long, tired sigh. "He can't help himself, Preston. What do you think he's going to do for you?"

"I don't know!" I didn't know what to do with my arms, my body. Everything about me felt big, bulky, and out of place. I jerked my arms across my chest, folding them tight. "He's the only one who can help me. No one else can."

She backed into the house and opened the door wider. "All right. Come in."

The inside of the house resembled a dark cave. The TV was paused on some action scene, the couches were empty, and the curtains were drawn. Snatches of memories flickered through my brain.

"I'll go see if he'll come. Stay here." Jaclynn left me in the living room, going down a hallway jutting off the back wall.

I paced the room. *It's going to be fine. This is what you needed to do. Think about Sammy. You almost killed him. You have to get help.*

Voices came from down the hall. I stopped by the front door.

Aunt Jaclynn came in, talking over her shoulder. "You don't have to do this."

"It's all right." The words were soft, broken. Troy's voice registered deep inside me in a connection I'd forgotten. I knew how it felt to come out of a panic attack and find him there, holding me and talking softly until I calmed down.

I'd arrived ready to fight, but my dad's voice took all the fight out of me. As he emerged from the hallway, the hate dried up in a puff of smoke, leaving behind an ache so sharp it pinched below my ribs.

He stood there in a baggy brown T-shirt and gray sweat pants. His light-brown hair had thinned on top, but it lay over his head in the same straight limp way that Sammy's did. Troy had a bit of a belly now and wore glasses.

His shoulders rose with a deep breath. "Come back here." He motioned for me to follow him.

We walked down the hall, past the room Sammy and I had shared, and the bathroom where Troy had taught me to hold my breath underwater. We stopped at the room that had been his and Mom's.

Troy pushed the door open. "It's quieter in here."

I didn't remember him ever yelling—couldn't recall being frightened of him. Only missing him like my body would break. Like the world had been ripped apart. Like I was the reason.

The small, dusty room was dim with the window shades closed, but I could make out a computer on a desk in one corner. A pile of dirty plates and cups sat on the dresser.

Troy closed the door and motioned me to the chair by the computer. "You can sit there."

I shook my head.

"Are you in some kind of trouble?" He waited for me to answer. And waited.

I licked my lips, too busy grappling with myself to reply.

"It's okay. Take your time." He sat on the edge of the bed.

He knew what it was like to run out of words. It was like facing my mirror—a mirror I'd avoided looking in for so long.

"You've grown." He pointed toward the nightstand where photos of Sammy and me from last year were propped up.

"You play football this season?" Troy said finally.

I almost didn't play because of his inability to hold down a job. My head nodded anyway.

"Good. Is Sammy still running?"

"No."

At the force behind my word, Troy raised his brows behind his black-framed glasses. Just the way Sammy did. "No?"

The conversation had moved too close to Bryan. I didn't respond.

"Has he had more heart problems?" There was real concern in Troy's voice.

I shook my head no and hoped he'd move on. *If he cared about that, he wouldn't have left the bills to Alex.*

His gaze followed me as I continued to examine the room: the dirty clothes spilling from the hamper, and the trash with an empty beer can inside. I stepped toward it and then really studied him again. Maybe he was drunk, and that was why he was talking to me.

"It's from last week. I'm sober," he said. "I thought you were getting better—your mom told me you were—but you still have a hard time talking, don't you?" Troy examined his hands. "I'm sorry you inherited it from me. I've been up and down the cycle enough that your mom must have told you at least a little bit about how bad it can be."

"I know a lot," I said. "I'm the one that had to pick up the pieces when you went down."

Troy's eyes shot to my face. "Your mom shouldn't have put that on you."

"She didn't. She tried to hide it, but she couldn't hide the bills, not all of them. I knew they'd be coming. I heard her when she cried." The words came bursting out of me, fast, sharp, and angry. "I've been picking up Sammy, too, every time someone whispered that it was his fault you never showed up, that he tipped things too far. I never have had the guts to tell him that if not for me, you'd never have been so close to tipping in the first place."

Troy swallowed. "It wasn't your fault, or Sammy's. I never wanted you to think that. I just wanted something better for you."

"I needed you! You were supposed to be my dad, and you were gone."

Troy's face paled, his eyes dancing away from mine. "It only makes it worse."

"What makes it worse?"

He was retreating, closing off to me again. His fast breath, the twitch of his fingers, the way he ducked his head—all signs I'd seen in myself a million times. "When I fall again, it only makes it worse if you've been pulled along that road with me. You are safer on your own, Preston, where I can't hurt you."

Safer. The word bought me up short. I'd been trying to keep Sammy safe.

"I know I've hurt you," Troy said, his voice trembling. "It kills me to think about it. I don't want to be like this. I didn't want to hurt you or Sammy or your mom, but I can't get over it. If I stayed, I'd have hurt you more. It would have been worse."

"You don't know that! You could have gotten help! You could have gotten better!" I paced the space in front of the bed, reached the trash can, and kicked it against the wall with a ringing thump.

"I tried." Troy whispered it on the silence that followed my outburst. "I was always introverted, but somewhere along the way it turned into this. It's life-crippling. I hoped it'd be different for you. I hoped if I gave you up—got you away from me—you'd be okay. When I heard your mom was getting married again, I knew it was the last piece . . . the last part of you I'd held on to. It was time to let you go. You'd finally be normal."

I wasn't normal. "It didn't help," I said, shaking. "It's getting worse for me too. How do I fix it?"

Disappointment flickered over Troy's face. He lifted his hands in defeat. "I don't know. This is me on a good day. On the bad days" —he shook his head— "I can't leave this room. I started a new medication, but it never lasts. I've tried more things than I can count. It always comes back." He lowered his head.

"I hurt Sammy today." The confession spilled out of me. "And my stepsister. I didn't mean to. I can't control it sometimes—the panic. I can't think clearly."

Troy's breath sucked in slowly. "That's why you came."

"Yes."

"I can't help you, Preston. The only thing I've done right was getting your mom and Sammy away from me before it was too late. I should have done it earlier. It might have made a difference for you. When it's hard, I think about how they are safe. I thought about you getting better, too. I'm sorry that you aren't." He leaned forward over his bouncing knees, pressing them down the way I often did.

This was it. What I'd become. I'd never go on a mission or hold down a job. I'd never get married or have kids. If I did, I'd end up doing to my own family what Troy had done to ours.

"Is he good? The man she married?" Troy said hesitantly, breaking the silence. "Is he taking care of her and Sammy?"

Images of Alex rushed in. Calming Bonnie or Sammy. Tickling Edith. Embracing Hannah. Holding Mom. Humming as he cooked, or painted, or hauled another box of trash out of the Karlon house.

"Yes."

Troy blew out a sigh of relief, and I could've sworn there was moisture in his eyes. "That is the only thing that helps. I'm glad for them. Is he good to you?"

My throat tightened with a sudden burning. I nodded.

"I'm sorry, Preston. I wish I could tell you it gets better. The best I can hope for is a break every once in a while."

A minute later I hauled myself into the truck. Half an hour had passed since I'd gone inside the house. I rested my head on the steering wheel and let my breath out slowly.

What next? No one could help me. And now I couldn't even blame Troy. The anger at him had gone, replaced with a painful hopelessness. I knew why he'd done what he did. It was exactly what I would have done.

I shouldn't have come.

I drove through Flagstaff and headed up the interstate. For the first time since getting in the truck in the grocery store parking lot, my thoughts turned to what might be happening in Kanab.

I fumbled with the phone I'd left on the seat and found twelve missed calls and five missed text messages. I dropped the phone without checking them. I was in so much trouble. Worse, if Mom found out where I'd gone, it'd hurt her, bring back all the pain of Troy, remind her how much I'd become like him.

What would Alex do when I hurt Mom like that? He'd lost it with me in the parking lot. I'd never seen him lose control before.

I pressed on the gas, increasing my speed. They couldn't know. I had to get home, give them my truck keys, and tell them I spent some time cooling off somewhere. I'd apologize. I could take pretty much any punishment they wanted to dish out, but I couldn't bear the thought of how my coming here would hurt Mom.

A grinding noise cut through the cab. I jumped, grabbing the steering wheel with both hands. The smell of burnt gears blasted from the vents. I tried to shift, but the truck groaned a protest. Merging to the right, I fumbled with the shift, clutch, and brakes, and managed to come to a halt on the side of the road. The smoky smell swirled around me as the truck shuddered and died.

Twenty-Three

The Arizona dust stuck to me, leaving streaks on my jeans and hands. I slid down the left side of the truck to sit near the front tire. I stared out into the desert for a while, then reluctantly pulled the phone out of my pocket. The dark screen was smudged by my greasy fingerprints.

If I called Mom, not only would she know where I'd gone, but she'd have to come here herself. She probably hadn't been to Flagstaff in ten years.

Groaning at the settling dark, I unlocked the phone screen and found Jesse's number. With all the times I'd gotten him out of stuff, he owed me. As long as he'd stopped holding the lake thing over me.

He answered on the second ring. "Preston! Where are you? Your mom's been here twice lookin' for you, and Alex and Dad are out tryin' to find you."

A heavy discomfort sank in my gut. "Look, keep it down, okay? I don't want to make it worse. I just need to figure out what's wrong with my truck. It broke down." I scrambled up and ducked my head under the open hood.

"You broke down? Where are you? I'll come help."

"There was a grinding nose and a burning smell. It won't start."

"Is there fluid on the ground? Did you crack something on your transmission? You probably need more gear oil. I can bring you some. I think I have some in the shed. If you didn't burn out or break anything, it might start up for us."

"I don't want you to come, Jesse. I want to fix this!"

Jesse was silent so long I wondered if he'd hung up—so long I *hoped* he had. Of course it was the transmission fluid. If I wasn't so stressed, I'd have figured it out myself. Who knew how long it'd been leaking and what else had been ruined. Maybe Sammy had damaged something when I forced him off the road. I rested my free hand on the hood overhead. *Take deep breaths and count.*

But I wasn't fooling anyone, because I was broken, just like my dad. The threads of his DNA snaking through me were permanent and loud. It'd all been a game, a false hope, trying to make myself something other than what he'd become.

"Preston, where are you?" Jesse's voice jarred my thoughts. "I'll come help you."

I refocused my gaze on the engine. "You can't."

"Yes, I can."

"I'm too far away for you to take off like that. You just started working things out with your parents. If you do come, you can't tell anyone where you're going. I don't want my mom to know."

"To know what? Where are you?"

"Flagstaff."

Jesse let out a hiss of surprise, but I plunged over it before he could speak. "It doesn't matter. I'll figure it out. Don't tell my mom."

"Like you didn't tell my dad about the lake and Melody?"

"Why are you bringing that up? I've helped you a million times. I'm asking for one thing. If you can't tell me how to fix the truck, at least you can cover for me."

"Preston, you need help. Let me help you."

"I'm fine."

"Where are you? Give me the mile marker or something. Are you on the highway?"

I hesitated.

"I'll take care of it, okay? It'll be fine," Jesse insisted. "Tell me how to find you."

"I don't want you to get in trouble again."

"Don't worry about that. I can handle this."

I gritted my teeth. Even if I walked to Flagstaff and managed to find a store still open where I could buy transmission fluid, the burnt smell and grinding sound pretty much guaranteed I'd ruined something oil wouldn't fix. I needed help. I rattled off my location as best as I could figure it and slammed the hood down.

"Okay. Give me three hours or so," Jesse said.

I wiped a trail of sweat from my forehead. "Thanks. I owe you."

"Don't do anything stupid while you wait, okay?"

Jesse ended the call. The guilt in my gut swelled. I'd dragged him into this now. What would his parents do when he disappeared for several hours in the middle of the night? Maybe we could say we were in the mountains. Any lie had to be better than seeing Mom's face when she realized I'd gone after Troy.

I climbed in the cab and sat behind the wheel, my heart boxing at my chest. With my phone out, I saw every time Mom or Alex called, a silent light on the seat beside me. I watched it until the battery died. By then darkness had settled, broken only by the occasional vehicle flying by, rocking Old Blue with the displaced air.

~

A tapping sound pulled me from sleep. I jerked up. A light flashed through the window.

"You okay?" A middle-aged cop with dark hair stood at the door.

I rolled down the window. "Yeah. My truck died."

He aimed the beam of his flashlight on the seat beside me, illuminating my dead phone. "You call for help?"

"Yeah. A friend is coming."

"That so? How long have you been sitting here? Have you called your parents?"

"No."

The officer directed the light on me again, then on my trembling hands holding the steering wheel. I dropped them to my lap.

"You want me to take a look under the hood?" he asked. "I know a bit about trucks. Or we could call a tow company."

I shook my head. *I already looked. I know about trucks too.*

"What's your name?"

My breath pitched into a rapid burn in and out of my nose. The cop wasn't giving me a ticket or arresting me, just trying to help. No need to get worked up.

"You're still a minor, aren't you? I couldn't quite figure it out at first. You're a big kid, but the ones who are under eighteen always get the most nervous. I don't care if you're in trouble with your parents, I can't leave you out here in the dark like this. So let me help you out. You got nothing to worry about, all right?"

When I remained frozen and wordless, he sighed. "Unless you've been drinking. Have you been drinking?"

A rushing in my ears muffled his voice. I had to talk. If I didn't talk, he'd assume the worse.

"Maybe you'd better give me your license and registration. You think you can do that?" He spoke gently as if I was a child.

I managed to peel my fingers from the dash, pop open the glove compartment, and snatch my registration. After handing it to him, I worked my wallet from the backpack Jesse had tossed onto the far seat. My hands left the black leather wet with sweat, and when I opened the wallet, they shook too hard to remove the license from the pocket.

"Can I get it out for you?" asked the officer.

My face burning, I passed the entire wallet through the window. He took out the license, handed me the wallet, and walked back to his vehicle. I counted to ten.

He left me there for a long time—so long another police car pulled up behind his. All the ground I'd gained during the wait was gone in a flash. They probably thought I was drunk after all.

Two officers made the return trip to my window.

"Well, Preston, you're a long way from Kanab, aren't you?" The first officer handed me my license and registration. "My name is Shawn. This is Luke. He came to help us figure things out."

The second man's stomach bulged at the buttons of his uniform, and his bald head reflected the light of the police car's revolving headlights.

"Can you tell us what happened tonight? How did you end up in Flagstaff?" Shawn fingered a radio on his hip as the sound of static buzzed and softened.

When I didn't respond, he glanced at Luke before turning back to me. "Let's have you get out, okay? Keep your hands where we can see them."

Blood pulsed through me, amplified by a sudden acute sense of my body—every beat of my heart, the shaking in my legs, the damp circles under my armpits, the taste of dust in my mouth. I'd never been pulled over before. Never gotten in trouble with a cop.

The first guy opened my door and backed up as I forced my legs to move. *Say something. Now. Or this is going to escalate.*

"The truck died." The words came out wobbly and scared, nothing to refute that I wasn't as drunk as the cops seemed to think I was.

Cold bit into my skin. My short sleeves and shorts from basketball practice didn't offer much protection against the winter air. My feet met the dusty gravel, but my legs didn't support me. I collapsed on the edge of the running board, my hands flying out to brace against the door and seat behind me.

Luke caught my arm above the elbow, half supporting me. "Preston, we need to know if you've taken anything." His voice was a deep rumble, raising with a sudden urgency. "It's really important, because you might need medical help."

I shook my head, trying to get my feet under me.

Oh no. Heavenly Father, please.

I sucked in my breath, the tears sharp as needles in my throat, my lids closing rapidly over dry eyes, my nose burning.

"It's all right, son. We're trying to help you." Shawn flashed the light in the cab again. "I don't see anything. What do you think he took? Should we look through that bag?"

"No." I slid down to the dirt, my fists clenched. *Don't do it. Don't do it.* It echoed in my head, a plea with myself not to fall apart, not to curl up and sob. *Talk!*

The static on the radio came again, followed by a voice. "Hey, Shawn, what did you say that boy's full name is?"

Shawn lifted the radio to respond. "Preston Troy Bensen."

The voice returned. "That's what I thought. I've had his dad, Troy, in here a few times. He has a really bad anxiety disorder. This is probably something similar, so step lightly. I'll call his aunt. I've got her number 'round here somewhere."

"No." I found my feet in the dirt and pushed myself up. "No." Luke's hand at my elbow tightened at my sudden movement.

Troy would never be able to help me. He'd send Aunt Jaclynn, who had enough to deal with already.

"He's not my dad. My dad is Alex. Alex Green." I spouted off the number I'd memorized after Hannah almost drowned.

The cops stared at me. I repeated the number.

"Fine, that's fine. I'll call it." Shawn nodded to Luke and pulled out his cell phone.

Why did I do that? Alex will tell them to call Aunt Jaclynn anyway. He's three hours away. Unless he tells them to take me into the station or something. I slid back down to the dirt beside the truck.

"Hey, is this Alex Green?" Shawn had switched into his cheerful conversational tone.

I let my head fall into my palms. If I was a mess now, I'd be ten times worse inside a crowded police station trying to make it through the night in a jail cell.

"This is Shawn Sharp, with the Flagstaff police station. We have a Preston Bensen here who said you were his dad."

My chest knotted up until it hurt to breathe. *Alex isn't my dad.*

"That so?" Shawn said into the phone.

I dug my hands into my scalp. The pinpoints of pain grounded me.

"Yeah. On the side of the road. He's not talking much. Really shaky. I think he's pretty scared."

I was rocking now. *Stupid, stupid.*

"Yeah? His birth dad? Did you know he was in Flagstaff?"

Luke crouched in front of me. "Breathe, kid."

I nodded at him and started counting in my head again.

"That right?" Shawn walked away from us, still talking.

I didn't know what was worse—the embarrassment of falling apart in front of the officers, or realizing Alex knew everything now.

The lights of a vehicle swerved across the road and stopped straight across from us, headlights shining a puddle of light on the truck. *Jesse. He's made it.*

He could talk enough for both of us.

Shawn crossed in front of me, his phone hanging in his hand by his leg.

A door slammed in the darkness, and my fingers uncurled from my palms.

"Preston?" a voice called from out of view.

My body stiffened, a ripple going up my backbone outward to my legs and arms. It felt like fingers strangling around my neck, stifling the vibrations from my vocal chords.

It wasn't Jesse.

It was Alex.

Twent/-Four

Jesse had told Alex. I should have seen it, but it blindsided me. Obviously Jesse was still mad at me, and this was his revenge.

I tried to stand, but Luke grabbed me. "You can stay here. Your dad will come to you."

No. I couldn't let Alex see me like that again. I pushed myself up and stood by the time he rounded the door and stopped in front of me.

The sleeves of his dress shirt were rolled up, and his hair was a mess. His bloodshot gaze pierced through me, his anger from earlier replaced by something impossible to read.

The officers told him everything, from the moment I turned into a shaking mute to when I slid out of the truck. Alex nodded to them periodically, but his eyes never left me.

Embarrassment as sharp as knives was shredding my guts into ribbons. I didn't know who I hated more, Jesse or myself, but if I started crying now, in front of them all, I'd never forgive myself.

Alex interrupted the officers. "Can I get him in the car?"

Both men nodded in unison. "Do you have someone to call for the truck?" asked Luke.

"Yeah. I'll take care of it." Alex reached for my elbow. "Give me a second to get him settled."

I jerked away, reflexes coiling, a voice in my head shouting not to let him touch me. "I'm fine."

Alex moved back. "Preston." His voice, solemn and tired, pulled on me. "Please stop fighting me."

The tension in me rolled forward like a wave. I circled around Alex to the car—he'd brought Mom's. I opened the back door on the right side of the vehicle. There'd be less pressure to talk if I sat there. Alex pulled me away and opened the front door. I climbed into the front seat, but only to get his hand off me.

He leaned over me and flipped on the overhead dome light. Then he popped open the glove compartment. My breath rushed hard against the back of his head, my body flattened against the seat, my hands curled around the cushion near my legs. The thickness in my throat rose up, and a small sound, almost a whimper, slipped out of my lips. I pinched my eyes closed.

Count. But I couldn't count when I didn't want to breathe. Alex smelled of rancid sweat and oil paint. The odor filled my mouth.

He pried my right hand off the cushion and wrapped my fingers around something. My eyes flew open. *A pencil.* He settled a new sketchbook in my lap, flipped open the first page, and then backed out of my space. Leaning with one hand braced on the door, he said, "I'll be back in a minute."

My fingers curled around the pencil, then unfolded, then tightened again. I shifted the drawing pad over my lap and brought the pencil to the paper. A line scratched over the surface. I sketched until Kanab formed on the page, crawling out into the valley the way it had this afternoon. I was only vaguely aware of the sound of tires on gravel as the officers pulled away.

Alex got in the driver's seat. I stayed hunched over the paper.

"I called a tow truck," he said.

My hand stilled. It'd cost a lot to get my truck home. "I'll pay for it."

"Okay. I'll let you know how much when I find out."

It was the first time he'd agreed to let me pay for pretty much anything since he'd gotten to Kanab. For some reason, his agreement added weight to the guilt already settled deep inside me. I rolled the pencil between my fingers.

"You need to call your mom." Alex slid my dead phone into the cup holder between us and shifted to remove his phone from his pocket. After unlocking the screen, he passed it to me.

I stared at it. Images of Troy wavered through my brain—the soft drawl of his voice, the moisture in his eyes, his worry about Mom and Sammy. I understood now. I was him. I always hoped I'd be something else if I tried hard enough, but it hadn't worked.

Frantic to draw, I put the phone next to mine in the cup holder and hunched lower over the pad.

Alex picked up the phone. Fear of him yelling at me again raced up from my stomach.

"I've got him."

I jumped even though his voice was calm. It wasn't even directed at me. He'd called Mom.

He listened for a moment and said, "Yeah. I think I better get a hotel room. I can't drive anymore tonight—I'm too tired. I'll text you when we are settled. You want to talk to him?"

I had to get out of the car. Now. I reached out. The pencil smashed against my palm, pinned between it and the door handle.

"Preston, stay in the car."

At the firmness in Alex's tone, my head turned and my fingers fell into my lap. The pencil rolled free. He passed me the phone.

I didn't want to do it, but my left hand didn't cooperate and placed the phone against my ear. Alex shut off the dome light and drove onto the highway, headed to Flagstaff. My breath rushed in and out, right into the speaker.

"Preston," Mom said, her voice breaking. "Baby, I'm sorry. I'm sorry I didn't tell you about the letter. I'm sorry I yelled at you. I just don't know what to do sometimes." A sob cut off her words.

The sound of her crying hit hard, breaking through to the place where my chest already ached. It peppered across my worry-bruised stomach and rattled around my frantically racing thoughts.

"I wanted to tell you—I was going to—but you were struggling and kept pushing me away." Now her tone was desperate. "I didn't want to add another thing to your load. I wanted to give you time."

The darkness rushed by as Alex drove. Too numb to even consider lowering the phone, I struggled to process Mom's worry. I'd never done something like this to her. Ever.

"Are you okay?" she asked me. "You went to your dad's, didn't you? What happened?"

I wanted to explain why I had to find Troy, but even if I could explain it, the sickness inside me would always be there, waiting. I was always going to hurt her. Hurt Sammy. It was in me. I could never be strong enough for long enough to change that about me.

"Preston, please don't push me away." Mom's voice broke into my thoughts. "Please. Talk to me."

But I didn't have any words. Just images. Pressed against my head, filling the spaces, swelling. Bryan pinned under a pile of four-wheelers, his neck broken. Mom on the floor by her bed, hiding from us while she sobbed, a divorce letter at her side. Sammy white faced, sleeping in a hospital bed. Troy standing cold and lonely in the hallway of Aunt Jaclynn's house.

Instead of words, a ragged, hollow echo filled my breaths. Instead of words, I blinked blindly at the passing lights.

The phone slid from my fingers into Alex's, and he wiped my sweat on his shirt before putting the phone to his ear. "Hey, Nat, hon, let me take it for a bit, okay?"

"I don't know what to do." Catching on another sob, Mom's voice carried through the car.

A writhing broke across my body. I slid down, working myself against the door.

"Nat. It's going to be okay," Alex said. "I'm with him now. I'll get him home to you, okay?"

"Promise."

"I promise. Give the kids a hug for me. We'll be home tomorrow. I love you." Alex lowered the phone to the center console, his gaze dragging across me before focusing on the road again.

I'd made her cry. Just like Troy had.

I wrapped my hands around the sides of my head. Everything I'd buried inside—the worry, the anxiety, the fear—surged upward.

JoLyn Brown

I hunched over, trying to stop the tears spilling down my face, trying to muffle the sounds escaping me, trapping them in the stale place between my chest and my knees.

A hand came to my shoulder. I ripped outward, unfolding like I'd been electrocuted.

Alex. I might as well have been naked. The tears and sobs ripped from me, tearing me open. I bit down on the inner part of my cheek and clenched my teeth until it hurt. The stupid tears didn't stop. I shifted away from him, tried to refold on myself, but even that wouldn't help me now.

The humiliation was drowning me. *Please help me stop crying.*

Alex drove down an exit ramp and stopped on the shoulder near a huge rock. The engine cut off. I shoved the door open and staggered out of the car. My body shivered with both the cold and my breath fighting through the tears. I backed against the rock and leaned over my knees. Alex stepped from the car and circled around to the trunk. My knees buckled, taking me to the dirt.

Alex slammed the trunk and crossed over to me. I willed him to walk away—to look away. Instead, he settled down four or five inches from me. I could feel the warmth coming off his body.

His hand settled on my shoulder and rested there until the silence reached all around me and ate up each sob. The car's headlights winked out, leaving us in a sea of dark.

I gave into Alex's silence, him being there without words. No words until I cried myself dry.

When the sobs subsided, my body jerked with shivers. My raw eyes blinked over the fatigue and salt. Alex shifted and passed me something. My coat. I slipped it on. My head sank against the rock.

The sound of my breath evened out little by little, and the chokehold around my throat loosened until I could whisper, "I don't know what to do."

"About what?" Alex's soft voice broke through the darkness.

I rubbed my hand along the hair at base of my neck. "It's getting worse. I had a panic attack last night, and lately it seems like I'm always about to have one."

The words came easier than expected. Since nothing I said could possibly be worse than the way I'd cried, maybe my body decided it was okay to talk now. "I'm just like Troy. I always have been. I'm going to hurt Mom again. I can't protect them. Not Sammy, not the girls. Not from accidents or their own stupidity, or even me. I'm going to make another mistake and it will hurt them again."

After several seconds Alex said, "If it truly was the end of all hope after we hurt our families, we'd all be unredeemable. I was driving the night Amy, Karen, and Adam died. It was my fault." The confession lingered between us before Alex spoke again. "God doesn't work that way. Families aren't about making sure bad things never happen to anyone we love. They are about helping the ones we love get through the bad things."

The darkness deepened. Even the interstate, winding away to the left, remained deserted. My head tipped back. Night cold had sucked the desert sky dry of clouds, painting an illusion of nothing between me and space. Stars burned across its inky blackness, more than I'd seen in all the camping trips I'd taken with Scouts or the Powells.

More words pushed out my dry lips. "But I can't even help the people I love."

"Yes, you can, and you do." Alex spoke with certainty. "You've helped your mom and Sam, and my girls and me, in countless ways since the day I met you. Just because you make mistakes doesn't mean you've failed."

He didn't know about Bryan. I'd never told anyone. "The day Bryan died," I began, "he asked Jesse and me if we wanted to go riding with them. We were so worked up about getting this truck fixed up that we didn't go. Usually when Sammy went off without me, I'd ask where they were riding. But that day I didn't. I just let him go."

I shivered, my body struggling against the memory: Sammy straddling the four-wheeler behind Morgan, Bryan on his own four-wheeler, waving to Josie as they drove off the edge of the lawn and down toward the Pit. The last time I saw Bryan alive. I shrank into myself, drawing my knees up. Alex shifted to run his hand over my hair, a few strokes before it stilled near my neck.

I exhaled hard. "I knew he was dead the minute Morgan said his name over the phone. The feeling was so strong. When I got off the phone, Josie and Jesse were standing there, and I couldn't say anything. I didn't say anything—not until we'd driven all the way out there and Jesse made us pull the four-wheelers off Bryan. I should have said something earlier, before Jesse did that. After I told them, all I could think to do was get Morgan and Sammy away from Bryan's body, away from Jesse screaming. Then I sat there and cried like a baby."

Lowering my knees, I swallowed. "My life is like that lately. I have all this stuff I should do but I can't. I keep messing it up."

Alex massaged at the tense muscles in my neck. "It's okay to cry, Preston, or to fall short. Even Heavenly Father weeps. And more than that, He is used to working with imperfect people. You haven't let Him down. Perhaps He wasn't so worried about you telling anyone that you knew Bryan was gone. Maybe He just wanted you to be able to focus on someone besides Bryan."

Knowing Bryan was gone *had* changed how I acted that day. I'd focused on making sure Sammy and Morgan were safe, rather than on helping Bryan. "I didn't think of that."

Alex sighed. "After losing Amy, Adam, and Karen, the enormity of my pain made it difficult to see any miracles at all. The miracle of having them with me again wasn't going to happen, so what else mattered? It's okay to feel that way. It's normal. The true miracle is that even while you are struggling, Heavenly Father keeps reaching out to you, even if you can't see it yet. It might help for you to look for that—the blessings you are grateful for that you might have overlooked. It's okay to start small. Those can be the biggest miracles."

"There's nothing." I couldn't think of a single thing.

"Sure there is. You like football. And drawing. How about Morgan? You get along really well with her. Aren't you grateful for that?"

I *was* grateful for all of that. Especially Morgan.

Then, as if the sky itself reached down and God's creations held some power over my tangled mind, new images emerged from the haze, sharp as the ones that had stopped my words earlier. Mom insisting I play football. Morgan holding my hand in the darkness outside the banquet hall. Sammy and Jesse pulling Hannah and me from the lake. Alex telling off Aunt Rhonda, stepping between Brett and me, and always showing up to press a pencil into my hand when I needed it.

My eyes shifted to Alex, sitting by me in the cold dirt on the edge of a highway. Less than twenty-four hours ago, I'd wondered if God put him in my life to help me. I visualized Troy, living alone in his room, letting us all go so we wouldn't be hurt by him. I liked my own space, liked the quiet, but I didn't want to live how he did.

"Troy said he'll never get better," I told Alex. "He said it always comes back, no matter what he does. Will that happen to me?"

"Do you believe he can't get better?"

"I don't know. It's been more than ten years."

Alex smiled at the sky. "Do you know what attracted me, in part, to your mother after I got to know her?"

"I hadn't thought about it." I tried *not* to think about it.

"She holds tight to hope. She never has given up on Troy. She never stopped believing he can get better. She realized that to help you and Sam and to take care of herself, she had to make changes, but she's never really decided Troy can't change."

"It's stupid, 'cause it hurts her every time he messes up."

"Then do you think your father is beyond the aid of Jesus Christ, that even our Savior cannot help him?"

"Of course He can." The words came automatic, left over from all my Sunday school lessons. Then what Alex had said hit me, penetrating into my tired, hope-drained body. The feeling blossomed, spiraling outward in all directions—the burn of the Spirit like a returning friend, filling the empty spaces my tears left vacant.

Of course Christ could heal my dad. It wasn't even a question.

"Centering our hope in Christ is powerful," Alex continued. "That kind of hope fills us up and lasts forever. That hope is what is inside your mom. It's what you need to keep going, no matter how many times you battle your anxiety." He shifted to face me. "It's what you need now. Trust that Christ both wants to and can help. Does that make sense?"

The warmth pulsed inside me. "I thought I believed that, but lately, it's like I forgot."

"That's a pretty dark place to be. It's also very normal. There's a reason one of the Spirit's jobs is to help us remember."

"I remember now." Even as I spoke it seemed I knew it more than before, like it had grown inside me.

"Good." Alex hesitated. "Preston, I told you all this because you need to come to terms with your real father and your fear of becoming like him. You needed to talk about that. Now I want to clarify a few things, okay?"

I pulled my coat closed against a sudden breeze, not sure what he was leading up too. "Okay . . ."

Alex placed both hands on my shoulders and turned me to face him. "It's okay to need alone time. It's okay to not like crowds or to feel uncomfortable around new situations and people. Being introverted isn't bad. You should never feel that not being as outgoing as someone else means you are less of a person."

"It's worse than that, though." I ducked my head.

Alex tightened his grip on my shoulders. "Yes, some bigger things are happening right now, things that aren't normal. What you've been dealing with is a reaction to a traumatic experience, not a permanent part of your personality that will make you end up like Troy. This is what is *happening* to you, not who you *are*. Do you understand that?"

I shrugged.

"Isolating yourself, letting fear keep you from doing what you enjoy, or trying to manage it all by yourself—that is what Troy does." Alex's voice grew intense. "Getting help is how you heal. It doesn't mean you're weak or flawed. It means you're human. You've helped everyone else for a long time. Give us a chance to return the favor."

I studied the dirt, unable to fully accept what he'd said, but too hungry for hope to dismiss it either. Maybe he was right.

Alex got to his feet. "Come on, let's go to the hotel. We can talk more while we drive. I'm freezing." He held a hand out to me.

I hesitated, then let him help me up.

Twenty-Five

Someone shook my arm and said, "Hey, it's 10:30. We've got to get checked out before 11:00."

I sat blinking over the residue of salty tears. *Where am I?*

I focused on the hotel room around me. A plate of hot food sat on the table in the corner, steam rising up. Alex pulled open the curtains and let the light spill in. I fell back on the bed and squeezed my eyes closed.

"The food is for you. I ate already," he told me.

I rolled over, pushed myself off the bed, and took a seat in front of the food. I hadn't eaten since lunch yesterday. By the time I finished downing the pile of muffins, eggs, sausage, and bacon, my brain had kicked on.

Ah, I've made such an idiot of myself. Scowling at the empty plate, I dragged my hands through my hair.

"You all right?" Alex sat down across from me.

I dug the plastic fork into the Styrofoam plate. "Sorry about yesterday."

"I accept your apology for what happened in the parking lot and for running off to Flagstaff without telling anyone. I won't, however, let you apologize for what happened last night."

He planted his hands on the table in front of him. "Preston, look at me."

I dragged my gaze up.

"You have nothing to be ashamed of. I'm not going to judge you. No matter how many times things like that happen. It's okay."

I stabbed at the plate again, my body torn between embarrassment and relief.

"You finished eating?"

I nodded at the table.

"Then let's go home."

⸎

Three hours in the car with Alex turned out to be the best way to get over my embarrassment. We talked art for a while and by then, the pressure was gone. I could sit in silence, or bring up Bryan, Jesse, or my worries about Sammy. I even talked about football. He didn't seem to mind any of it. When we reached the outskirts of Kanab, the tension leaked back into me.

Now I had to face Mom.

The car pulled into the driveway, and Alex shut off the engine. "Take a few slow breaths, Preston."

"I'm trying."

"It's going to be okay."

The front door opened. Mom stopped on the top step. The rest of them spilled out around her.

I groaned and slid down in the seat. "I can't do this." What if she started crying again?

"I'll take care of the kids. All you need to do is talk to your mom. That's it." Alex climbed out and grabbed his bag from the rear seat. He intercepted the kids, herding them up the stairs. At the top, he spoke to Mom and pointed down at the car.

She took each stair with deliberate slowness. The front door closed over the rest of them.

I got the door open and inched out. *It will hurt her more. I'm going to hurt her all over again.* My head lowered and I kicked at the gravel.

She stopped in front of me.

"I'm sorry." My voice cracked and I scrambled to pull back the rush of emotion inside me.

"Are you all right?" She reached for my hand.

I shook my head at her. The flaring anxiety blocked my thoughts and strangled my voice. I grasped for the car behind me. A tear splashed to my cheek.

"Preston." She breathed my name, her arms sliding around me.

"I thought I was turning into Troy." I moved into her embrace, pressing one hand to my eyes to stop the tears. "I didn't know what to do. I've been having panic attacks. A lot."

Her hands rose up my back to pull me against her. "Oh, honey. It's going to be okay."

"I thought if I told you, if you knew, it would remind you of Dad. I didn't want to hurt you. I didn't want to make you cry. Not like he does."

She released the hug and cupped my face, rubbing over the stubble growing there. "Of course you remind me of your father. You have his compassion, his patience and protectiveness, even his sense of humor. You have all his best traits, but you are more than just Troy. You also have a strong loyalty toward your friends and a focused sense of responsibility. When someone needs help, you forget all about yourself in your effort to make sure they are okay. You are a blessing to me, and you are a blessing to our family."

Embarrassed, I pulled away from her hands and fidgeted with the door knob behind me. "I've got his flaws too, Mom."

She slipped her arm around my waist. "We all have flaws. I'm not always as patient as I should be. I say the wrongs things at the wrong time. Having some of Troy's flaws won't make you him any more than having his good qualities will. If you make a mistake and I cry, it means I love you. It means I want to help you but don't always know how to do it. It means I'm your mom and maybe a little too emotional. It never means you are going to end up like your dad. Can you believe that?"

Alex's words from the night before stirred inside me. *It's what's happening to you, not who you are.*

"I think so," I said. "I got sort of wrapped up in my own head."

A tiny smile touched Mom's worried face. "I noticed. What can I do to help?"

"I don't know. I feel overwhelmed sometimes. There's nowhere I can be alone to think. I'm always on edge."

Mom rubbed my back. "You don't really have a space of your own here. We should do something about that."

"Really?"

"Sure."

I relaxed another fraction. "I worry about Sammy all the time. I have dreams about him dying. I dream about Bryan, too. Other times, random things remind me of the accident. I don't know how to deal with that. I lose my temper or have panic attacks. Like I did yesterday."

"Worrying about Sammy is natural," Mom said. "What happened to Bryan affected us all. You don't have to hide that from me." Her hand stilled. "Are you comfortable with me asking Alex for advice? He's dealt with stuff like this before, so he might have some ideas."

"Yeah. That's fine," I said.

Mom tipped her head in surprise. "Really? I thought you'd . . . I was worried . . . what happened last night?"

A flush heated my skin. "It's a long story."

She studied me and then pulled me away from the car. "Why don't we go inside? We can talk in my room."

I followed her to the house.

At the sound of the door, Bonnie darted out of the kitchen and sped straight at me. Alex called after her, but she kept coming and rammed her head into my gut, wrapping her arms around me in a fierce embrace. "I thought you weren't coming back." Her voice cracked and hard sobs broke through.

Alex strode down the hall toward us. "Bonnie, I said you needed to wait. You can talk to Preston in a little while."

"It's okay, Alex." I pried her fingers loose, then held them as I squatted down to her level. "I'm sorry. I didn't mean to scare you."

She shook her head at me, tears rolling in a flood down her face. "I already lost Adam. I don't want to lose you, too."

My right knee came to the floor. I pulled her to my shoulder. "Hey, it's all right. Didn't you already know your dad would track me down if I tried to break a rule?"

She spoke into my shirt. "I didn't think you'd come. Sammy said you don't want him to be your dad. I thought he couldn't make you come home if you didn't want him to be your dad anymore."

Hannah and Sammy crowded into the hallway behind Alex, waiting to hear what I'd say next.

My dad *anymore*. It made sense in a way. Alex had been more of a dad to me in the last few months than Troy had been in years, but it wasn't that simple. Especially now. The image of Troy burned in my head, clearer now that I couldn't hate him.

I smoothed Bonnie's hair and forced a smile. "What? You really think he'd let me off the hook 'cause I said I didn't want him to be my dad? You think it's that easy to get out of this family? It's not. I think you're stuck with me."

Bonnie backed away from me, a tiny smile on her lips.

Pushing between Sammy and Hannah, Edith said, "Hey, I can fix him. Let me through." She shoved a container of peanut-butter ice cream into my chest.

The condensation soaked through the front of my T-shirt. My fingers slid around the carton.

Edith pressed a spoon against my free hand. "See, that's better."

A laugh escaped my chest on a rush of relief. I tapped the top of the carton with the spoon. "Eddie, you're brilliant."

She grinned. "I know."

Twenty-Six

The next morning, I went running with Alex. It was one of the suggestions he said might help. We didn't talk, which was fine with me. I had a hard enough time keeping up. Running was Morgan's thing, not mine. But after my body warmed up and moved into the rhythm of the motions, I thought maybe I caught a glimpse of why Morgan loved running so much. It didn't crowd my head the way football or basketball did, with thoughts of the next play or move I needed to make. It just *was*. Simple, repetitive, and in a way, calming.

Not long after we got home, Jesse drove up in his dad's white double-cab truck and offered to drive us to school. Grounded from driving, I couldn't really think of a good reason to say no—other than being uncomfortable about it. I hadn't talked to him since Monday night. I got out at the school without having said a word.

He jogged after me. "Wait up, Preston."

I stopped, facing the glass doors.

"Are we cool, about, you know?" he said.

"Yeah."

"I wasn't trying to get back at you."

"I know."

"I was trying to help."

"I know." I hesitated. "Thanks."

Jesse huffed in surprise. "So it worked out all right?"

"Yeah."

"I guess Alex ain't so bad." Jesse pulled open the front doors. "Are you coming to basketball practice after school?"

"I'll be there."

"Sweet."

We walked by Bryan's memorial display and headed to class.

~

When I got home from practice, Hannah was sitting on my bed. She perched on the edge, her knees bouncing and her lips down in a worried frown. I'd told her sorry on Tuesday. She'd brushed off the apology and hadn't said a word about any of it since.

I dropped my bag on the floor by the closet.

She scanned me up and down. "You're always crabby."

I let my arms swing free. Basketball had been a little stressful. *Probably not the best way to handle my anxiety after all.* "You're always happy. It's annoying. Except for right now. It's weird—I can tell when you're worried ever since you took that plunge. What do you want?"

Hannah grinned. "That's what happens when you pull someone out of a lake. Unfortunate side effect of being so protective."

"I guess I'll have to deal with it. Someone's got to keep an eye on you and Sam. Did you want something?"

She took a deep breath. "Just so you know, I'm not asking for your permission. I don't need it and neither does Sammy. I asked Natalie and Dad, and they said okay."

That was a bad start. What was Hannah going to do this time?

She stumbled on, her gaze dancing away. "I'm telling you because I don't want you to freak out when you find out we're gone."

I crossed to her and crouched by her bouncing knee. "Hannah? What are you talking about?"

She looked at me straight on. "I'm taking him into the Pit. To the place he used to go with Bryan. We're going Saturday."

A hard breath caught in my throat, and it was all I could do to keep the blind panic from taking over. The edges of my vision blurred. The thought of the Pit felt like fire, burning through every shred of hope and control I'd harnessed in the last few days.

"We are hiking in—nothing too dangerous," Hannah explained, talking faster now. "Sammy knows the place like he knows his own house. He needs to go back. I'm going with him because you maybe can't yet. He needs a friend to take him. Not a parent. Just a friend."

I sank to the floor. "No."

Her hands wrapped around mine and she knelt in front of me. "I know how it feels. It's like getting in a car after the accident. If Dad hadn't let me go on my terms—if he made me wait until Bonnie was ready—it would have taken another month. Sometimes when I'm afraid, I realize the waiting is worse than doing it. I do stuff so I can get over being scared. When you are ready, Sammy and I will go with you, too. You don't have to do it alone."

Hannah got up and left me there.

I didn't remember charging out. I didn't remember going up the stairs, or pretty much anything else until I'd cornered Alex in the kitchen. I had enough presence of mind not to tackle him, but I really wanted to. He caught my shoulders, pushing me around the counter and into the hallway. I shoved his hands away and said, "What's wrong with you? You can't let them go in the Pit!"

His hands wrapped around my biceps, steering me backward. "Let's talk in the room."

"There's nothing to talk about!" I ground my feet into the carpet.

"Preston," Alex said gently and pushed again. I stumbled into his and Mom's room. He closed the door behind us. "Okay. Let it out."

"You aren't his father! You have no right. You've never been in there. You don't know what it's like. Are you *trying* to get Sammy killed?" The words came louder and louder until it felt as if I stood outside myself, watching along with Alex as I yelled.

And yelled.

Until I couldn't anymore.

I dropped onto the edge of the bed, my chest heaving. A rawness clawed at my throat. *Why did I do that?* I hunched over, locking my hands behind my head.

The creak of the rolling chair from Mom's desk stopped in front of me. Alex sat down and asked, "Have you calmed down a little?"

"Yeah."

"This is going to be one of the hardest things anyone's ever asked you to do, but I know you can do it."

"No, I can't. I'm doing all the right things. Praying, reading my scriptures, getting exercise, talking about stuff. I still can't breathe when I think of it. I almost tackled you."

"I appreciate that you didn't." A trace of humor hung on Alex's words.

"I used to pray when I got scared or panicked. Heavenly Father used to calm me down. I can't feel Him anymore. I can't find Him. I can't do this without Him." The urgency picked up in my voice, and Alex wheeled his chair a little closer.

"He's still there, Preston. He hasn't left you. The anxiety makes it hard to hear Him, so He's using the people who love you to remind you that you're not alone. If you look up you'll see someone who may just understand a little of what you are going through."

Focusing on the bits of green paint stuck to Alex's tan socks, I said, "You didn't want to let Hannah get in a vehicle."

"No."

"How did you let her?"

"I did a lot of yelling first. I used to be really good at that. Then a lot of walking and thinking and praying. My father-in-law gave me a blessing. Ultimately, I realized riding the bus or walking everywhere was impractical and life-crippling. I didn't want to cripple my girls or myself. So I did it. I was stronger than I realized. It got easier after that."

I was starting to doubt my own ability to be that strong. Maybe Troy was right after all. Yet that thought wouldn't stick to me. I couldn't afford to let it. I closed my eyes and swallowed.

"Will you give me a blessing, Alex?"

His hand tightened a fraction. "Yes, I will."

The next day when Jesse showed up to drive us to school, I told him I wasn't going to play basketball.

Sam and Hannah went silent in the back seat.

Jesse's eyes flickered to me and then back to the road.

I stared out the window. I hated telling him that, but I needed to let basketball go. Running with Alex for the second day in a row only helped me realize the contrast in how tense basketball made me. It would never help me the way I wanted it to.

"Is it basketball you hate?" Jesse asked, his voice careful.

I glanced over at him. "No."

He sighed. "Okay. You still want to practice with me? I'll come to your place. We can play at the park down the road. In the evenings."

"Is something wrong with the hoop at your place?"

"No."

"Why don't I just come over there? Alex would drop me off."

"If you are willing to come over, I can come get you."

Oh. I'd been avoiding anything that reminded me of Bryan for so long, I hadn't really thought about what it meant for Jesse. "That's fine." I didn't have to do the basketball team, but I did have to stop hiding from the memories. "I'll come. Every night, if you want."

"And me," Sammy interjected. "I'm coming too."

A grin spread over Jesse's face. "Sure. You and anyone else who wants to come. Hannah, you play basketball?"

"Yep." She settled into the seat behind Jesse, smiling at me over the backpack clenched in her arms. "As long as you promise not to knock me in any lakes."

He laughed. "Deal. I won't make any other promises, though. I have four brothers running around. Things get crazy pretty fast."

After dinner that night, I told Alex about going to Jesse's. He settled a stack of plates in the sink, dug his van keys out of his pocket, and passed them to me.

"You're letting me drive?" I said in shock.

"Sounds like this is pretty important to Jesse. It doesn't make sense to complicate things." Alex looked over at Mom. "Nat, is that okay with you?"

Mom, who hadn't eaten much, was still sitting at the table. She stared at her plate, her eyes distant.

"Nat?"

She refocused on Alex and me. "Huh?"

"Are you ready to let Preston drive again? He wants to take Sam and Hannah to Jesse's house tonight."

Mom frowned. "Isn't that bad parenting? We did say he was grounded from driving for a week."

Alex chuckled. "Yeah. It's pretty bad. And you know Preston. He'll probably take advantage of it."

Mom smiled, then raised her brows at me. "You think you can overlook the flawed parenting just this once?

"I guess. As long as you don't make it a habit." I winked.

As she and Alex laughed, I ran my thumb over the digital key, letting my muscles relax. If I could get myself to go to Jesse's house without Morgan there, I could drive Alex's van.

Mom pushed her chair back and stood, reaching for rice casserole in the center of the table. "Where are the rest of the kids? Shouldn't they be helping?"

"I sent them to clean up Bonnie and Edith's room," Alex said, trying to sound casual.

Mom's eyes went wide. "What happened?"

I'd only got a glimpse of the water-soaked carpet and walls. The water fight had happened while I was reading in the laundry room.

Alex took the casserole dish from her. "You don't want to know. Trust me."

"Alex," she moaned. "What happened to trying to rein in the chaos a little?"

Leaning over, he kissed her forehead. "Consider it reined. I've removed all water guns and squirt bottles from the house."

When Mom still looked stressed, I circled around her and Alex. "I'll go help, Mom. It's just water."

She nodded at me, her hand sliding to her stomach and staying there as she watched me walk to the hallway. Halfway down the hall, I stopped short and went back. Something about that motion . . .

In the kitchen, Alex slid his hand over Mom's and pulled her against his chest, his hand and hers now cupped against her stomach. "Nat, it's going to be okay."

"Is it that obvious I'm worried?"

"Yeah. You were pretty zoned out at dinner." Alex leaned around her and kissed her neck.

She closed her eyes and rested her head against him. "Are you sure we can handle another one?"

He laughed. "It's a little too late to be second-guessing."

I braced myself against the wall as cold sweat drenched me.

A hand touched my elbow. Jumping, I whirled to see Hannah, arms piled with damp towels. She took in my shocked face, then glanced around me into the kitchen. Snagging my wrist, she pulled me after her as she went in. "You know, if you aren't planning on making a general announcement," she said loudly, "you've got to stop talking about being pregnant while the rest of us are close enough to hear."

Mom flushed bright pink and pulled against Alex's arms. He drew her back in. His eyes traveled to me and Hannah. He smiled. "Maybe we need to have a family discussion about eavesdropping."

"I didn't mean—I just—" I stuttered, stopping to sink into the closest chair.

Hannah dropped her towels and sat next to me. Mom and Alex released each other and crossed to the table to find chairs by us.

"You okay?" Hannah asked me.

A whirlwind of emotions battered around in me. For a moment I couldn't speak, and the three of them sat there waiting.

I focused on Mom. "Did you want another baby?"

She scooted her chair until she sat in front of me and took my hand. "Yes. I'm just worrying about the details."

"What details?"

"Just details. If I'm going to quit my job. If we'll be moved into the Karlon house by then. How you and the other kids will react."

"When? When are you due?"

"In the summer."

Summer. I would be eighteen by then. Old enough to go on a mission. Old enough to be moved out. Old enough that this shouldn't be making me panic so much.

Alex's hand on my back took my attention from Mom. "Tell us what you're worried about, Preston."

"I don't know." My heart was racing.

Hannah leaned toward me. "You want to know what scared me the most when I found out last week?"

"Not really."

She grinned at my answer. "I'm going to tell you anyway."

"I know." I pushed her head back and she laughed.

"The thing that scares me the most is the idea that something might happen to Dad or to Natalie or both of them, and I'll end up trying to parent three kids before I turn twenty."

"Yeah, that sounds terrifying," I muttered. *Only it won't be just you left with an unexpected parenting job.*

"It's the worst-case scenario," Hannah said. "I think about the worst thing that could happen and decide if I could handle it."

"Sounds really comforting."

She shook her head. "Not really, Preston. Do you even realize how hard it is to get Bonnie to do stuff? I don't want to be fighting with her through her teenage years."

I laughed as some of the tension eased in my body. "I'll take care of Bonnie, if you change the diapers."

Hannah wrinkled her nose. "Yuck." Her eyes brightened. "I know, Sammy will do the diapers. I'll be in charge of Edith."

I thought of Edith's latest adventure with food coloring and sponges on the back deck. "Deal." I held out my hand to Hannah.

Schooling her face into a solemn expression, she grasped my hand and shook it. "Deal."

"You do know that Alex and I fully intend to be around to raise *all* of you children," Mom put in, her eyes sparkling.

Hannah smiled at her. "I know. We're just making Plan B. Plan A is to leave you guys to raise the baby and the other kids while I take photography classes and almost fail my math class, and then after I graduate, travel the world doing semesters abroad. By then Preston will be married. To Morgan. They'll make a bunch of babies of their own."

I choked. Alex pounded a hand against my back.

Hannah kept going. "Of course, first he'll go on a mission and all that."

My body froze. The panic returned in a blind rush, crashing over me. I flew to my feet and reached the door to the stairs before Alex caught my arm. Mom pushed between me and the stairs, and Hannah's hand grasped my wrist. My breath rattled in my ears. Instead of pulling away, I let them draw me back into the kitchen.

When I sat, Hannah released me and said, "I think we found it."

"What?" I whispered between ragged breaths.

"What scares you. You're aren't afraid of another baby. You're afraid of going on a mission and being gone when the baby is born. You're afraid of not being around to protect us all."

I'd been wrong about Hannah. She wasn't chill or easygoing. She was terrifying.

Mom slipped an arm around my shoulders. "Preston, take slower breaths—in for five seconds, hold for five seconds. Then release."

I looked at her and worked my breaths back down to a normal pace, one inhale at a time.

Alex crouched at my knee. "Are you worried about a mission, Preston?"

I nodded.

"About not being here to take care of your mom and Sammy?"

I nodded again.

"And about your mom having a baby, and me maybe taking off and leaving her while you're too far away to get back to help her?"

My eyes flew to Mom and then back to Alex. For the first time my fears shifted and something hit me. "You won't leave her."

"No. I won't. Not her, or Sam or the new baby. Not my girls or even you. I'm in this for eternity."

I relaxed a bit. "I know." I stared at my hands. "I'm just not sure how to always keep that in perspective. Lately I've had so many panic attacks, and I'm still not sure how to stop them on my own. You or Mom or even Hannah won't be there when I'm on a mission. The last thing anyone wants is a missionary like that."

"It would certainly be unwise to send you on a regular mission before you feel like you've got a handle on your anxiety." Alex grabbed a chair and pulled it between mine and Hannah's, forcing her to scoot over. He sat next to me. "But that doesn't mean you can't serve or that there isn't another, better option for you."

Mom rubbed at my palm in small circles with the tips of her fingers. "Do you want to serve a mission?" she asked.

The desire lingered under layers of complications, a soft pulse of love for God that hadn't been burned out yet. "I do. I just panic thinking about it. I know Heavenly Father will help me talk. I know He can and will take care of you when I'm gone. I know all that, but I can't control the anxiety. Even if I talk myself out of worrying during the day, it comes back at night."

Mom lifted my chin so I faced her. "You don't have to leave right when you graduate. There is no rush. You have time to figure the anxiety out. You have time to heal. I know that Heavenly Father wants you to take the time you need to take care of yourself. Alex is right. There are different things you can do. Not all missions are two years. Not all missionaries leave as soon as they are old enough."

"I know. But it feels like I'm letting God down."

"You aren't," Hannah interjected without warning. "Would you tell Sammy he was letting Heavenly Father down if he can't serve a full-time mission? Do you think the work God has for Sammy, wherever Sammy goes in his life, is any less important that the work God gives to someone without Down syndrome?"

The fire in Hannah's eyes pierced me. She might be as defensive of Sammy as I was. And she was right. "No," I said. "God is always sending Sam places no one else can get."

"Right." Hannah pointed her finger at me. "And He's doing the same with you. No matter what kind of mission you serve and no matter when you go, if you serve Him with at least as much commitment as Sam would, the Lord will do crazy awesome stuff with you too."

An electric silence settled around us, as if the air itself was charged with Hannah's words. A slow smile tugged at my lips. "So, Hannah, are you going on a mission before you travel the world?"

"I guess we'll see. God hasn't told me that part of Plan A yet."

In the days after going to Troy's, I spent more time thinking about and talking to God than I had since Sammy ended up in the hospital last January. I learned a bunch of things, but didn't find any peace about Sammy going in the Pit. Long after he turned out his lamp on Friday night, I wrestled with the panic.

Finally I rolled out of bed onto my knees. *I can't let him go in there.* I'd told God that several times. I didn't really expect a response. Still on the floor, I grabbed my phone off the nightstand and opened my scripture app. I couldn't focus on what I was reading, but my breathing slowed down. I settled with my back against the bed.

Maybe I should draw.

I dug through the bottom shelf of the nightstand, searching for a sketch pad. I had several now. Alex kept passing new ones along to me. He must've had a box of them.

A pocket-sized notebook slipped onto the floor. I scooped it up. A sketch of Sammy filled the first page, his eyes unfinished. It creeped me out. I grabbed a pencil and sketched them in. Working the rest of his face, I pulled in lines and shading, until I noticed the similarities between him and Troy. The curve of his jaw, the fullness through his cheeks, his unparted, stick-straight hair, flattened toward his forehead.

But Sammy's eyes were different. Confident. He didn't doubt himself at all. What gave Sammy that? He had plenty of struggles. Was it his own will? Or something else? How could he be ready to go out into the Pit again? He'd been with Bryan, alone, for a good forty minutes or so. He sat there holding Bryan's hand.

Something he'd told Hannah filtered through my head. *I was scared, but then I prayed. I knew Bryan was okay, even though he wasn't alive anymore.*

If my dad could find God, would that help him? Would he be more willing to try? Warmth dried up my anxiety, spreading through me with a penetrating calmness.

Did God want me to keep trying to help my dad?

Holding onto Troy would've kept Mom from moving on, finding Alex, having another baby, and being happy. Holding on to Troy would've kept Sammy from his dream of a family complete with sisters and a dad who loved and knew him. But holding on to Troy wouldn't do a thing to hurt me. Alex was already more my dad than Troy. An adoption paper wouldn't change that. Alex wouldn't treat me any different, but it would change everything between Troy and me.

I needed to keep Troy's last name and let him know he would always be my father. I'd been through all of this anxiety, panic, and worry, and in the end, I'd not only forgiven my dad but understood him now.

I sat there burning with the clarity of my decision. I'd been worried about sealings and eternal families. The worry had gone. God would work it all out. One day I would take someone to the temple, a girl willing to take a chance on me, and we would be sealed together. We would start something eternal of our own.

And maybe Troy might want to be around to see it.

If I picked up a Book of Mormon, I could send it to him.

I sank against the bed, surprised to find my anxiety gone. I looked heavenward. *Thanks for helping me figure out what to do about Troy, but I really was trying to figure out what to do about Sammy.*

I sketched until sleep tugged at my eyelids. Hauling myself into the bed, I collapsed face first into the pillow. As I dozed off, a thought drifted through my fogging brain.

Go with him.

Twenty-Seven

I woke to Sammy packing his hiking bag in the dark. I threw the covers off and flicked on the lamp next to me. "I'm coming too," I told him.

He went still and then shook his head. "No. You only want to go so you can tell me to not do stuff."

"Sammy, let him come," said Hannah, stepping into the room.

"He'll boss me around!"

I yanked on my jeans. "Hannah, you need to knock."

She rolled her eyes. "I don't care what color your boxers are. I've seen them before. Or did you forget about the mouse?"

My face went hot. She crossed over to Sammy, who plopped onto the bed with a growl.

She sat beside him. "You know you're just like him when things get dangerous. Sammy's mouth dropped open and she laughed. "You both get crazy protective. It's what I like and hate about having you for brothers." She glanced at me. "Let him come. He needs this too."

Sammy pressed his lips tight and studied his hands in his lap. I braced myself. I didn't want to fight about it.

He jumped up and snatched his bag. "Dad's making breakfast." Sammy's grin focused on me. "You can come too."

I was pretty sure he meant I could go in the Pit, not just eat breakfast with them. I grabbed my shirt, a sweater, and hiking shoes, then followed them upstairs.

The Pit gave up its skin-scorching heat in late November. The shadows cast by the narrow passages and winding paths snaking down into its belly left cold pockets of white frost. Walking to the trail that started down the road from our house in Karlon, we passed the stone markers Brett, Jesse, and I had set up for Bryan's runs.

I expected the panic, the rush of memories, the pulse of fear. I thought I was ready, but when it hit me in my center, I stopped only feet into the Pit, watching with a terrible sort of helplessness as Sammy and Hannah got further away from me.

I can't do this.

Hannah turned back, saw me standing there, and sent a reassuring smile. She didn't stop walking—just left me as if she didn't care whether I came or not. It was up to me.

It triggered something stubborn inside me. I might not be able to do this on my own, but Heavenly Father built worlds and a whole sky of stars. He could get me in the Pit.

Please help me.

At first I couldn't feel the Spirit at all. The anxiety tightened my chest until I felt dizzy and sick. I started with breathing. *In for five seconds. Hold. Let it out.*

Everything was fine. Sammy and Hannah were laughing. The trail markers were still visible, and we were on foot, not ATVs. I had my cell phone in my pocket, and Hannah had a bag that had to have at least one first aid kit inside.

And even if the worse possible thing happened, God wouldn't leave me to figure it out on my own. Beneath the anxiety, a calmness worked inside me, warm and reassuring.

I took a step forward. And then another. I descended into the Pit, one slow footfall at time. I lost sight of Sammy and Hannah, but I could still hear their voices. Sammy knew the Pit better than anyone. They were safe.

After weaving through the twists and turns, the passage opened into a bowl-shaped valley dotted with lumpy rock structures. We used to go there a lot—Jesse, Bryan, Sammy, and me. We brought the little boys sometimes, too. And once this summer we ate lunch there with Morgan. The wider paths and rocky obstacles made for fun four-wheeling.

Sammy and Hannah sat on a sloping rock near the edge of the valley. I climbed up and joined them on top. I'd made it. Breathing out, I let the better memories chase away the one that had been haunting me. There were so many, it was almost easy to not think about the place on the other side of the Pit where Bryan died.

Hannah slid off the rock and looked around. Sammy stayed beside me, quieter than normal. Something in his face seemed older, grown up. Was it really less than a week since he'd driven my truck? Jesse's voice trickled into my thoughts. *"He's pretty good at it."*

"Sam?" I said suddenly.

He twisted toward me. "Yeah?"

"When did you learn to drive?"

He grinned. "Bryan was teaching me." The grin faded. "Are you mad at him for doing it?"

"Why was he doing it?" I tried to keep my tone neutral.

"He read this stuff online about kids with Down syndrome getting their licenses, and he thought I'd have a pretty good chance of doing it myself. We were worried about what Mom would say. He decided to teach me and then we'd show her and hopefully she'd see I could do it."

Sammy frowned. "Back then we were more worried about Mom keeping me from doing stuff. Bryan actually thought you'd help us convince her. Now you're worse than her."

Back then. My mind flipped to before. How Mom hated when I let Sammy drive the three-wheeler, but I knew he'd be at least as careful or more so than Jesse and I were. How I trusted his sense of direction when we helped look for lost hikers. How I convinced Mom to let him run on the track team, even though she'd been worried about his heart.

Sammy being able to do stuff always gave me hope. Like if he could do things people said he couldn't, I could do all the stuff that scared me.

Coach Mendez's voice broke through my thoughts. *You need to make passing lanes, not just block.* Somehow, Bryan's death had pushed me from being the person who fought for Sammy to do what he wanted, to being the person who blocked him—to not believing he could do hard things.

What did that mean I'd decided about myself?

~~~

When we got back, I dug the three-wheeler key out of the box under my bed where I'd hid it. Then I slipped into the laundry room and turned the new door lock I'd helped Alex install earlier in the week. He'd apologized about the lack of a better private space for me, but I didn't care about the dirty clothes, just the ability to keep people out when I needed to.

Sinking in the frayed green armchair Mom had wedged next to the washer, I let out a long breath. A rustling noise came from my left. Luna popped out of a basket of folded laundry with her flattened and frayed mouse toy in her crooked jaws. She loped over to me and jumped at my leg until I lifted her into my lap, where she promptly curled up in a ball with the mouse under one paw. My fingers brushed over her white fur, snagging on what seemed to be a clump of dried pink paint.

For a long time, I sat listening to the sounds of everyone else in the house, distant beyond the locked door. Sammy's voice carried through over the rest.

I pulled my phone out and opened the scripture app, my mind rolling over everything that had happened since August. I still stood on a brink, but some things were clearer now. I wanted to serve a mission and go to college, but I wasn't ready yet. It sounded nice to have some room to breathe, time to heal the stuff inside me. I knew it was the right thing to do, but sometimes I still felt like I was letting God down.

I forced my thoughts toward the words on the screen and read until I came to the story of a man named Enoch. One day while he was traveling, the Spirit came to him and told him about a job God wanted him to do. Enoch didn't understand. "Why would the Lord want me?" he asked. "I am young and slow of speech."

I'd been asking God that same question. Why would He want me? What good could I do? How could I help Him with anything when I couldn't even help myself?

The Lord said he would fill Enoch's mouth with words—that Enoch would turn rivers from their course and move mountains. "Walk with me," the Lord told him, as if it never mattered how weak Enoch was, as long as he walked with God.

I slid the key to the three-wheeler from my pocket. It might not be a real mountain, but it sure felt like one.

Was I enough the way I was? Broken, a little scared, and still so far from getting over my anxiety? Did I have it in me to make another passing lane for Sammy? Or would I stand in front of him forever?

Heavenly Father, help me do this.

I climbed to my feet and put Luna back on top of the laundry.

God had jobs for me to do. He'd told me about Bryan so I could take care of Sammy and Morgan that day in the Pit. God let me experience anxiety so I could understand my dad. God sent me a bigger family so I could get help when I needed it. He gave me Sammy so I would never stop trying hard things.

I wasn't alone. Heavenly Father loved me the way I was.

I pushed open the laundry room door, a prayer pleading on repeat in my head. *Walk with me.* My feet took me upstairs.

Alex and Mom were at the center island in the kitchen. He was chopping onions, the blade a flash of steel on the cutting board. Mom balanced on a bar stool, her own knife forgotten on a second cutting board covered in green peppers. She leaned on one hand, watching him work while she talked.

He held up his hand, pausing her in midsentence. "You need something, Preston?"

My skin went cold with perspiration. At the same time, the key in my palm grew heavy, as if it could pull my hand to the floor. *Please, help me do this.*

I stood still for another moment. The Spirit pumped through me like blood. The feeling grew so strong that I half expected to see the Savior next to me. With a last deep breath, I crossed the room. My hand shook but I lifted it and let the key clatter to the counter. I pushed it around the cutting boards until it sat dead center between Mom and Alex.

It was time to move my mountain.

About the Author

JoLyn Brown was raised alongside a peach orchard where she worked with her family. Some of her favorite memories are of listening to stories told by her relatives. These stories and her own experiences provide inspiration for her writing.

JoLyn's first novel, *Run,* tells Morgan's story and introduces readers to Preston Bensen and the Powell family. JoLyn's other published works include *You Are Worth It: Eternal Perspectives for a Young Woman, Values-Centered Activities for Young Women, Home Evenings for Newlyweds,* the compilation *A Circle of Sisters,* and several short stories. She is currently working on a fantasy novel and plans to write a follow-up to *Run* and *Break.*

JoLyn lives in Utah with her husband and two children. When she's not writing, she sews, scrapbooks, reads, and spends time with her family. Learn more about JoLyn and her books by visiting www.jolynbrown.com.

a novel

RUN

JoLyn Brown

One summer will change everything.

When Supermom joins Dad on his latest project, sixteen-year-old
Morgan is left with her aunt. Instead of dating the cute boy from her
high school track team, Morgan will spend the summer in a small
town near Kanab, Utah, five hours from home and all of her friends.
Her plan is to keep a sane distance between herself and her aunt's six
boys. What Morgan doesn't expect is being attracted to the neighbor
kid who hangs out with her cousins. How can she like two guys at
the same time?

Just when her life couldn't get more messed up, Morgan stumbles
across an abandoned house and learns she lived there when she was
small. The house and its secrets haunt her—it turns out she's been
dreaming about the place for years. All she wants is to hold onto what
she loves. But as the summer passes, she wonders if she's going to
lose everything.